Gillian ('Gill') Mather has b
and at various times has w
covered by general practi   , family,
employment, civil litigation, v   ... and property). Gill
ran a small solicitor's practice from her home near Colchester
until 2020. She is a member of several writers' groups in Essex
and Suffolk, and is also a member of Dedham Players. Some of
Gill's novels were previously published under the pen name of
Julie Langham.

Gill has published eight novels on Kindle, the first five,
including *The Ardent Intern*, being a series of romantic-cum-
crime novels set in Colchester around the same fictional law
firm and featuring the same main characters over a number of
years. *As The Clock Struck Ten* is the sixth novel. The seventh
novel *The Unreliable Placebo* is a humorous account of a
woman's struggle to come to terms with her sudden single state
after her husband leaves her. Gill's latest novel, *Class of '97*, is a
psychological mystery.

A series of six novellas have been published in booklet form for
local distribution.

Gillian Mather – October 2021

THE ARDENT INTERN

GILL MATHER

This paperback edition published in 2021 by Georfre
Publications
georfrepublications@aol.com

A CIP catalogue record for this book is available from the
British Library

Paperback ISBN: 978-1-8383806-7-0
ebook ISBN: 978-1-8383806-6-3

To Donald Coleman

For helping a teenager take her first steps in the law with
kindness, consideration and circumspection

And to Dan
For his exceptionally thorough proof-reading.

PROLOGUE

THE TWO small boys, one fair-haired, one dark-haired, hovered outside the house on the rough estate, stamping their feet in the thick snow.

"I can't go in," said the dark-haired boy, tear stains streaking his flushed cheeks. "My new stepdad'll kill me for losing the sledge. It was a Christmas present. It cost loads."

"Course he won't. It's not your fault," said his friend.

They both had strong cockney accents and were big boys for their ages, six and nearly six.

"He will."

"I'll come in with you and tell him. Then he won't do anything."

The fair boy went in first, the other dragging his heels, near to tears again. They walked into the lounge where the stepdad sat watching the football.

"I'm sorry, Mr. Harris. But some big boys came and stole the sledge. It wasn't our fault. They said they'd hurt us if we didn't hand it over."

"You what? Where is 'e? Come over here you miserable brat. I'll give you what for. You can't be trusted with anything without busting it or losing it. Your mum and me work our fingers to the bone to provide you with a decent home and what do you bloody go and do?"

The dark-haired boy walked slowly over to the man, trembling. He squealed as the man caught him by the ear and started to take off his belt with the other hand.

"Stop it. You're hurting him," shouted the other boy.

"And you can bugger off or you'll get the same," the stepfather said to the fair boy who stood his ground, torn between getting away and helping his friend.

But when the man snarled at him like a lion he ran for his

1

life, so he thought, to the front door and out of the house where he crouched under the window and sobbed for his friend whose screams he could hear each time the heavy belt bit into his backside.

After a time, the door opened and the dark-haired boy was thrown out bodily into the snow. His friend went over and comforted him, pulled him to his feet and they both hurried off to the bus shelter down the road. They often went there although it smelled of pee and had pale-coloured, slippery, balloon-like things strewn across the surface of the concrete floor.

The dark-haired boy could hardly sit down. The fair one didn't know what to say or do for the best so he offered his friend a pinky swear, something they'd seen on American TV and had done before. The two of them linked little fingers. The fair one said:

"Best friends forever?"

The other sniffed back his tears. "Best friends forever."

CHAPTER 1

Mid- January – Approximately Twenty Three Years Later

THE AGEING rock star lounged in the stand. He was beginning to fidget and twitch. The young solicitor defending the rock star's accountant and manager, who'd been charged with swindling twenty-five million pounds out of him, had been waiting for this, knowing the rock star to be a sixty-a-day man and that nicotine patches were no substitute.

The solicitor had already broken down the forensic accountancy witnesses and thrown doubt on the carefully laid out evidence tracing the money in a number of tranches several times round the world via different banks and investments, some of it ending up in the accountant's coffers. Enough doubt to result, hopefully, in the jury being unwilling to convict the accountant.

He had also induced the rock star to admit to spending small fortunes on drugs and high living and to having failed to keep any records at all of his expenditure or outgoings.

"So, Mr Anston," the solicitor was saying with a faint smile, "which of your several young girlfriends did you say was staying with you in your Cannes villa on 3rd April 2009 when you allege that Mr Seaford got you drunk and used undue influence to obtain your signature to the management agreement of that date?"

"I think it was Patsy. Patsy Taylor."

"But in your evidence earlier, I thought you said that it was…" The solicitor looked down at his notes "…Sophie Naughton. Which was it?"

"I can't be sure. But does it matter? The fact is I signed the agreement without knowing what I was signing."

"Actually, yes, it does matter. You apparently had relationships with each of these girls for several years. They were fairly long-standing relationships. If you expect the court to believe that in April 2009, you were duped into signing an agreement substantially increasing Mr Seaford's management fee retrospectively, then it isn't unreasonable to expect *you* to recall something as significant in your life as which girl you were having a serious relationship with at that particular time.

"The girl who was there with you in your villa when Mr Seaford came to stay with you for one of his regular consultations with you."

"Well, I don't know."

"There *was* a girl staying with you at the time wasn't there?"

"I think so."

"So, is the girl, whoever she was, here today as a witness to support your account of events?"

"Er, no."

"Why is that?"

"I don't know."

"Mr Anston, if the Agreement dated 3rd April 2009 was genuine and wasn't entered into using undue influence, then that accounts for at least half of the money Mr Seaford is accused of stealing from you. Doesn't it?"

"I don't know. I'm no good at the maths. That's why I have someone to manage my financial affairs."

"That's what the expert witness Mr Thompson conceded in his evidence, didn't he?"

"Maybe. I'm having trouble taking it all in."

"Mr Anston, what is your current worth in total?"

"I'm told about two hundred and twenty million. Pounds."

"And what was it when Mr Seaford became your financial manager fifteen years ago?"

"I can't remember."

"In fact, the records show that it was about twenty five million pounds. Mr Anston, have you released any new records or gone on tour in the last fifteen years?"

"No."

"Have you produced any records or other material for other artists in that time?"

"No."

"Have you actually done any form of work in that time?"

"Not really. I've made the odd TV appearance. And I've received royalties."

The solicitor looked at his papers.

"The royalties are said to come to about three hundred thousand pounds a year. A huge income by most people's standards but hardly enough to have amassed a fortune of two hundred and twenty million pounds, after deducting your substantial living expenses. So, you're no good at maths yourself. Where do you think your money has come from?"

"The investments I suppose."

"Who made those investments for you?"

"Mr Seaford."

"Therefore, do you agree that Mr Seaford built your wealth up from twenty-five million pounds to two hundred and twenty million pounds in fifteen years, that's nearly two hundred million pounds, without you having to do anything?"

"I suppose he must have, yes."

"And he did it partly by moving your money and investments around to the best advantage including to minimise your tax liability. Isn't that right?"

"I suppose so, yes."

"Do you think it's possible, Mr Anston, that there hasn't actually been any theft here at all, just a very complicated investment structure which made you a very rich man and for which Mr. Seaford was paid a relatively modest amount of remuneration?"

"I just … I don't know."

"Thank you, Mr Anston."

IT WAS the following day. The judge and jury were out, the accountant Seaford having given his evidence calmly and clearly and the jury having been addressed. Hugh Sutherland had turned round and was facing the back of the courtroom, leaning against the bench. "I'm going to get a coffee. Want one?" he asked Ali and she followed him out to the machine.

After chatting briefly they took the polystyrene cups back into the courtroom and Hugh looked at his notes.

Hugh was just about the coolest person Ali had ever come across. She thought her dad was pretty laid back, but he could afford to be. It was her opinion that his generation had had it rather easy. Economic growth, plentiful jobs, high pension expectations, not much regulatory stuff to worry about. Her dad was due to retire soon and was in the 'winding down' phase and he wasn't yet sixty-five, whereas it looked like Ali's generation were going to have to work until they dropped.

Compared to her dad, Hugh was positively glacial. Despite the strains of the job, he never got flustered or in a temper. He never got in a flap. Nothing seemed to faze him. He just single-mindedly and usually successfully dealt with criminal cases.

When Ali said something stupid which, she had to admit, wasn't an especially rare event, he'd make some mild, dry remark, but he never made her feel a complete fool. When the other partners had tantrums, as they fairly often did, particularly the men, Hugh either walked off or he'd point out the realities with a sabre-like logic or come out with a veiled put-down and they'd bluster and harrumph and have to calm down.

And now, a quality assurance scheme for criminal advocates was on the cards, and Ali was researching into it for Hugh. If Ali ended up being only half as good a solicitor and advocate as Hugh, she'd consider she'd done extremely well.

The somewhat portly older QC representing the prosecution was chatting up the junior, a pretty young female barrister. It was a fairly big money, complicated, high-profile case that the prosecution obviously thought merited a QC. The defence just had Hugh and Ali, and she was only there to take notes and try to pick up anything important Hugh might have missed.

Ali's musings were cut short as the judge and the jury returned. Ali and Hugh hurriedly put their cups on the floor under their bench.

"On the charge of theft of twenty-five million pounds or thereabouts from Rick Anston, do you find the defendant guilty or not guilty?"

"Not guilty."

"On the first charge of false accounting, do you find the defendant guilty or not guilty?"

"Not guilty."

"On the second charge of false accounting, do you find the defendant guilty or not guilty?"

"Not guilty."

The false accounting charges were sample charges but it was unlikely any further charges would be brought in the circumstances.

There was a small cheer from Seaford's entourage in the gallery, the jury were dismissed, the judge left the courtroom and Seaford, Hugh and Ali went out to face the press.

ON THE return journey to Colchester, Hugh and Ali chatted in a desultory fashion mainly about the case. Ali knew very little about Hugh despite having been with the firm three months now, so subjects for conversation were quite thin on the ground.

She knew he was best friends with a businessman in whom the tabloid press took an interest and who was facing an unpleasant charge at the moment, but there was very little left to say about that case.

Hugh never asked about her personal or private life outside the office, presumably because he was too polite. And she certainly didn't want to bore him by bombarding him with unsolicited details or risk a rebuff by asking him about himself.

So after a time, Ali turned and looked out of the window at the mostly uninspiring, mid-January landscape adjoining the A12 flashing past, and wondered what to wear for Baz Trimble's forthcoming Burns Night do.

CHAPTER 2

Two months earlier – November

ALI trudged through the deep snow along the seemingly never-ending drive as it curled gently away from Baker's Lane. The silence was unnerving, and the high hedge on one side and the wooded area on the other had already cut off her view of the road.

She started to feel vulnerable and scared but at least it wasn't too dark. The moon was up and illuminated the snowy landscape visible through the gaps in the hedge.

Just as she was seriously wondering whether to abandon her mission as a fool's errand, the big Georgian house at last came into view. It looked inviting and Ali immediately felt reassured.

There was a fir tree near the front door, though the Christmas lights wound around it weren't on, nor was the light over the door. A warm glow came from some of the windows. Thank heavens someone was at home. A faint humming sound could be heard from somewhere, possibly the back of the house.

Just as she was reaching out to knock on the door, it opened and she nearly fell into the hall. It was Graham Spellings showing someone out.

"Hello?" said Mr Spellings.

"Oh. I ... I'm– "

"Goodnight, Graham," said the older woman leaving the house and she nodded to Ali as she stomped past. Graham Spellings turned his attention to Ali, smiling enquiringly.

"Hello. I'm Ali Barratt. From Patterson Watts? We've spoken on the phone. I just came to t–"

"Come in. Please," offered Mr Spellings. "You can't stand there in the cold." And he led her through the cavernous, unheated hall into a large kitchen at the back. The kitchen was much warmer and it was all wonderfully cosy after her two-mile hike this freezing evening.

"Do sit down." He had a definite cockney twang despite the smart clothes and gentlemanly manner.

What was she thinking. Gentlemanly manner, indeed! Ali mentally scolded herself. Just because she was re-reading Pride and Prejudice for the umpteenth time, she didn't have to think like a fictional Georgian heroine. Graham Spellings sat down at the table and took up a glass of wine. He offered Ali a glass but she shook her head.

"Sorry, I can't. I have to get home, Mr Spellings–"

"Graham, please."

"OK. The thing is ,Graham, your purchase can't go ahead tomorrow. We've been trying to get hold of you all day. The sellers' removal firm won't move them tomorrow. Obviously because of the weather. So I just wanted to let you know that you won't be able to go and collect the keys tomorrow. As I was passing on the way home, I thought I'd call in and tell you. If you want to claim interest and anything else, you'll have to talk to Mr Watts tomorrow."

"Oh no. I wouldn't bother with making a claim. A few days won't make any difference. It's not their fault after all and it's only a buy-to-let."

"Oh well, good. Mr Watts'll be relieved. Er, there's a lot on at the moment what with the weather et cetera," she added, laughing slightly nervously. "Anyway," she stood up, "we'll keep in touch with you. Well. If we can. There was no reply from any of your numbers today."

"Yeah," he sighed, "the phone lines are down, and the mobile phone mast and there's no electricity."

Ali looked around her questioningly.

Graham laughed. "The Aga's solid fuel and I've got a generator in the yard at the back for the lights. It's a bit of a relic though. I just hope it lasts until the power comes back on again."

He stood up too and loomed over her. As she'd heard, he was stunningly attractive, dark-haired with an upturned mouth that made him appear at ease all the time without looking smug. And not that old either. He looked maybe late twenties, early thirties. The firm were dealing with his divorce as well and hoping the pre-nup would hold up. She couldn't think why Petunia Spellings had run off with a fat banker. Ali had sneaked a look at his file and Graham's statement said he was devastated, especially as they had been trying for a baby.

"I'd better get going or I'll be late."

"Right. I'll pop into your office tomorrow to see how things are going if the phones are still down," he said. "Oh, um, how did you get here? I didn't see a car. The roads are virtually impassable anyway aren't they?"

"Yes. I've been walking into work the last few days. I live in Braiswick. It's not that far, about two or three miles. I'm quite enjoying it."

"Look, I can't let you walk back on your own in the dark. I'll get the car." He walked off towards the back door. "I'll meet you at the front of the house," he said, glancing back at her, and then he was gone in a wave of cold air as the back door opened and shut.

The journey home in Graham's Range Rover didn't take long. Ali had been wondering where the older woman had gone on foot but as they travelled along the drive, she saw a small house set back in the wood not far from the main house. The lights were on now but it must have been in darkness before.

Following her gaze, Graham told her it was where May lived. He said she worked as his housekeeper.

"Unfortunately she hasn't got a generator. She's having to use Tilley lamps. But she's got her own Rayburn and a wood burning stove. And I'll look after her for anything she needs."

Other than that there wasn't much conversation.

Graham dropped Ali off at her house, repeated that he'd come to the office tomorrow if the phones were still off and, with a brief wave, he drove away.

CHAPTER 3

IT WAS another freezing day. The snow and ice showed no sign of abating. Ali's younger brother Ed and his mates had laid their hands on snow boards from somewhere or other and had made off to terrorise the smaller children in the park. School was closed. Boilers not working, teachers huddling at home, icy conditions making slipping accidents too likely.

Ed was being particularly obnoxious since Ali had come back to live at home after finishing uni. He disliked Ali's boyfriend Rob whom she'd met at Bristol, and he had hoped that the larger second bedroom would become his. His hopes were dashed when Ali came to live at home as Rob had decided to stay on and take a fourth year. Otherwise the plan had been for Ali and Rob to get jobs and live together.

And now, apparently, Rob needed to stay on for a fifth year to study for a PhD. Ali had argued with him about that. Who needed a PhD in management accountancy?

Ali was having trouble living at home with her parents again and the difficulty getting a job, any job, came as a bolt out of the blue. She must have written seven or eight hundred letters to firms of solicitors everywhere seeking a training contract. The minimum salary for trainee solicitors didn't help. When only rejections or silence resulted, she'd lowered her sights to clerical fee-earning jobs. Still nothing.

Then suddenly about five weeks ago on her afternoon off, she'd made her weekly round of phone calls to all the firms in Colchester and, completely unexpectedly, Patterson Watts & Trimble's receptionist had put her through to Sandra who was the senior partner, Mr Victor Watts's, senior secretary.

Later the same day, she'd attended a five-minute interview with Sandra, on meeting a cross between a rugby forward in drag and Mary Poppins. Sandra had smoothed down her flared skirt, asked a few questions and, when it appeared that Ali could string a sentence together, offered her an 'internship'.

"The position is of course unpaid," said Sandra, not meeting

Ali's eyes. "You'll receive training however, and there's the possibility of a small travel allowance. You'll be assisting Mr Watts, though I'm afraid he can't see you now. He's extremely busy since his previous assistant left to have a baby."

"What area of law does Mr Watts practise in?" Ali asked. She hadn't had a chance to look at the company's website and Mr Watts's profile in her anxiety to get to PWT's office as soon as possible in case someone else was offered the prized position. She hoped it would be something glamorous; maybe acting for celebrities in privacy cases, or dealing with high profile murder trials.

"Mr Watts deals with residential and commercial property transactions."

Ali's spirits plummeted for half a minute. It wasn't exactly what she'd been hoping to do. Ever since she was a child she'd been riveted by legal TV dramas. She'd dreamed of being involved in rich people's divorces, of striding into court to successfully defend those accused of heinous crimes, wrapping up complicated company cases and achieving record damages in personal injury claims.

She'd followed civil rights issues in the media and considered the police to be bullies and thugs. That was until her older sister, Jan, married a detective sergeant, the divine Matt, who'd turned out to be one of the nicest men Ali had ever met and she was only too pleased that he'd turned inspector recently. This, however, only strengthened Ali's resolve to go into the law.

Being awarded her law degree had been the most wonderful experience of Ali's life. She spent the day floating on air. And not even Ed's jibes about her looking like a witch in her hired academic gown, or Rob being unavoidably unable to attend the ceremony, could penetrate her euphoria. It was like a dream.

It had taken a while to come down to earth. She'd kept in touch with her friends from Bristol and they were all having a hard time getting on the next rung of the ladder, with the exception of a few whose families 'knew someone'. Contacts seemed to be everything and Ali hadn't got any.

Still, being offered an internship with PWT was better than nothing. Actually, it was more than better. It was fantastic and she was opening her mouth to accept when Sandra stood up.

"Well, of course if you don't want the job, we'll leave it there," she said huffily. "I've got a lot of work to do."

"But I do," Ali insisted. "When can I start?"

"Oh," Sandra seemed mollified and sat down again. They discussed a few details and as Ali left the office, she couldn't help skipping a few steps along the pavement in her excitement, convincing herself that it would all work out wonderfully well and lead to great things.

But no training materialised and her predecessor's baby turned out to be possibly a fiction, the assistant having walked out without warning due to pressure of work the day before Ali telephoned.

Ali was expected to learn 'on the job' by reading through completed files. After three weeks at Pattersons, she had knocked on Mr Watts's door and asked him if she could possibly spend some time with some of the other partners, say one or two days a week, seeing other areas of the practice. She'd barely spoken to Mr Watts yet and he turned out to be fairly OK, just a touch harassed.

He looked up at her from his desk, then down at her details in front of him and said what she'd heard at least a million times before:

"Hmm. Aluisha Clayton-Barratt. I'm surprised you didn't get a job at the BBC with a name like that."

Ali laughed anyway. "Yes. My parents named me specially."

Mr Watts seemed to realise he'd been caught out making a very obvious remark and went slightly pink in the face.

To cover the moment, Ali sat down and asked again about spending time with other partners.

Oh dear, he said, Ali had turned out to be quite good at drafting documents and dealing with the clients and, honestly, the conveyancing department needed her.

Prepared for this, Ali pointed out that she had lost her earnings from her previous employment by coming to work for the firm and couldn't carry on any longer without pay and would have to leave unless there was a good reason to stay on.

She wanted to get some experience in civil and criminal litigation, or company law or family law, not just ordinary residential conveyancing. If necessary she'd do some extra conveyancing work at home if she could just spend a couple of days a week with another partner.

Mr Watts sighed and said he supposed it was only fair and Ali was left to approach the other partners.

Since Mr Trimble, the corporate partner, was far too busy doing 'fucking great takeovers', according to him, to drag a wet-behind-the-ears law graduate around with him, and Alison Atkins, the family law and civil cases partner, was working on a big money divorce at the moment and couldn't risk upsetting her 'finely balanced team', Ali started to spend Mondays and Tuesdays with Hugh Sutherland. There was also a Wills and Probate department but Ali hadn't asked about that.

Hugh Sutherland was a mainly criminal solicitor. He had an HRA award certificate. That meant he had rights of audience in, that is he could appear in, higher courts than solicitors normally had. There weren't so many solicitors who had an HRA certificate. It was a significant accolade.

Hugh was quite remote and professorial. But he taught Ali a lot. He was a superb advocate and very much sought after by the dubious characters who practised and plied their trades all over Essex and the adjoining counties and indeed increasingly further afield. He was also in demand by the company directors who got caught speeding. And in other fixes.

This was all the more a tribute to him since there were plenty of larger firms in Colchester and other nearby towns and cities who could have catered for this demand.

In fact, he was increasingly regarded as the local 'Mr Fixit'.

The Mondays and Tuesdays Ali spent with Hugh were

either in court, usually the mags and Crown Courts, where she took copious notes of the proceedings, or in the office with clients talking over the case or taking statements. He'd started to entrust to her taking statements, a task which she found fascinating. Many people were evasive and difficult even though she and Hugh were on their side. She quickly learned to cajole the women and charm the men into relaxing enough to be more forthcoming.

When the stories didn't quite add up, she smiled nicely and moved onto another topic and filed the discrepancies away in her head to bring up with Hugh later and leave him to iron out. It didn't occur to her for a moment that this might be at all morally wrong. She was firmly of the view that solicitors should be impartial and that everyone was entitled to a defence. A view Matt, her brother-in-law, didn't entirely agree with. But, give him credit, Matt acknowledged that a good defence kept the police on their toes and prevented the odd miscarriage of justice.

BUT this was a Thursday and Ali wasn't shadowing Hugh today. She was working for Mr Watts and, due to the weather and the delays it caused, nothing much was going down. Very little post had been delivered and Pattersons and other firms were seriously undermanned so that the phone wasn't ringing and there was hardly anything to do.

As a result, Ali spent most of the day with the paralegals and secretaries (or PAs as the younger ones now liked to be called – the older secretaries didn't seem to care) who had made it into the office, swapping but mainly picking up gossip.

She especially liked Samantha, a blonde-haired, green-eyed would-have-been model who had become pregnant and, instead of heading for London, had stayed in Colchester and married. She worked for Basil 'Baz' Trimble.

Married or not, Sam liked a girls' night out and they regularly hit the town together. They also spent lots of lunch hours in a huddle together. It was nice to have an ally.

Otherwise her relationship with the PAs, particularly the conveyancing PAs, was fairly fragile. The thing was, Ali wasn't a proper fee earner and she wasn't a paralegal or a PA. She didn't really fit in anywhere. She had a law degree, a good one, which the PAs and paralegals didn't have, but she lacked the practical knowledge of the PAs.

As it was so dead today, at lunchtime they all piled over to the Sod `n` Shovel.

CHAPTER 4

"SO HOW are you getting on with Hugh, then?" said Amanda, Alison Atkins's PA. Ali caught a slightly sarcastic edge to her voice. Cathy, Alison's paralegal sitting next to Amanda, nudged her so her drink spilled and they both started giggling.

Ali chose to take the words at their face value.

"He's a brilliant lawyer. I think I'm really lucky to be able to work under him…"

More giggling.

"Sorry. What's the joke?" said Ali in as straightforward a manner as she could muster.

Samantha broke in. "Hugh's the archetypal eligible male and he's pretty fit into the bargain. This pair of clowns can't imagine that he might be coaching you in anything innocent. Their minds are way below their navels most of the time."

"But I only spend Mondays and Tuesdays with him," Ali said, realising as it came out how pathetic it sounded so, as she finished the sentence, she put her head on one side, raised one eyebrow knowingly and smiled, she hoped, enigmatically.

This seemed to take the wind out of their sails and they didn't say anything, their expressions thoughtful. Ali wasn't certain it was the right impression to have given. Still, she couldn't have these two habitually teasing her. They were nice enough, but cocky and a bit bitchy and she could see they could become bullies in the right circumstances.

Paul, a trainee solicitor working in Baz Trimble's department at the moment, looked her up and down as well and Ali hoped she hadn't started the rumour machine going. She knew almost nothing about Hugh but he came over as serious and quite stern and she rather feared that he wouldn't be at all understanding if any stories about their non-existent relationship got blown out of all proportion and found their way back to him.

"Sheila," she said by way of a change of direction, "why hasn't Hugh got LLB after his name? He must have a law degree. Even I've got an LLB."

Sheila was Hugh's slightly more mature secretary who had listened to the exchanges with detached resignation, like a mother dog watching puppies misbehaving.

"I don't think he does actually. He doesn't say much about himself but I think he got a degree in medicine. I suppose he could put BM or something after his name but I don't think he's bothered."

"He can take my blood pressure any day," said Amanda.

Ali took a sip of her drink, brushed her long dark hair behind her ears and decided to change the subject completely.

"Talking of fit, I went to Graham Spellings's house last night." And she explained why.

"You should hear what his ex, or soon to be ex, has to say about him." Cathy winked.

Ali raised an eyebrow again, this time quizzically. The others were riveted.

"Well," said Amanda pausing dramatically and gazing around, "she says he couldn't keep his hands off the hired help."

"Hmm. I saw one last night and she couldn't have been a day over sixty-five!" said Ali laughing. "His tastes are obviously very wide ranging." The others laughed too.

"Oh yeah. Very clever." Amanda was much put out. "Petunia was talking about the stable maids actually. She's taken her horses and the stable staff away with her, only today apparently. She says Graham tried to stop her – although he doesn't ride – but Barry got his security staff involved."

"Do you believe it?" said Samantha. "After all, she's bound to paint the worst possible picture of him isn't she? And the tabloids don't actually portray her as little Miss Innocent, do they, when it comes to playing around?"

"Well, Petunia's legal team are saying it wasn't just the hired help he tried it on with. They reckon Graham was always at it with someone else. He denies it all of course, but Petunia says he was just discreet and managed to charm the other women into keeping schtum.

"In fact," continued Amanda, "she's made some rather sensitive allegations. Rather close to home actually–"

But she stopped when Cathy gave her a warning glare. The others were silent, hoping for more.

"Well," said Paul, "there's always been stuff about him in the business world. Although nothing, er, sexual. Just astute, some might say ruthless, financial dealings. Nothing actually dodgy though."

"I'd better get back," said Ali looking at the time on her mobile. It was well past 2 pm. Graham would want to see her if he came to the office. And of course any other clients of the firm.

"Oh well. If Professor Clayton-Barratt thinks it's time to leave, I s'pose we'd *all* better make a move," said Amanda, looking archly at everyone.

IT WAS like a morgue at the office. Mr Watts had left. Sandra was still filling in as receptionist since Tammy, the regular receptionist, hadn't made it in. Sandra was sniffing her disapproval.

"That girl is *so* disorganised. Look at the state of this drawer!"

The others dutifully peered into it. It had to be said that there was little in the way of conventional stationery in there. Some magazines, chewing gum and assorted items of makeup. Plus a pack of condoms, what might have been a strip of morning-after pills and what looked like a pregnancy testing kit.

"Well, really," huffed Sandra.

"She's only nineteen," said Samantha trying not to snigger. "And going equipped is just sensible these days!"

Sandra pursed her lips. "Someone will have to look after the phones while I go and powder my nose."

Ali offered and Sandra seemed to be placated. Everyone else cleared off to their assorted tasks and Ali sat and doodled.

Sandra didn't come back. Ali started to leaf through the magazines. Just one call came through from Mrs Green who telephoned at least once a day, usually more. She tried as usual to speak to Mr Watts but when that wasn't possible, she started on Ali, wanting an update.

"Actually we're getting almost no calls in," said Ali. "There's been no faxes or emails either. I did try to call the other side this morning but I couldn't speak to anyone who could help. It's the weather, you know?"

"Well in my day we didn't let a bit of snow bring the country to a halt…"

And off she went. Ali read an article about the female orgasm as Mrs Green ranted on and finished that she'd expect some definite progress tomorrow.

At three-thirty Amanda walked round and said that Alison, the only partner in the office, had announced that they could all go home.

Ali spent a few minutes recording a suitable greeting about the weather in case there were any more calls by which time everyone had left. She'd no idea that lot could move so quickly.

Ali hadn't noticed Alison leaving. Presumably she was still here. Good. Ali wasn't sure how to set the alarm in spite of having had it explained to her quite a few times. She checked that Alison was still in her room then got her things together. Just as she was walking towards the exit, the door flew open and Hugh almost fell in.

"God's truth! The bloody weather out there's atrocious! I'm nearly frozen to death."

Well, if he would go out in just a suit with no coat or scarf…

He strode past Ali and off to his room, taking no further notice of her.

Ali hesitated. He was obviously in a bit of a mood, nevertheless she decided she'd go and ask if she could shadow him the following day, Friday, as all the completions had been deferred to next week and she had nothing to do.

He was already sitting down dictating away and he didn't look up when she went in.

"Er, Hugh?"

"Hmmm?"

"I was wondering, if you're working tomorrow."

"I think it's a fair bet I will be."

"Yes. Of course you are. Well, could I shadow you tomorrow because there's nothing to do at our end. The weather's stopped people from moving."

Hugh was poring over some papers and not responding.

"Er. Even Graham Spellings's purchase isn't going through."

Why she'd picked that case in particular, she didn't know. Just because Graham was so well-known presumably.

"He ... um ... I have told him. I called in yesterday evening when I was walking home because we couldn't get hold of him on the telephone.

"He was OK about it," she blundered on. "Some clients have gone berserk when they've been told about the delay. There's no post coming in and nothing to do so–"

Something seemed to catch Hugh's attention. He looked up sharply and stood up.

"Did you say you went to Graham Spellings's house last night?" he barked.

"Er, yes. Yes. We couldn't get hold of him on the–"

"Yes, yes, I heard. That wasn't very sensible was it!"

"Wasn't it? Why?"

Hugh frowned, momentarily non-plussed.

"Well, it wasn't. Er, it's a bit remote. I hope you told someone you were going there!"

"Well no, not really. It was a spur of the moment thing. But it's all OK. He–"

"All OK? Are you mad? Going to a strange man's home in the middle of nowhere at night and not telling anyone!"

Visions of Mrs Bennet asserted themselves, though come to think of it, wasn't her sense of propriety somewhat lacking if it meant one of her daughters getting off with a wealthy young man?

"I'm not a teenager, you know," Ali said crossly, "And he's

a client of the firm. Trusted client I imagine."

"Yes. *But* he's been arrested for sexually assaulting one of the stable maids at his place on Tuesday evening this week. Allegedly. I've just spent most of this afternoon at the nick with him being questioned."

Hugh was staring at her keenly. Ali could only stand there gawping.

"Yes. His estranged wife got the horses and stable staff out of the place today and then the stable maid felt safe enough to make the allegation to the police. Well, that's the story."

"I don't know what to say." Ali's tone hardened. "You sound as though you believe he did it. Surely there can't be any definitive evidence already. Not forensic evidence."

"Haven't you read the firm's code of conduct. It expressly forbids staff from visiting premises or meeting someone without telling someone else." Hugh sighed. "I'm just trying to point out that it isn't sensible. Or safe. Graham's obviously OK, but you can't go wandering around in the dark on your own. And if this thing did happen to the stable maid then there might be someone lurking about in the area."

He was looking down at her, serious blue-grey eyes full of concern, thick fair hair still damp from melted snowflakes. Despite the way the others went on about him, Ali hadn't really taken a good look at Hugh before. Actually, he has quite a sensitive face, she decided. In fact, quite girly looking if you ignored the broad shoulders and five o' clock shadow. Maybe he wasn't such a cold fish after all.

"Yes. You're right of course. I wasn't thinking. But surely you don't think he did it do you? You'll be trying to get him off won't you? What does he say about it?"

"He denies it. Obviously. Look, he's my oldest friend. We grew up together. I know him back-to-front. I don't think there's any question that he didn't do it. But somehow or other this has happened and just being charged with something like that can be enough. Anyway, of course I'll do my best to avoid a charge or get it dropped if he is charged, otherwise obviously we'll certainly be defending it."

"He may be a bit of a lad by all accounts, but actual assault! I've only met him once but, well, I wouldn't have thought he'd need to resort to assault."

Ali immediately regretted that last bit. Hugh's expression was sardonic with a touch of exasperation.

"Your assessment is very valuable, Ali. I'll bear it in mind. And the answer's yes."

"What? Sorry?"

"To your shadowing me tomorrow. *And* next week. I'll need the help if I'm to put the hours into Graham's defence. Watts'll just have to pull his finger out and heave his carcass into the office and do a bit of work himself. See you at nine."

And Hugh turned his attention back to his papers. Ali felt duly dismissed and crept out into the now raging blizzard. Then a thought struck her. That comment about Watts getting some work done must mean that at least Hugh had noticed how hard Ali was working.

She unconsciously stood up straighter, thrust out her chest and pulled her shoulders back, then immediately lost her footing. She only narrowly missed going 'arse over tit' as Samantha would have said. She peered around furtively to see if anyone had noticed, but there was hardly anyone about, and those that were had their heads well down. Sensible them.

CHAPTER 5

DARREN SUMMERS was eyeing up the girl on the other side of the desk. He presumed she was a solicitor. Although he'd turned up early, he had chatted up the young receptionist, and charmed her into getting him seen straightaway. He'd shot his cuffs in, he thought, a manly, professional way, giving her a sight of his expensive watch. She was obviously impressed and her bosom was heaving as she hurried off to speak to Ms Barratt.

Darren looked down on solicitors who, as far as he could see, tried to bugger up transactions by raising stupid enquiries and rejecting his schemes to save stamp duty as illegal. Nonetheless, his strategy was to try and keep on the right side of everyone so he threw Wattsey a few crumbs of conveyancing cases occasionally and if he wanted a decent solicitor for his pet clients on big transactions, he still sent them to Watts.

He decided he wasn't going to be bossed about by this slip of a girl, even if she was a solicitor. She was quite pretty. Very pretty in fact, but dark and earnest-looking. Not his type at all. He went for blondes with high heels and short skirts and large boobs. Like his Sharon. Just a pity Sharon was 15 stone after having the kids. He'd hoped she'd go back to work and smarten herself up once Perry started school and Larry went to nursery school. There wasn't much sign of it, Darren thought morosely.

"Well? Did she?"

Darren realised the girl was asking him something again. He was here because he'd been clocked doing 130 mph down the A12 at eight-thirty one evening.

"Sorry, I didn't catch that."

The girl sighed. "You said you'd been on your way home because your wife had telephoned you and was worried about an intruder. Didn't she think to phone the police?"

"Oh. No. She was too het up."

"Obviously it took you some time to get home after being pulled over by the police. What did Sharon do when you didn't get home straight away?"

"I don't know." This was exasperating.

"Darre,n I'm sorry but this is *your* evidence. You have to tell me what happened."

"I don't know," he barked. "The babysitter had arrived and Sharon had gone out by the time I got back."

Darren's mind turned to the sixteen-year-old babysitter's firm young breasts showing through her jumper and her sweet unlined young face looking at him while he'd regaled her with riveting facts about the housing market as they waited for her father to come and collect her and take her home.

"No. It was late by then. By the time I got home."

"How late?"

"I dunno. Eleven or something."

"The police report says they'd finished with you by nine o' clock. So what did you do in the meantime?"

Darren considered this. "Well, after popping back home and seeing everything was OK, I went back to the office and shuffled some papers about. Y'know?" Worker to worker!

"Weren't you worried about Sharon?"

"Well, she didn't phone again so I reckoned everything was OK."

"Will Sharon back up your account of calling you about a suspected intruder? Would she go to court and give evidence?"

"Leave it out! I'm not getting her involved. She'd be – she wouldn't want to appear in court."

"OK. Then will your home phone records show she called you before you set out for home earlier on?"

"She called me on her mobile."

"It should be possible to access the mobile phone company records."

This was too much. "Look, can't we just go with my evidence. I was dead worried when she called. My kids, everything. Sharon's … not very strong … mentally. Lots of things upset her. She probably just imagined she heard someone, you know?"

"You said she'd gone out when you got back. Where did she go?"

"Round her mum's. It's not far. That's why we live there. So she can be near her mum."

THIS was tortuous. Like pulling teeth.

Ali had been twirling around in Hugh's big leather chair and tinkering with the expensive fountain pens on the leather-covered desk (only there for show, she knew – Hugh always used a cheap Parker) when Tammy had burst in and said that Darren had arrived and was demanding to be seen immediately, he had such a full schedule that day. Tammy was obviously impressed by such masterfulness and her bosom was heaving.

So Ali had to comply. Since he was early, she'd had no time to read the papers and had to go through them as she interviewed Darren.

Her job was to take a statement from Darren about his speeding charge. Hugh had already determined that Darren couldn't get off the charge and so the job was to try to prevent him from losing his licence.

Darren was an estate agent and very much fancied himself. Ali had seen his new Beemer ostentatiously parked outside the front of the agents' office even though they had a big car park at the back. Mr Watts automatically hated Darren and his company and indeed all estate agents. In the good old days, Summer Homes had put a lot of business the firm's way in return for just an invite to the New Year's party and a bit of other entertainment throughout the year. Watts had secretly hated the agents even then, but at least they'd had their uses.

However now, a few short years later, Summer Homes had expanded and opened a string of offices over Essex, Suffolk and Hertfordshire and did what all the agents did, or those that hadn't set up their own conveyancing outfits. They demanded huge fees from solicitors' firms to 'recommend' solicitors to house buyers and sellers. Mr Watts refused to pay the fees and developed a reputation instead for quality and for dealing with the high end of the market. He tried to look loftily down on the likes of Darren. It worked up to a point but the ups and downs of the market and the fluctuating income had shattered Mr Watts's nerves.

Darren had sounded peeved so far by her questioning, as though he expected *her* to make up his story for him. He looked uncomfortable and Ali wasn't at all sure he was telling the truth.

She'd been about to query the expense of a babysitter just so that Sharon could visit her mother, which she could do at any time, but cast an eye over Darren's expensive suit and haircut, large, showy Rolex, and his faintly bored expression and reckoned that the cost of an evening's babysitting would be peanuts in Darren's household.

"OK then. How would you get to work and get around generally if you lost your licence?"

"Easy. I'd get one of the girls to give me a ride. No double entendre intended." Darren laughed.

Ali felt mentally winded. Wrong answer. He'd lose his directorship. His company would collapse. He'd go bankrupt. Those would have been good answers.

"Sorry, Darren," she said. "But we're going to have to go over it all again."

"BLIMEY, that was an effort," Ali said to Tammy once Darren had left the office. "How these agents make so much cash is beyond me. You'd think the man wanted to lose his licence. Still, perhaps he does."

"What was the story?" Tammy wanted to know.

After Ali had gone over the interview for Tammy, she thought about it some more and put forward the theory that Darren couldn't care less if he lost his licence. He was just trying to put up a case to satisfy his wife Sharon that he was doing something about it.

Secretly, he might find it a positive advantage to have to depend on an office floozy to drive him about. If Darren was in the habit of playing around, which it sounded as though he might be, he could use the excuse to Sharon that he couldn't get home at such and such a time because he hadn't got a driver until later, leaving Darren free to pursue other, er, activities.

"Fine," said Tammy warming to the subject, "but if he simply wanted to lose his licence, why didn't he just get himself done for drunken driving? It'd be a cert then."

"I suppose," Ali considered it. "Only, the thing about that is that you could drive around half cut for months, years even, and never get caught. And into the bargain you might injure or kill someone. Now that wouldn't be good for business. Not at all. While losing your licence when you were driving a good car on a relatively empty dual carriageway and didn't actually harm anyone, if anything, might get sympathy. The story about rushing home to your vulnerable wife and family! Certainly it'll get publicity. And you know what they say about that. I don't suppose he planned to get stopped, but now that he's in danger of losing his licence, well it may seem quite attractive in many ways. And it'd only be temporary.

"Hmm. We'll have to keep an eye on our Darren. Perhaps he's not as thick as he seems."

And Ali went off to type up her notes for Hugh.

And Tammy filed all this away for future reference.

CHAPTER 6

HUGH was back in the office, having had a mammoth session with Graham.

"How're you getting on with Graham?" said Ali as Hugh glanced through the transcript of her statement from Darren. Instead of answering, he shook his head.

"You'd better brief junior counsel. I'm not going into court with a concoction like this."

"But Darren expects you to present his case!"

"You must be joking. It'll make the firm a laughing stock."

Ali tried to put forward her theory that Darren was only using the intruder story to save his marriage and as a publicity stunt to gain sympathy, not to mention the advantages to him of being free of the matrimonial chains for six months. Hugh cut her short.

"Well, he can use someone else to promote his business and further his shenanigans. My name isn't going in the papers in support of a pack of obvious lies. Instruct counsel and tell him it's the best thing for him."

"But *does* he want the best thing for him?" argued Ali as she cleared up her papers and prepared to walk out. "Maybe he wants the kudos of being represented by Hugh Sutherland."

That had come out wrong!

"Thanks for the vote of confidence, Ali. You'll still have to instruct counsel and sell it to him that it's the best thing for him because I'm not presenting that bundle of hokum!"

"Right," said Ali, and traipsed off to her room.

'ROOM' would be a kindness, actually, to describe the broom cupboard that had been assigned to Ali on her first day at Pattersons. The romantic appeal of a possible career in the law had eclipsed the realities of the situation during her first week at the firm and she had started to set out the 'room' to its best advantage. Ignoring the fact that it had no windows, she filled it with plants and brought in an ultraviolet lamp to keep the plants alive.

She had christened the room 'The Privy' and attached to the door a paper sign in fancy writing using one of her calligraphy pens. However, Sandra had quickly turned up and told her that the lamp would use too much electricity and had taken it away.

So Ali had acquired some colourful posters and tried to cheer it up that way. They were starting to look tawdry and it was beginning to sink in that all the firm wanted out of her was the maximum work for the minimum outlay. Sure she was getting training, but they didn't care about her at all. She started to feel tearful, and realised that the only way to retrieve the situation was a session with Sammy.

She was reaching for the internal phone to ring her when it buzzed insistently. Picking it up, she heard Hugh telling her to get her coat. They had to go to the station. The DI was ready to interview Graham, and Hugh wanted her there to take notes.

AS ALI dashed into the car park, Hugh was yanking open the driver's door of his old four wheel drive.

"Don't you lock it?" Ali asked.

"If I have time. C'mon. Get in."

Ali, tears forgotten, jumped in and slammed the passenger door shut as he pulled away. She just had time to clock with surprise that the car was a bit of a mess inside. In fact, there was stuff everywhere. Old coats, shoes and boots, boxes and bags of stuff. He'd had to move a box off the front seat as she was getting in.

Blimey, she thought, for someone so precise and meticulous with his work, he was a bit of a slob with his stuff. She remembered being told he'd just bought his first house not long before. He was just the junior partner after all. Perhaps that was it. He was moving things. But the inside of the car clearly hadn't been hoovered for ages and the clutter had that look about it of a long-standing committed sloven. She should know. She'd come across enough of those types sharing houses at uni.

She nearly asked him if he slept in the car. It looked as though someone did. But she didn't think he'd take jibes lightly, so she buttoned it.

Typical bachelor she thought. It was rather endearing really. Anyway, her mother always said you can't trust a man who's too tidy. What he needs is a good woman, thought Ali. She wasn't her mother's daughter for nothing.

She'd just had time to get a couple of writing pads (that was all she could find – she hoped it would be enough) and some pens together. She knew Hugh didn't like to be kept waiting. He was driving furiously considering the conditions but since there weren't many people about, Ali hoped they might avoid hitting inanimate objects instead. The car was sliding and skidding somewhat. Hugh didn't seem to notice and very shortly they were parking at the front of the nick in an area that wasn't meant for parking. Hugh wasn't going to bother about that.

They waited about for more than a few minutes while Hugh paced up and down, making Ali feel nervous. At last they were told to come to the interview room and found DI Hunter and another younger detective checking the recording equipment. The younger man was introduced as DS Mason. DI Hunter smiled pleasantly enough, though when Ali tried to read the officers' body language, she concluded that they were both rather tense.

After what seemed a long time, Graham was brought in. His face was ashen, his hair dishevelled, he had a day's growth of beard and his clothes were creased. Despite what she had heard about him, Ali felt sorry for him. It was all rumour anyway. In actual fact, she knew nothing concrete at all about him.

Graham nodded to Ali and she smiled at him, she hoped encouragingly. His eyes travelled round the room and landed on Hugh, saying better than words could express: *Please get me out of here*. Ali wondered how she'd feel if she had been arrested suddenly and had to spend a night in a police cell. But, she supposed, arrest wouldn't be all that unexpected if one had carried out a serious crime. But had he?

CHAPTER 7

DI HUNTER turned on the recording equipment, introducing those in the room. He explained that Graham Spellings was there for questioning in connection with the alleged assault of Angela Cadman at The Old Lodge, Bakers Lane, Colchester. The date was given as last Tuesday. It was understood that Graham had agreed to answer some questions. DI Hunter cautioned Graham who said he understood and the questioning started.

The questions were substantially pre-prepared and went mundanely through Graham's background for some time. Ali had to restrain her normally generous sweeps of the pen in order to cram in as much as possible. At this rate, she'd have finished a pad before they'd even established what Graham had had for dinner on the day in question.

She also had to will herself to concentrate properly after a while and not keep drifting off. Graham was still stunning-looking despite being so tired and worried. In fact, it rather added to his appeal, made him look more vulnerable. Hugh, on the other hand, was leaning forward, eagle-sharp, making the occasional note of his own, his fair hair ruffled from passing his hand through it from time to time. She told herself to cut it out; she wasn't there to produce an article about the relative physical appeal of client and solicitor.

Graham was taken through his domestic situation, the separation from Petunia, and was being asked to outline the staff situation at The Old Lodge.

"So you still had your wife's horses at The Old Lodge? Do you ride yourself?"

"No."

"Could you explain why were they were still there."

"Well, firstly they weren't strictly my wife's. I'd bought them, at her request, for her to ride. She didn't know much about horses but she took to riding quite well so…" Graham shrugged.

"For the audio record, Mr Spellings has shrugged his shoulders," said DI Hunter. "Could you explain what you mean by that."

"I thought Petunia might get sick of the riding and that it was just a gimmick, like a status symbol, to keep up with the rich friends she'd started to make. Having horses and riding seems to be de riguer for her crowd." Graham paused, apparently uncertain whether another question was coming, but carried on. "As I say, I thought she might get tired of it but she seemed to want to keep it up – provided someone else groomed and fed them et cetera so..."

He went to shrug again, but obviously thought better of it. "So I thought what's the harm in it. Except, she liked a lot of night life and I wasn't sure after she left whether she'd look after them properly. So yes, initially, I wanted to keep them, but Petunia and her solicitors made such a fuss about it that I gave in and the horses were taken away and went to Pet's place. There are some stables there and a bit of land." Graham finished rather lamely.

"When was that?"

"Last Thursday."

"And Miss Cadman went with them?"

"Yes. She had to. And the part-time day staff. Someone had to look after them."

"Going back to the situation prior to last Thursday, we established earlier that Miss Cadman had accommodation in an annexe to the house. Presumably you had keys to the annexe."

"Yes, of course."

"So you could let yourself in at any time."

"Theoretically yes, but I wouldn't do that unless there was an emergency. While Angela was with us, it was her home and she was entitled to her privacy."

"Where do you keep your keys?"

"Apart from the ones I carried about with me, that is my car and my own house keys, they're kept on a peg board just inside the back door. I suppose that doesn't sound very secure but the house is a bit remote. We've never had any burglaries or any trouble with intruders or anything like that and the back door's kept locked. Sometimes. Trouble is if they were put away somewhere I'd forget where and never be able to find them," Graham said defensively, and then more defiantly, "I'm not prepared to live in a fortress."

"So what keys are kept on the board?"

"Spare house keys, spare annexe keys, garage keys, stable keys, spare car keys. I think that's it. Oh and spare keys to Mrs Allan's house."

"As you say, it's not very secure," cut in Hugh. "So it is true that anyone could have taken a key and for example copied it?"

"Yes but–"

"Thank you, Mr Spellings," said Hugh.

DI Hunter carried on.

"Please describe your movements during the evening of Tuesday 24th November."

"Well, Mrs Allan always goes to visit her sister on a Tuesday. She lives in Basildon – the sister – and Mrs Allan doesn't normally get back till late, so I always cook my own evening meal on Tuesdays. Because of the weather, Mrs Allan was going to stay overnight at her sister's. After dinner, I looked at some papers, watched a bit of telly just to relax and went to bed, er, about ten pm."

"Isn't that a bit early?"

"No, I don't think so. I generally start work about six am so I've got used to having early nights."

He's sounding a paragon of virtue so far, Ali thought. Hard working, worried about the horses, conscious of the staff's privacy. He'd sprout wings and curly golden hair soon and fly off to perform a few miracles before sitting at God's right hand. DI Hunter clearly thought so too.

"You've been separated for three months now. Have you formed any relationships with anyone else in that time?"

Graham laughed without much humour.

"Relationships. I'd be lucky to find the time for just one relationship. We're involved in a takeover at the moment and I barely have time to take a breath. This is incredibly inconvenient." He became suddenly stressed and anxious. "I hope I'll be able to leave after this?" His earnest look of appeal covered both Hugh and DI Hunter.

"All in good time," said Hunter. "So no relationships?"

"No, not unless you count a stray cat that wandered in a few weeks ago." And he crossed and re-crossed his legs and folded his arms over his chest, in a gesture of suppressed energy. Even through his shirt sleeves his pecs were pretty obvious, at least to Ali, as were his muscular forearms where the sleeves were rolled up. Everyone else was wrapped up warmly. The ambient temperature in the station she had noticed wasn't exactly tropical. Graham, however, exuded good health and vitality and looked ready to spring into action.

Again she dragged her thoughts back to the matter in hand.

DI Hunter hesitated over his notes. Ali supposed he could hardly quote the tabloids to challenge Graham's account of his private life.

"OK. So you say you went to bed at 10 pm. Did you go to Miss Cadman's annexe at any time during the evening?"

"No. Not at all."

"How can you be sure? Miss Cadman didn't make her allegations for another two days. Can you always remember exactly what you've done several days ago?"

"That evening, yes. I was supposed to go to a meeting about the takeover. But it was called off at the last minute."

"Why? Because of the weather?"

"No. The wife of one of the blokes involved went into labour early. He had to go to the hospital. So the meeting was cancelled."

"So you went into Angela's flat at other times?"

"I never visited Angela's annexe in the evenings or any other times normally. She was employed to look after the horses. She was paid well. She did it very well. She normally gave them a last feed and look-in about nine and if she was going out she did it earlier, and then looked in at them when she got back. I'd usually hear her. And if it was late Jake, my dog, would sometimes bark and wake me up. I didn't go to the annexe because I didn't need to."

"Miss Cadman says that on Tuesday evening at about 10.45 a man came into her annexe and assaulted her. What were you doing at 10.45 on Tuesday 24th November?"

"I was in bed asleep by that time. I go to sleep very quickly. I had to be up early."

"Did you hear anything?"

"No, I was asleep."

"Did your dog bark?"

"No."

"When did you wake up."

"When my alarm went at 5.15 the next morning."

"What happened after you got up?"

"I got dressed. Grabbed some breakfast and went outside with Jake so he could have a run around."

"Did you notice any footprints or tracks?"

"No, it had been snowing hard overnight."

"Did you find Angela's mobile phone anywhere?"

"Yes, it was on her doorstep. It was clear of snow because there's a small porch."

"So what did you do with it?"

"I took it into the tack room and left it on the table. I put a post-it note on it saying where I'd found it. Then I went to work. I took Jake with me because Mrs Allan wasn't going to be at home."

"So are you saying that a girl gets assaulted in the annexe to your home and you don't wake up and you don't hear anything?"

"Yes. Or at least if Angela says she was assaulted, then she must have been. She's a sensible girl. I don't think she'd make up something like that or waste police time."

"Miss Cadman is a pretty girl, wouldn't you say?"

Graham sighed, apparently exasperated. "I haven't taken any notice of her. She looks as nice as any other young girl."

"Did you know she was hoping to go into modelling?"

Graham was silent for a few seconds, then he looked from Hugh to DI Hunter and back again with a worried frown.

"What in heaven's name does that have to do with … whatever I'm being accused of doing?"

"Did you know Miss Cadman hoped to become a model?"

"I don't think so," Graham put his hand to his forehead and looked at the DI strangely. "If it's of any relevance at all, Petunia looked after the stable maids. Whatever the girl's ambitions might have been, it was nothing to do with me."

"Apart from Miss Cadman's account, there is physical and forensic evidence of an assault." DI Hunter left it there. Graham's eyes widened. "Miss Cadman … resisted. She screamed. Are you seriously saying that all that went on within literally yards of where you were sleeping and your dog was there too and you didn't hear anything?"

"I really heard nothing. Er, the walls are pretty thick. The annexe is on the ground floor at the opposite end of the house from my bedroom which is on the first floor."

"And yet you've said you heard her and your dog barked if she came home late and went to the horses."

"That was different. It was outside. Jake would hear her car and her footsteps on the concrete."

"Doesn't the dog sleep in the kitchen or somewhere that's near the annexe?"

"Actually, since Pet left, Jake's slept on my bed." Graham frowned, perhaps embarrassed. "Petunia didn't like him much. I gave him some food about nine and let him outside for a time. He didn't stay out long."

"Did you see anything unusual or anyone about when you let him out and let him in again?"

"No. Nothing."

"Did you go into the annexe between Tuesday and Thursday?"

"No."

Hugh again cut in. "But you might have."

"Yes, I might have, but I didn't."

Wrong answer, thought Ali. If he'd admitted to being in the annexe on some innocent errand, any DNA or other evidence left behind could be used later to throw doubt on his having been in the annexe on the night of the attack. Though, of course, he must've been in the annexe previously at one time or another. It was his house.

Ali chided herself to stop this analysis. They'd pick over it all later. She had to concentrate of the interview. And the DI was speaking.

"There's forensic evidence of the presence of a man in the annexe and on Angela's clothing and bed clothes. It's being analysed for DNA and if it matches your DNA, how would you explain that?"

"Well, I do own the house. I must've been in the annexe before, but I can't remember when."

Ali mentally applauded this; just what she'd been thinking. She needn't have worried.

"Are you aware if Angela had a boyfriend?"

"I wouldn't know."

"Did she ever have visitors to the annexe?"

"Well, yes, I think she did. It was her home. She could have who she wanted there within reason."

"Did she have male visitors?"

"How would I know?" Graham spread his arms in exasperation. "I didn't monitor her movements. I took almost no notice of her and what she did. Petunia looked after her when she was there and I … well … maybe I should have taken more notice after Petunia left, bearing in mind what's now happened, but I didn't think. I mean I just carried on as before paying Angela and letting her get on with the horses. Obviously if she needed anything special she came to me but she had authority to do all the basic necessary things like order the horses' food, get the vet in, arrange for the farrier to come. All that sort of thing. I didn't need to be involved. Obviously I should have taken more interest. A girl on her own in an annexe."

Graham shook his head. If it was a performance, it was a

damn good one. An appropriate level of concern wout being dramatic about it.

"Did you know Miss Cadman had a girlfriend to stay with her on Wednesday night and during the day Wednesday and Thursday?"

"No."

"Can you account for the fact that when we examined Angela's bedroom, we found a coat, believed to be your coat on the bed?"

Graham gasped. "I have no idea," he said frowning.

DI Hunter produced a bag.

"Is this your coat?"

"Well, yes. It's an old one. I haven't seen it for ages."

"Miss Cadman says it was you that entered the annexe, entered her bedroom and attacked her and tried to rape her. Why do you think she would accuse you of the attack?"

"I haven't the least idea."

"If it wasn't you who attacked Angela, Mr Spellings, then who do you think it was?"

"I haven't any idea."

"Mr Spellings, does the house have a CCTV system?"

"Yes. Normally"

"What areas does it cover?"

"The drive at the road end. Then there's two cameras at the front of the house and two at the rear. And movement sensitive lights as well."

"So why wasn't it working that Tuesday?"

"Because of the weather. The power kept going off and I was having to use a generator."

That was true, Ali thought, *at least on the Wednesday night as she'd been there.*

"But the CCTV was turned off wasn't it."

"Yes. And the lights. In fact I turned them off that Tuesday night. The generator would only work so many appliances at once. So I turned the lights and CCTV off."

"Our tech guys say the generator was powerful enough to

run the CCTV *and* the lights. So why did you turn them off?"

"Well, if I wanted to have lights on in the house, watch the TV or wash some clothes or dishes or use my PC, there wouldn't have been enough juice for the lights and CCTV as well. And I wanted to do the other things. I didn't think the surveillance cameras or security lights were that important."

"So if someone else turned up and got into Angela's flat and assaulted her, there would usually have been a recording. But that night there wasn't. Because you turned the outside lights and CCTV off. Is that right?"

"I told you it was because of the weather."

"And if it was you who went to Angela's flat and assaulted her, the CCTV would have recorded your movements wouldn't they? But you'd turned the CCTV and lights off. Did you turn them off to hide your movements that night?"

"No."

"Isn't it the case that you'd been due to go out that evening but it was called off. Mrs Allan your housekeeper was away. Your wife had left you. So you thought you'd liven up your evening by going next door and trying to have sex with your stable maid. And you turned off the lights and CCTV in case anything came of it later. Isn't that what really happened?"

"No," said Graham with emphasis.

"Mr Spellings, did you attack Angela Cadman on Tuesday 24th November in the annexe to your house at approximately 10.45 pm?"

"No I did not."

"Interview ends at 6.45 pm."

The recording equipment was turned off.

"Thank you for your co-operation," DI Hunter's words seemed to extend to Hugh and Ali as well. He turned to Graham. "You're free to leave." Then again to all of them: "We'll be in touch."

AFTER Graham had been processed, they all stood shivering outside on the forecourt to the station.

"Can I give you a lift?" Hugh offered Graham.

"No, that's OK. I think I'll go and stay at my sister's this weekend. She only lives up there as you know." He gestured towards Lexden Road then shook his head. "I can't stay *there* after what's happened. I'll get May to run Jake over and my things and put the cat in kennels and tell her she can have a few days off if she wants. You can get me on my mobile if you need me."

And with hunched shoulders and head down, he strode off forlornly towards the roundabout.

CHAPTER 8

SATURDAY dawned with no sign of a thaw. Ali decided to have a lie in but it didn't work. She couldn't go back to sleep for thinking about Graham's interview and wondering what would happen next. After trying to watch breakfast TV for half an hour, she got up and made a cup of tea for herself and her parents who were stunned to see her about at such an hour at the weekend. Poxy Ed could make his own tea. She could hear him whining for a cup in his room.

Normally she'd spend at least part of Saturday at home hoping for a call from Rob which mostly didn't materialise (either too much work or too bad a hangover were the usual excuses, the latter of which always seemed the more plausible). However today, Ali felt too tense to sit about pining and decided if possible to go into the office and make a start on Darren Summers's brief to counsel for his speeding hearing, though she hadn't told him yet that Hugh wasn't doing it.

Hugh sometimes went into the office on Saturdays and since she didn't have her own set of office keys, with some trepidation she dialled his mobile.

He sounded surprised to hear from her though not too unhappy about it. Yeah come on in, he said, he was in the office already .

Only 9.15 on a Saturday and he's already in the office. Hasn't he got a life? Oh shucks! I'm going in too. Better squash that thought.

The buses were running again and Ali got there easily enough. Actually it was quite a hive of activity. Mr Watts was there and Baz Trimble. Paul had turned in as well obviously wanting to impress, smarmy git. They were all dictating away furiously so Ali went off to The Privy and started her brief. She was typing it herself since she had no one to dictate to, or at least the secretaries always found a way to avoid doing her typing. It seemed to be a matter of principle with them.

Darren's case was of course rivetting, but Ali would've liked to discuss Graham's interview with Hugh. The only excuse she could think of to visit his room was to go and offer to make him a cup of coffee. Just in time, she remembered the cardinal rule: if you were a girl trying to get on *don't* offer to make the tea and coffee or you'll get lumbered with it and people won't respect you. Typing your own stuff was different. A lot of fee earners did it these days.

So she sauntered past Hugh's open door in the direction of the kitchen hoping he'd see her and come out or call her in; he didn't even look up.

Instead, she found a sulky Mr Watts in the kitchen squeezing out a tea bag with unnecessary aggression.

"Glad to see you can put in the hours for the criminal department," he said.

"Oh, but it's for the general good of the firm," Ali replied innocently.

Harrumph, he went.

"*And,*" Ali continued, "of course I'm not being paid and therefore it's only fair that I get as wide a range of experience as possible."

He must know she was teasing but, oddly, Ali found it easier to employ a bit of backchat with old Watts than she would have with any of the other partners. She knew he had teenage children so perhaps he was used to it.

"Actually I'm surprised that conveyancing isn't on the way out as a legal process. The government is still trying to widen the types of organisations that can do legal work. It may yet lead to most of it being done from call centres in India or China." It had been suggested in some quarters, though she didn't believe for a moment that it would actually come about. Nevertheless, she warmed to the theme. After all it was necessary to have a bit of fun on a cold early December Saturday morning when she had nothing better to do than go into the office. "In fact–"

She stopped because Mr Watts had turned purple and she was seriously worried she'd gone too far.

She hurried on, "But it doesn't seem very likely does it and anyway the editorials are saying that it's very unlikely that big business would want to pile into mass conveyancing since it's such a complicated process." What she didn't say was that one of the reasons it wasn't attractive was because the fees people were prepared to pay were far too low relative to the amount of work involved and that the work could only be standardized up to a point. The risks of claims were high. Cyber fraud was becoming a big problem. Lots of reasons.

Mr Watts seemed mollified, thankfully, and stomped off to his room with his tea. Ali returned to hers with her coffee and a mental promise to herself not to push Wattsey too far in future. She didn't fancy having to perform CPR and mouth-to-mouth on him any time soon – or preferably ever. She hoped he'd wait to have his coronary until after she'd left the firm.

Finishing up and printing off the brief, Ali left the letter to counsel's clerk until the Monday when she'd be able to fix up with the local chambers who would do the case. Despite Hugh having said it should be a fairly young barrister, Ali felt that it would be disrespectful to send someone wet behind the ears and less mature.

Anyway, Darren had plenty of dosh. Why not go for a middle ranking barrister at the very least. Hopefully the right person could put things over to the magistrates with style and panache so that they would deal with him as a concerned family man and pillar of the community.

She walked round and said goodbye to everyone who was in (Hugh had just grunted). She was taking her coat from the rack, when Hugh suddenly came round the corner and unexpectedly offered her a lift home, with maybe a stop off at the Pink Elephant on the way. She'd put in some decent hours this morning and deserved a reward. He was even smiling.

Ali was so surprised she agreed straight away. It would be a way, maybe, of discussing the Spellings case. And Hugh's fair hair *was* all tousled and in need of a trim.

By the time Hugh brought his car round, his mood seemed to have worn off and as usual he was entirely preoccupied. I'll have to thaw him out at the pub, Ali thought.

The Pink Elephant was quite near Ali's home, although she hadn't been there many times. She'd tried to get a job there during holidays without success. Her impression was that it was an older person's pub, but the custom was mixed that lunchtime. Hugh seemed to know a lot of people or, more to the point, they seemed to know him. There were "Hello's" and "Nice to see you's" as they threaded their way through the drinkers to a table in the corner.

People were looking at Ali curiously, their expressions clearly clocking whether Ali might be a possible romantic interest.

As they sat down with their drinks, Ali was wondering whether to bring up the subject of Graham or talk about the firm generally or try to draw Hugh out about his private life. She had to doubt whether the last of these would get anywhere.

She was saved the trouble as Hugh was already asking her what she thought about Graham. They didn't know in any detail what the prosecution's case was going to be yet, that is *if* he was charged. But if he was, what did Ali think about it?

"You mean do I think he's innocent or guilty?"

Hugh looked pained. "We don't talk about innocent or guilty. We don't *care* about innocent or guilty though you know what I think already. We just care about whether we can get him off or not. OK? So given that we don't know much yet about the prosecution case, what do you think about the thing so far?" He studied her intently, oblivious to the interested stares of the other patrons.

"Well, he's very convincing. He may well sway a jury. You would think though that the girl Angela would know whether it was Graham who attacked her or not. He may not have taken much notice of her, but you can be sure she would have taken a lot of notice of him. Rich entrepreneur, often in the press, good looking, married to a celebrity wife. If she was a good girl like he says, why would she make something up. If the DNA shows up as his, I think it'll be difficult for him to avoid a conviction. And it's bound to really, isn't it, if his coat was there?"

"I suppose so. But I've been wondering why he hasn't been charged already. As you say, Angela must have known him well. If she's a credible witness, then why wait. I got the impression yesterday that the DI wasn't sure of his ground. I think there's something there that makes them unsure." Hugh chewed his thumb nail thoughtfully, though not breaking eye contact with her..

"If he was there in the annexe," Ali reflected, "and Angela *saw* him, there couldn't be much doubt about it. Perhaps the lighting was pretty low in the annexe. Low enough for Angela not to be able to see properly who came in. Anyway she was in bed. Or at least the DI said he'd entered her bedroom. Perhaps it all happened in the dark. In which case…"

Ali took a sip of her drink, conscious of Hugh's eyes on her.

"If that's the case," she continued, "it'd only be what she could hear that would make her certain it was Graham. His voice. Presumably. Apart from the coat of course."

Hugh nodded. "I've been thinking about it and I've come up with the same conclusion. I just wanted to know what you thought."

"It'd be a lot flimsier if it was just her impression that it was Graham's voice. I think a jury would be a lot less likely to convict him with that. Unless the DNA stacks up against him. Like he said, he must've been in the place before, but not on that bed and those sheets." She sighed. "It doesn't look that good for him. But I know you'll do your best. I'll do a bit of digging around if you want."

"Like what?" Hugh was obviously alarmed.

"I don't know. His background. Her background. Something might turn up."

"I don't think that's a good idea. We're not private detectives. This isn't a TV legal drama. In fact, actually, I'd have to forbid it. It's not at all professional. If we *do* do it, we'll get a professional enquiry firm involved."

"No. All right. Of course I won't. It was a silly idea."

"Good." Hugh relaxed. "Anyway drink up. I'll get you

home."

This was disappointing. They'd only just got here. The dolled-up middle-aged women in the pub could hardly contain their interest as Hugh and Ali walked to the door.

"I hope we'll see you at the golf Christmas dinner," one called out to Hugh as they passed, with a meaningful look at Ali as well.

"Yeah. I'll definitely try to make it Trish." Hugh quickened his pace.

"God. They're like vultures," he said as soon as they were outside. It was the nearest she'd seen him to flustered and over something so pathetic. "They remind me of my mother. Always trying to worm their way into my brain. It's horrible." He shivered and frowned.

Ali however laughed. "That's what mothers do. Mine certainly does. Still, I'm sure with your tactical skills, you could outwit any over-enthusiastic parent. Not to mention a walking advert how to dress not to impress and how not to try and surgically improve one's appearance."

Hugh laughed too and shook his head. "Yes, well. Trish is very nice actually, just a bit desperate. Come on."

CHAPTER 9

ALI and Sam had decided to have a mid-week girls' night out and to start at six o' clock straight after work without going home. Sam and her husband weren't going out anywhere so he could hardly refuse to look after the children that evening.

As usual they went to the Sod 'n' Shovel. It wasn't very full when they arrived but it would liven up later. At six, a few business people went there to prop up the bar before going home.

They bought their drinks and sat fairly near the door.

"So how's it going with Rob?"

"How isn't it going," sighed Ali.

"What d'you mean?"

"Well, I can never get hold of him. Ever. He doesn't reply to my emails or texts even. I mean, when I was at university, I was like that with my mum. Now I know how she must've felt. I don't even think I'll see him over Christmas!"

"Baz sometimes organises a bit off a bash later in the New Year. Maybe you could persuade him to come up for that. There'll be a lot of influential people there, businessmen who might be interested in someone with his qualifications or talents."

"Yeah maybe. Actually that's a good idea. When is it? I'll feed him a line about an entrepreneur who's looking for a budding management accountant. Maybe he'll take the bait."

A familiar voice butted in.

"Well, if you were the bait, I'd be caught hook, line and sinker." And Darren sat down at their table. He was his usual cocky self. The comment was addressed to Sam. It was quite clear to Ali that she wasn't the target.

"Aren't you going to introduce us?"

This *was* addressed to Ali, and she visibly wilted.

"Hmm. This is Samantha. She works with Baz. Sam, this is Darren Summers. The, er, brains behind Summer Homes."

Sam seemed impressed. She knew of him of course, Sam

said, but it was a pleasure to meet him at last. Oh God no, thought Ali. She'd better do something.

"We're dealing with Darren's speeding case. It's coming up next week isn't it, Darren? How does Sharon feel about you possibly losing your licence? You won't be able to run her and the kids around then will you?"

"So long as she gets her designer dress allowance, she's not bothered," said Darren airily, grinning at Sam.

Sam was smiling back. Ali wondered if it was an act but it looked pretty genuine. Looking at Darren's cheerful face, she could see he was fairly attractive in a laddish sort of way. Not having met Sam's husband yet, perhaps, Darren was Sam's type. There was no accounting for tastes.

"Actually, if the worst happens, I might have to take a bachelor pad in Colchester. Very inconvenient and all that. But one has to make sacrifices for business." Darren showed a set of gleaming white teeth Ali was sure couldn't be natural. Sam was unfortunately lapping it up. If eye contact was anything to go by, they were in bed with each other already.

Ali rolled her eyes and muttered that she'd go and get another drink for them. Darren didn't want anything. He had to be off in a minute and didn't want to add being over the limit to his sins. What Ali had come to think of as his characteristic leer implied there was a long list of them.

Ali stayed at the bar as long as possible hoping that Darren would have left by the time she got back. When she couldn't wait any longer, she wove her way over to the table. The pub-cum-nightclub was beginning to fill up. She was glad to see Darren standing up.

"So, um, are you both coming to Summers' Christmas party in a couple of weeks? It'll be a wild night you can be sure!"

"We'll see–" Ali began.

"That sounds great. We'll make it a date. It's going straight in my diary," Sam said.

Darren gave a gallant salute. "Look forward to seeing you ladies then." And he was out of the door.

"Gee thanks! I was hoping to avoid the grope of the century

actually. I've heard about their do's. I thought Pattersons were personae non gratae, if my Latin serves me correctly, for refusing to pay referral fees."

"Well, he obviously recognised qualities other legal firms can't provide," said Sam archly, getting out her compact and touching up her lipstick and eye makeup.

"Seriously Sam. You've got two lovely children."

"They may've looked lovely when my mum brought them to the office but really they're little horrors."

"*And* a wonderful husband who loves you…" Here Ali was fishing a little, floundering as it turned out.

Sam sighed and looked away. She leaned her chin on her hand and peered at Ali.

"It's all right for you. Young and fancy-free. After a few years of marriage things … kind of pall. You just think there must be more than this. I got married too young. I'd advise you not to do the same."

"But that's awful. You don't want to dump your marriage just because you're bored do you? What if a second marriage got boring. And a third. And a–"

"Yeah. OK, I get the message. But it's not just boredom you know. Den is, well, he's not very nice sometimes."

"Sorry?"

"He can get a bit aggressive."

"You don't mean he's violent?" said Ali, appalled.

"No. no," Sam hurriedly backtracked. "He just … I think for some reason he thinks I'm better than him and … I could have had a better career and … well he resents it."

"What does he do?" Ali was confused. "How does this resentment manifest itself if not in actual violence?"

"Well. He'll push past me. Bang doors. Slam out of the house." Sam swallowed.

"So what brings this on then?"

"If he's had a few drinks. It doesn't take much then. I forget to agree with him all the time. He thinks he's being got at and … Boom," Sam raised her arms, "up he goes. Just like that. There's nothing I can do then but shut up completely. Luckily the kids are usually in bed by the time these episodes happen."

"Oh." Ali was shocked and didn't know what to say.

"Look, all I'm saying is, if wotsisname isn't that keen, honestly try and look at it as a happy escape. Anyway, I want to forget my marital situation for one night. C'mon. Let's play LLI." It stood for 'lewd legal innuendo', a fairly unsubtle game they with which they amused themselves sometimes.

"Well, OK," said Ali, "let's start with Hugh. He runs rings round the opposition. He's really good on his feet you know."

"I wonder what he's like on his back then!" mused Sam, "Perhaps you can start your own investigation into that subject."

Ali tried to look po-faced and failed.

"Well, if I can ever give him my endorsement, you'll be the first to know!"

"Yes. You'll have to issue a memorandum of satisfaction."

Ali giggled. "Hmm. I'll be the judge of that. I'll have to collect a sufficiently large body of evidence. *And* I'd have to see his *bona fides* first."

"Just so long as you don't get caught *in flagrante*. If things get really desperate, you'll have to issue a writ of *habeus corpus*."

"Well, if I just have to have that body, I'll have to find a way of getting access to it."

"Just so long as he doesn't effect egress too early on…"

And they both fell about and dissolved into paroxysms of hopeless laughter.

Suddenly there was a cough from behind. Both girls straightened up quickly as Hugh came round and sat down where Darren had been sitting fifteen minutes earlier. Ali wondered how much he'd heard. He gave no indication. He looked around, then, ignoring Sam, he told Ali that the police were going to charge Graham in the morning. The DNA results were back and there was a match with Graham's DNA. Plus DNA from another unknown male. And there was other forensic evidence such as fibres from his clothing including dog hairs.

Ali didn't like to ask but couldn't help it.

"Is it alleged he actually tried to rape her?"

"Well, the charge is going to be just sexual assault, which of course is bad enough. There isn't enough forensic evidence for attempted rape. She says the man was distracted or disturbed by something and left before anything serious could happen. She doesn't know what disturbed him. It was pitch black in the annexe because he'd switched the trip switch off. She says she knew it was him by his voice. And now there's the forensic evidence."

Sam was riveted by this information and Hugh seemed to notice her suddenly and said quickly to Ali:

"I'll need you to come to the station tomorrow and take notes again. And at the hearing after he's charged when we'll ask for bail. Be in the office early. OK?"

"Yes, of course." And Hugh got up and started to leave.

"He will get it won't he? Bail, I mean."

"Yeah. It should be a formality. He's not likely to do a runner is he? And it's not as serious a charge as it might be." And he was gone.

"God I wish I had your job," said an envious Samantha. "I could probably even put up with married life if I could deal with exciting celebrity cases like this. All we get at our end of the office are crappy leases and rotten company takeovers and sales of newsagents' shops."

"It's not a celebrity case," chided Ali. "Don't be so dramatic. Anyway my role is minor. Taking notes isn't exactly highly skilled. In fact it's pretty tedious."

She wasn't sure why she was so tetchy. She'd been looking forward to going out with Sam but suddenly she didn't want to stay much longer, though she couldn't let Sam down.

Rescue came in an unexpected form. Without warning, a grinning face deposited itself opposite them as Darren Summers sat down and asked them what they wanted to drink. He'd had a reprieve he said. He'd returned to the office and phoned home to find that his wife had gone to visit her mum *again*. The babysitter was looking after the kids and they were already in bed. Darren was free for the evening to entertain "you lovely ladies" – looking only at Sam as he said it.

Sam readily accepted a drink. Ali still had most of hers left untouched so she declined. Darren bounced off to the bar.

"Ali you look done in. I wouldn't mind if you went home and got an early night you know," Sam said, her eyes wide and innocent.

"Thanks, you're so kind and generous."

"No, I mean it. You could catch the last bus rather than having to take a taxi later."

"What and leave you here on your tod with Leering Larry? What sort of friend do you think I am?" Ali said with mock concern.

Briefly, Sam looked worried. Then she gave Ali an unnecessarily violent nudge and giggled. Ali regarded her and surmised that she was already half cut. She wondered if she really should stay and keep an eye on Sam. But her instincts told her that she would be wasting her time and just end up playing gooseberry while they pawed each other. Sam seemed intent on debauchery and she can get on with it as far as I'm concerned, thought a resigned Ali. Anyway who am I to sit here all evening and try to protect my friend's honour? Some nineteenth century chaperone.

"But you would cover for me, wouldn't you?"

"Sorry?"

"Tell everyone you and I were together all evening."

"What lie for you? Just so that you can shag Darren? He's such a wanker!"

"Yes, but will you?"

Ali sighed. "I suppose so. I *am* tired. Or at least for some reason totally pissed off and I don't fancy staying – especially not to have to chaperone *you* all evening. You don't deserve it." She stared at Sam's exposed cleavage where she'd been wearing a scarf a few minutes earlier. "You could at least put the Brontë sisters away."

Sam took no notice.

"Anyway it might not come to shagging. Not yet. The Darrens of this world might expect a bit of girlish resistance, a respectable period of courtship. Like one or two dates at least!" and Sam was already beaming away at a self-satisfied Darren weaving his way towards them with the drinks. In fact he looked totally delighted by the turn of events. Cock-a-hoop. Like a little boy who'd got into the sweet shop.

"Well, I'll be off then." Ali stood up and, as she walked away, nodded at them; or more accurately at Darren's back as he put his arm along the top of the chair and leaned towards Sam while adding the mixer to her drink. She couldn't see Sam at all.

Suddenly, Jane Austen came to the fore. "Don't think I'm condoning this you know!"

And Ali flounced off. She could hear Darren saying "Ooh! Who sprinkled Bisto on her latte!" to Sam and they both laughed. And then Ali was out in the dark cold evening, dashing to the stop as the last bus drew to a halt.

CHAPTER 10

THEY were standing in the lobby of the court building. Graham had been charged and been bailed without difficulty. He was, he said, going to go home and face his empty house. Ali called a minder from Graham's company on her mobile to bring the car round and she and Hugh shielded Graham from the assembled press outside the court.

Cameras were flashing and microphones were poked in Graham's, Hugh's and her faces with a barrage of questions. Ali had never been in such a situation before and tried to look professional and serious at the same time as conveying the impression that this sort of thing was not an uncommon event as far as she was concerned. In fact, she found it almost mind-numbing. She didn't notice if there were any TV cameras there. No doubt she'd find out later. Hugh looked noble and above it all. Graham appeared suitably pissed off. He was, of course, used to dealing with the press.

None of them said anything and they hustled Graham into the waiting car as quickly as possible. With its engine already running, it sped off leaving the ravening hordes behind, and dropped Ali and Hugh at the office. They knew there would be more press waiting at Graham's house but Graham would have to sort that out. He had enough cover.

The rest of Ali's day was dull in comparison. Sam wasn't in and hadn't telephoned to say why. Ali tried calling her home and mobile numbers and texting her with no luck. Perhaps she and Darren had eloped together, she speculated wildly! But she heard Tammy putting Darren through to Mr Watts. Just before lunch Den, Sam's husband, phoned in and said she had a stomach upset. Sorry he forgot to call earlier. Ali wished she could go round to see her at lunchtime but it was too far away and Ali had no car, not on the money she didn't earn!

DARREN was very pensive for him. His secretary was trying to jolly him along and interest him in the arrangements for the office pre-Christmas bash without much success and so gave up in the end to go and thumb through some brochures for furniture etc for the company's new branch office.

Darren swivelled his chair and stared out of the back window. The view wasn't too bad. He'd had the rear garden, formerly a wilderness, landscaped for the staff to use at lunchtimes. He was proud of it. It had lots of seating, a summer house, some children's play equipment and a barbeque area, all covered in snow at the moment of course.

He'd even had the old small but adequate swimming pool restored. In the summer, they regularly had Sunday get-togethers for the staff of the Colchester and other offices and their families. These and other events and outings increased staff morale, especially in difficult times, created loyalty and cemented relationships.

He liked to regard himself as a hands-on, forward thinking, enlightened boss. It was partly self-congratulation but also he genuinely wanted to be friends with the staff and get to know them, put faces to names. Without the outings and so on, he'd certainly have barely any real, meaningful contact with the staff in the branches further away. He could well remember the feeling as a school-leaver in his first jobs of being constantly overlooked, never having his ideas taken seriously.

Increasingly though, he thought glumly, he seemed to be the only one at these gatherings without a spouse or family to accompany him. He wondered if the others noticed. Sharon usually didn't want to come and since he had to spend his time circulating, his kids didn't come either. Sharon was bored at these events. She just got to look after the kids she said and might as well be at home. Darren tried to tell her that the kids all had a whale of a time together while the mums and dads stood and watched and gossiped. If Sharon would just enter into the spirit of the thing she could have fun and get to know the others.

It would have helped Darren immensely to have had his wife backing him up and reporting back to him on the staff's concerns. In the informal atmosphere, they were likely to be relaxed enough to say what they thought. 'Yes' people weren't necessarily the best for the company. Sadly, Darren had no partner there to help him both enjoy these events and sound out the staff.

While Darren may have projected a laddish image, he was in fact quite conservative. He might smile and make suggestive remarks, but in fact he'd never actually strayed into a relationship with another woman. He wanted his marriage to work. He didn't want his kids to be the products of a broken marriage.

Sharon was making it so difficult though. She didn't seem pleased to see him when he got home every day. He'd try to start a conversation but she'd just grunt and shrug, the picture of disinterest. Often there was no meal ready for him. She just slopped around in old clothes and, he presumed, spent all day eating cakes and biscuits from the look of her.

He'd tried flowers, accounts with expensive clothes shops, offers of meals out and offers of long weekends away without the kids (God knew she spent enough time at her mother's – Mum could certainly be pressed into service to give Darren and Sharon a few days away together). Nothing worked. Sharon just largely ignored him. Sex was out of the question. She wouldn't even have a cuddle. It was inexplicable to Darren and very hurtful. He'd put up with her sloppiness around the house and overeating if she'd just be a companion to him. But she wouldn't.

And, horror of horrors, he had started to have the added worry that Sharon was neglecting the kids. They were always getting bruises and bumps and he'd put it down to the fact that they were, well, kids. Lately he wasn't so sure.

The night he was pulled up for speeding for example, he *had* had a call from Sharon. That much was the truth. But it wasn't about an intruder. Sharon wanted to go to her mum's *again* and didn't want to wait about for Darren to get home and couldn't be bothered to get a babysitter. She was going to go and that was that. If Darren hurried, the kids'd only be on their own a few minutes. It wouldn't kill them. Darren couldn't believe he was hearing this. So he hunted through is mobile for their regular babysitters and managed to find one who lived nearby and then legged it back to Witham.

Unfortunately, Her Majesty's Constabulary saw to it that he was held up and when he was pulled over he just said the first thing that came into his head, which was that his wife was worried about an intruder. He wasn't going to tell this arrogant know-it-all copper about his family situation. Nor did he want it aired in court and plastered all over the local press, therefore he stuck to his story about the alleged intruder.

And of course the police hadn't bothered to follow up the intruder allegation so it seemed best to stick to the story. Ali obviously thought it was a complete concoction. Well, let her.

Nonetheless Darren had never been unfaithful. But he was thinking about it.

Last night when he'd put Samantha into a taxi at midnight and taken one himself, he'd wondered if Sharon would mind him getting home so late. In fact, she'd been fast asleep and rolled over so as to face the other way when he got into bed. He'd lain there thinking about Sam and her liveliness and interest in his career and everything. He badly wanted to see her again but she was married too with children and he knew what it was likely to lead to. He'd sighed and resolved to try to speak to Sharon seriously about the marriage as soon as the opportunity arose.

He swung round in the revolving chair and looked at the desk clock. Christ it was time he got on with some chasing up. Got to keep those solicitors on their toes. He picked up the phone and asked Susie to get hold of old Watts for him.

CHAPTER 11

HUGH didn't want to discuss the case, so Ali spent most of the afternoon going through the evidence so far on her own. It was very damning. Graham's fingerprints on Angela's mobile, otherwise no fresh prints in the annexe. But hair taken from Angela's bedclothes matched Graham's DNA. And fibres from his coat on the bed as well as the coat itself.

There was DNA from another man's hair, sweat and saliva on the bed clothes, but the lab hadn't come up with a match.

Angela's statement was long and detailed and took Ali ages to go through, especially since she kept having to go over points again and highlight key parts.

Angela said that she was in bed nearly asleep. She was tired from cleaning out and exercising the horses earlier, especially as it was so cold outside. Suddenly a large form was on top of her trying to pull down the bedclothes between them. To begin with, she thought for some reason it might be Graham's dog that had somehow got into the annexe or been there from earlier on and leapt onto the bed. Then she realised it was too heavy to be a dog.

It was pitch black and she began to be frightened and asked who it was. When there was no reply she started to scream. All the time the man was trying to get into the bed with her and pull up her night shirt and pull down the knickers she'd worn to bed. He put one hand over her mouth when she started screaming. It seemed to have a glove on it. Possibly a leather glove. She tried to bite it and struggle but it didn't make much difference.

The man told her to shut up. She realised it was Graham's voice and said that she sort of froze. She was really surprised. She thought if she got him talking he might stop. She thought maybe he was drunk, but she couldn't smell alcohol.

She asked him why he was doing this but the man didn't reply. She began to think there was nothing she could do and went limp.

Suddenly he stiffened and turned away. He seemed to be listening to something. She couldn't hear anything. Abruptly the man turned her over on her front, fumbled about and she felt her hands being tied behind her back and her legs tied together. And something else was going on that she wasn't sure about.

While the man was fumbling about behind her, he said that if she told anyone what had happened or even thought about going to the police, he'd make sure she'd be dealt with so that there was no possibility of modelling. Who'd want a fashion model with a face like a burn victim? She'd better watch out. It was Graham Spellings's voice. She was sure of it.

He got off the bed and she heard him padding softly to the door and out of the annexe. She heard the door being locked from the outside.

Angela wriggled herself to the side of the bed, felt about and tried to turn on the bedside lamp. When that didn't work, she noticed there was no display from the digital clock on her bedside table and decided the electricity must be off. She couldn't remember where she'd left her mobile.

She wriggled off the bed and towards the bedroom door on the floor and out into the hall. Suddenly she was pulling against something which wouldn't give. She reasoned that her feet, as well as being tied together, were tied to something heavy so that she couldn't move any further.

She lay there for a time sobbing in the dark until she pulled herself together and made an attempt at untying her feet from the back. It turned out to be not too difficult and she realised the knots were quite loose. Soon she was free of the bonds on her feet. She managed to curl up and get her feet through her arms, bringing her arms round to her front and, using her teeth mainly, she untied the yarn around her wrists.

After that it was easier. She felt for the hall light switch but the light didn't come on. Running her hands over the walls and furniture, she made her way through the annexe to the entrance door, trying light switches as she went. Nothing. At the door, she touched the small table and she made out the shape of one of the torches left there ready for night trips to the stables in the dark. She shone it onto the fuse box near the door. The trip was down. She turned it back up and light suddenly flooded the rooms.

She checked the door to make sure it was locked. It was, but the intruder had obviously had a key therefore she dragged a heavy chest of drawers from the lounge, pushing it against the door. It took her a long time and several stops. She put some of the lights off since she felt too visible from outside and drew all the curtains.

She tried to decide what to do. She thought it had been about an hour since the man (she still found it difficult to believe it was really Graham) had left. She started to think that no one would believe her if she reported an attempted rape to the police. She still couldn't really believe it herself. She daren't go outside. Normally she wasn't afraid of the dark since she spent so much time outside at night tending to horses in all seasons. It was her job. She still couldn't find her mobile and the annexe didn't have a land line. She felt mentally frozen.

She couldn't make up her mind what to do but since the man hadn't come back, she decided that she hadn't much alternative but to try to go back to sleep and tell someone in the morning. She went into her bedroom and found a strange coat on her bed and loose rope tied to the leg of her heavy bed. That was obviously what had held her back. She left the rope where it was. She wasn't sure about anything but, at the back of her mind, she knew that if she did decide to approach the police, they would want the scene undisturbed as far as possible.

Not wanting to sleep in the bed where she'd been attacked, Angela dug out a sleeping bag and watched the TV in the lounge and eventually drifted off to sleep.

After a fitful night, she was woken by the sound of Graham's car driving away. She turned on the TV to find out what time it was. About 5.30 am. She knew Graham normally left early. She watched the TV for a while, tried to eat some breakfast and then decided she'd better get out and see to the horses. She hadn't had a lot of sleep and felt disorientated.

She washed and dressed, hunted again for her mobile, still couldn't find it and went off to the tack room. Once in there, she quickly saw her mobile on a table with a post-it note from Graham saying he'd found it next to the back door. Her head felt clearer in the cold air and she was coming round to deciding that maybe she should report the incident. She put on a pair of gloves, removed the SIM and put it in a plastic bag.

She dealt with the horses as quickly as possible. She had keys to the house in case she needed to go in when Graham wasn't there. She returned to the annexe to get her keys to the main house in order to phone out from there. She hurriedly looked up Petunia's number. All the numbers most in use were on a board next to the phone in the kitchen. Petunia was the first person she thought of calling. She knew she couldn't leave without making some provision for the horses and they were Petunia's horses as well. She got through straight away.

Barry, getting ready to go to work, answered and called Petunia. When Angela told her what had happened, Petunia had been desperate to help her and she had felt quite a lot better. She had told Petunia that she wasn't prepared to make any formal complaint to the police while she was still living at The Old Lodge. Petunia had said she would order her solicitors to put pressure on Graham to hand over the horses, which he had so far failed to do. And Angela would then go with them. It might take a few days. Could Angela wait that long? Angela had said that she couldn't leave without the horses. She felt responsible for them. She'd try and get a girlfriend to come and keep her company. Which is what she did.

Her friend was only too pleased to come and stay with her in a house owned by a couple of tabloid celebs. She didn't speak to her friend about the attack in case it put her off or worse in case she went to the press. She made the excuse to her friend that she had been spooked by a seance she'd been to and set up a couple of camp beds for them in the lounge.

She bought another mobile in which she installed her SIM.

The following day, Graham called her mobile while he was

at work and told her that he was sorry, but the horses were going to have to go to Petunia's place. If she wanted to go with them, she could. Or she could stay in the annexe. Either way he'd understand. If she went with the horses, he'd have to sort out the details of her pay et cetera later as this had happened so quickly.

She gladly left The Old Lodge with the horses on the Thursday. Petunia had been very kind. She had encouraged Angela to report the incident to the police. After getting away from The Old Lodge, she was so relieved she would have put it behind her as she wasn't hurt but Petunia persuaded her that reporting it was the right thing to do. In fact it was her duty to save any other girls from the same experience.

Petunia was so supportive. To begin with, she wanted to get another girl in to look after the horses. Angela had refused, assuring Petunia that she was all right and was more than happy to do it. She was given a bedroom with an en suite and a huge salary rise and made to feel very welcome. They, Petunia and Barry, were going to sort out some separate accommodation as soon as possible so she could be independent. For the time being, Angela had felt secure and happy where she was.

That was it.

There was also a statement from Mrs Allan, Graham's housekeeper. Hugh had been against her giving a statement to the police but Graham had made it clear that he wanted the police to be given full co-operation. So Mrs Allan had reluctantly gone to the station when asked.

She confirmed that she wasn't at home on the night of the alleged assault. She had left much earlier in the day to visit her sister as she always did on Tuesdays and stayed the night due to the weather.

She was asked some general questions, how she'd come to work for Mr Spellings and how long she'd been his housekeeper. Details of a long-standing relationship emerged. She had lived near Graham when he was a child. She was a widow with no children of her own and since Graham's mother wasn't always well, Mrs. Allan often looked after him. He was like a son to her. When he had become successful and asked her if she'd like to come and be his housekeeper, she'd jumped at the chance.

That had been five years ago. She implied that Petunia was no better than she should be and hadn't liked an almost live-in housekeeper resident in the grounds but it was the one thing Graham had insisted upon. Normally he let Petunia have her own way about everything. More fool him, her words implied.

When pressed about Graham's mother and home circumstances generally as a child, she said she wasn't willing to speak ill of the dead and thought it was irrelevant to the current case and it was left there.

No, she didn't know what Graham's movements were or were supposed to have been on the night of the incident. She wasn't his diary secretary. The electricity was off. She had none at all in her house but she made do with lamps and fires and was quite comfortable, thank you. If she had wanted anything, Graham would have seen to it.

Did Graham ever make advances to the stable girls or any other women employed, for example, as temporary cleaners or anything like that? Certainly not, said Mrs Allan. He had appeared to be very attached to Petunia and very upset when she left, goodness knew why.

Had Graham ever shown an interest in Angela, the girl who had been assaulted? None whatsoever. What did Mrs Allan think of Angela? She was a sensible, pleasant girl who did her job well and sometimes spent time in the kitchen with Mrs Allan. So if Angela said she had been assaulted by Graham, did Mrs Allan think she was telling the truth? She must have been mistaken regarding it having been Graham was the reply.

She was asked about the key situation and confirmed what Graham had said.

No, Mrs Allan hadn't noticed any signs of intrusion the next day. She hadn't seen anything of Angela before she left to move in with Petunia. Hence, she wasn't in a position to comment on whether Angela behaved any differently.

Ali also went through Graham's interview notes again and noted that he'd been born and brought up in Basildon. Hadn't Hugh said something about having grown up with Graham? Well, who would have thought it? Hugh was an Essex boy!

ALI considered what she'd read. It didn't look good for Graham. Ali wasn't sure about him herself. There were a lot of derogatory things written about him in the tabloids. It was mostly generated by 'sources close to Petunia' since their separation; and mostly unsubstantiated accounts of his philandering.

Graham had maintained a stout silence in the face of the onslaught.

Ali couldn't see why he would risk a prosecution for sexual assault. Angela had said he'd threatened her with violence and disfigurement. In the police interview DI Hunter had suggested Angela wanted to be a model so she would have been especially frightened about being disfigured. But Graham had no known associations with the underworld or the sort of thugs who'd carry out such a threat. He was a businessman and, apart from adverse publicity concerning his love life via Petunia, the only other stories about him related to his business dealings. Perhaps the strain of the separation was telling on him. But an ordinary person didn't just go and do something like that, did they?

Again, Ali considered digging further into Angela's background, then rejected it. Hugh would never allow it. So how else would they get Graham off? Hugh was a great advocate, but he wasn't a miracle worker. If Graham didn't assault Angela, the possibilities were that either someone else masqueraded as him or that it didn't happen at all and Angela had made it up and used stuff from Graham's house to ensure his DNA and fibres from his clothes were present on her bed. She had a key to the house. She could have done it.

Again, though, why? Perhaps Petunia paid her to concoct the story or offered her some other inducement such as a modelling introduction. That didn't really add up as far as Ali was concerned. Both of them would have had to be certain sort of single-minded, ruthless, very unpleasant people to do such a thing to an innocent man. And they would have risked prosecution themselves. It seemed very far-fetched.

On the other hand, girls and estranged wives had done that sort of thing over the centuries to advance their causes. It wasn't impossible. The question was, would a jury believe Angela had made it up and, more than that, had manufactured the evidence. Ali thought she'd have to get Hugh to agree to some sort of investigation into her background.

The other alternative was someone else masquerading as Graham. The question was, who and why? Perhaps Graham could supply some leads in that respect.

Graham had the resources so they ought to be getting a good firm of investigators onto the case. In a determined frame of mind, Ali marched off to Hugh's room.

HUGH was on his private line. He looked faintly irritated when Ali stayed there and sat down, and he turned to face the window. He seemed to be having a bit of a set-to with someone. Sounded like perhaps a female who was being too pushy. Hard to tell, though whoever was the caller was certainly getting the brush-off in Hugh's aloof restrained manner. Ali stood up and had started to leave the room when Hugh slammed the phone down.

"What is it?" he said shortly.

She told him what she thought about the Spellings case. He rubbed his eyes and said, actually fairly kindly, that he'd already discussed it with Graham and some investigators had already been appointed.

So she asked what Hugh thought about May's statement. If she was called, what she said about Graham's mother suggested that she wasn't a good mother. It could make a jury think that Graham might have a grudge against women and strengthen the prosecution's case.

"Well, I'm not going to call her, and if the prosecution do so and start up some psycho-babble argument, I'll just have to nip it in the bud."

"But once it's out it's out, isn't it?"

"Maybe we'll take some preliminary point about it. At the moment, we need to wait and see if they want to use her statement first or call her."

"You must know her pretty well yourself. You know, having grown up with Graham."

"Yes. She's a very dear old thing. She's devoted to Graham and he'd do anything for her." He looked out of the window. "Without her, his childhood would have been appalling. She and my own parents protected him from a series of unsuitable stepfathers." He looked back at her. "And that's strictly confidential. And I mean within these four walls. Please don't even tell anyone within the firm. Not even your bosom pal Samantha. I shouldn't really have said anything about him, but I trust you, Ali."

"Of course. What about Graham's dad then?"

"No one knows who he is and that's totally confidential too."

"I was just wondering if you're not too close to the case. Maybe you should hand it over to someone else."

"Don't think I haven't raised it with Graham, but he wouldn't hear of it. And I couldn't let him down."

"But that's part of it isn't it? He may not realise what's best for him or ... what's appropriate for you. Just because a client wants a particular thing, doesn't mean we have to go along with it if it's inappropriate."

"Ali please don't imagine I mind you questioning me. Not at all. It's good. But if it's not illegal or unprofessional, then I have to act for him if he wants me to. There's no two ways about it. Thanks for bothering though."

"Oh. Well. OK. Do you think there's anything else I can do?"

"Not for the time being. It's late. Why don't you go home."

"Yes. Fine." She felt immensely stupid. Of course he'd have matters in hand and have thought about anything relevant. She was getting overwrought with the case.

"Thanks a lot, Ali. You've been a lot of help," Hugh called after her as she left the room.

CHAPTER 12

WHEN Ali and Sam showed up at the offices of Summer Homes, they found they were not early arrivers, in fact the crush was well under way. Darren had obviously recruited the prettiest girls from his various branch offices to run around with trays of drinks and eats and the ploy was working as quite a few people were already fairly merry.

No one actually pinched anyone's bums these days. Far too risky, but there was a lot of general bonhomie in the girls' direction. Sam, having made a considerable effort with her makeup within the confines of Patterson's ladies' room and poured herself into a new strapless, sequinned dress, soon had an admiring crowd around her.

Ali was using the opportunity to pump a trainee solicitor from another local firm about how he had secured his training contract. It didn't sound too promising. The answer seemed to be a first from Cambridge, a public school background and a family with contacts in just about every field you could think of. He hadn't fancied architecture or accountancy or banking, so his father had called in favours in the legal world instead.

No, Jeremy hadn't got any suggestions how Ali might secure the treasured training contract on her own merits alone, he freely admitted. His own contract was nearly at an end and then he planned to call in more favours and get a job in London where the family had a flat he could doss in. And no, he didn't think his current firm were planning to take on any more trainees just now.

Ali looked around and wondered why Darren wasn't taking the opportunity to chat up Sam. Sam obviously thought so too as Ali noticed her glancing over at Darren from time to time. She was getting a friendly smile in return but nothing more. He didn't go over and Ali could tell Sam was disappointed, though she hid it well.

Jeremy had ditched her by this time in favour of someone

more likely to further his career rather than the other way round, therefore Ali scanned the room. She saw Tammy flirting unsuccessfully with Darren. Then her eyes alighted on Hugh who had just made an entrance. However, he ignored her and went over to old Wattsey who was happily helping himself to another drink and a portion of canapés the size of a small car.

Trouble was, not having previously been part of the legal and/or property fraternity of Colchester, Ali knew almost no one here who wasn't a member of Patterson Watts. The only other person in the room who appeared to have no one to talk to was Summer Homes's oily office boy who was standing by the phone in case anyone important called. So it was a choice between inveigling herself into Sam's group or the ignominy of lurking by the wall or going off to powder her nose. At that moment, Sam looked over, smiled and beckoned. Ali was only to pleased to be summoned.

"James here is dying to meet you," gushed Sam as soon as Ali was within groping distance. James looked innocent enough as he quaffed his punch so Ali smiled at him pleasantly and was rewarded by a lurch in the general direction of her bosom, though it was hard to tell as she realised James was at least nine parts hammered.

"Well, you two get to know each other," Sam said, as she sashayed off towards a group of girls Ali hadn't met before.

James, it turned out, was a surveyor, not quite chartered yet but getting there, he told her as he made assiduous attempts to chart the contours of her bottom without any apparent sense of what was or wasn't politically incorrect. He had a healthy country glow and white, perfect teeth that, unlike Darren's, looked totally natural. The product of generations of good living and a privileged background.

Though clearly plastered, he proved to be easy, undemanding company and Ali found herself laughing at his accounts of his tussles with planning officers and the trivialities of party wall disputes. She even silently forgave him when he started on about the shoot his family was putting on over Christmas on their estate and the riding to hounds soon after, not even considering that she might not approve of field sports – which she didn't. It just seemed too churlish to bring it up at this pre-Christmas bash when there was so much good cheer about.

Instead, she told James about her attempts to get a training contract and he said his old man knew a lot of bods in the legal business; he'd see if a word couldn't be put in for Ali who was overcome by this generosity from an almost total stranger. By now three parts cut herself, Ali grovelled her thanks, not even considering that James might not remember a word of this unexpected offer the next day.

Without Ali noticing, the room had filled up with even more people and since it was gone five, the door had been locked (late-comers were directed to the rear of the building according to a small sign on the window), the blinds and the lights had been lowered and burly blokes were bringing in large speakers and other equipment. There was going to be a disco realised Ali with unnecessary delight.

Soon enough, strobes were flashing and the latest hits and some oldies were being belted out to introductions from (Andy) Nutts About Sound.

Since James had disappeared to the loo (Ali thought he might have been going to hurl actually), Ali accepted an offer to dance from Jeremy who had realised belatedly that Ali was far more beautiful, talented and intelligent than he had noticed earlier, and they and others cavorted on the dance floor for what seemed like hours.

Taking a breather, Ali went off to try and find Sam. Perhaps she would be snogging with Darren by now in one of the typists' rooms upstairs and if so, thought Ali drunkenly, she'd tell them just what she thought of it. Which was? Christ, it was hard to recall. What did they put in that punch! In fact she saw Darren, to her surprise, in animated conversation with Wattsey and found Sam in the cloakroom re-touching her makeup.

"So how's it going?" said Ali, expecting Sam to be as high as she was.

"You tell me," came the reply. "You seem to be having a

ball!"

"Well, you could've had James to yourself," said Ali airily, "but you just had to palm him off on me. He's quite nice actually. You should try to see the good in people."

"Gee thanks," snapped Sam, shutting her compact with unnecessary aggression and flouncing out.

"Who's getting Bisto sprinkled on *her* latte now!" shouted Ali after her and dissolved into giggles.

"Good on you," said a voice from one of the loos and Ali's arch-enemy, Amanda, emerged. Ali grinned and linking arms, sisters in search of mischief, they staggered together back to the dance floor, collecting James on the way who was only too delighted to be commandeered by "two lovely ladies". He said he felt much better having had a "bit of a break".

"You must have the constitution of a horse," said Ali. James grinned and showed his large white teeth in reply. His laugh came out as a sort of bray and for some reason, Ali and Amanda thought this was hilarious and collapsed onto some ringside seats.

Without warning, a wet flannel approached in the form of Hugh. Out of the corner of her eye, Ali had clocked him just now talking to Pandora (Pandy) Simmonds, a newly qualified solicitor who did crime and family at Selwyn Ashe & Mason.

"It's rather late," said Hugh, apparently stone cold sober. "I'll be leaving soon. Would you two like a lift?"

They both said with varying degrees of incoherence that they'd prefer to stay on just the same.

"Actually, the disco's packing up and people are leaving. Hadn't you noticed?"

Regrettably, it was true. Some background music was playing on a CD player, and the same burly blokes were starting to manhandle the outsized speakers towards the back of the building and the lights were going up.

Ali and Amanda lolling on their chairs shoulder-to-shoulder looked at each other. Amanda shrugged in an exaggerated manner.

"Well. S'pose we'll have to then." Ali knew her words were

coming out slurred but couldn't do anything about it.

Hugh, smiling slightly, helped them both onto their stiletto-heeled feet and shepherded them towards the front door which was now open. The blast of icy air that hit them was refreshing rather than shocking.

"I'll call you next week after having a word with the old man," James said as Ali went past. Blimey, he'd remembered, though there was hardly going to be any of next week. They broke up Wednesday for Christmas. Broke up! Just like school. Ten whole days off. Like many solicitors' firms, they were closing down from the day before Christmas Eve through to the next working day after New Year's Day. Suddenly she realised she was going to miss going into the office for nearly two whole weeks.

Sam, too, was waiting at the door for a lift which appeared to be just arriving. She ignored Ali. As Hugh guided the girls out into the picturesque snow-covered High Street, Ali glanced back and caught sight of Darren, looking round Wattsey's ample torso, gazing after Sam. The expression on his face was ... what? Ali suddenly realised with surprise it was wistful. Not lecherous or lewd, but sad and full of unrequited longing. She wished she hadn't seen it. She really didn't want to be burdened with Darren and Sam's unresolved attraction. But somehow she felt that she was.

CHAPTER 13

THE following day, Saturday, Ali sent out more CVs and begging letters to firms who might just be prepared to offer a training contract or even some form of training or experience coupled with actual remuneration. Also, with remuneration in mind, she called some pubs and clubs in Colchester enquiring about jobs, anything, over Christmas. Amazingly, her favourite watering hole since she'd started at Pattersons, The Sod and Shovel, needed bar and waiting staff urgently and could she start that evening. When she heard the rate of pay over Christmas, she wondered why she'd put so much effort into trying to become a solicitor. She'd be better off opening a town pub. At least they could afford to *pay* their staff.

Ali agreed immediately, despite a raging hangover. She'd just have to drink loads of orange juice and dose herself up with aspirins.

She called Rob to tell him the good news. He said huffily that if she was going to be tied up all the holiday letting drunken businessmen peer down her front, there wasn't much point in him taking a break from his studies to come and spend a few days.

Ali tried to hide her disappointment. She was distracted by a female voice in the background at the other end of the line yelling something about hurrying up. Rob quickly put his hand over the mouthpiece and there was silence for about ten seconds.

"Who was that?" Ali asked, when Rob's flustered voice came back on the line.

"Just one of the others with a bedsit upstairs. Some of us are going out for a lunchtime drink."

"Oh." Ali couldn't think of much to say. Of course, he obviously had a life of his own down there in Bristol and she said, "Well, have fun."

"Yeah. And you."

This seemed somehow a bit final. Did he mean today, or the

Christmas break or, and this was the thing, the rest of her life?

"Rob, don't put the phone down yet. Er … look, we haven't seen each other since the summer. I know long distance relationships can sometimes work, but do you think this one is?"

It just came out. She'd been thinking about what Sam had said on their night out before they'd been accosted by Darren.

"I don't know. I hadn't thought about it." He paused. Ali heard a door slamming in the background at his end. The other bedsit occupant no doubt.

"Though you obviously have," continued Rob and left it there.

Here we go. Ali mentally kicked herself. After making all the running herself for months, she'd given him the perfect let-out. She was tempted to start ranting at him but found she hadn't the energy. Instead she said:

"Look, Rob, you've neglected our relationship for months. If you really want to go somewhere with it, call me by Wednesday about coming up here. I'm only doing bar work because I need the money. But you're not working. You could spare the time surely."

"Gee, thanks. So your career is so much more important than mine. Is that what you're saying?"

"Rob, you're deliberately twisting what I said. No one said your career wasn't important too. But I've got the possibility of earning a few quid over Christmas and I've got to take it because basically I'm flat broke," she ended, almost in tears.

"I'll have to see what I can sort out," said Rob non-committally.

"Well. Good. Call by Wednesday. If you don't I'll assume it's over. I'd better go now. I've got to go and have a short interview at the club."

"Yeah. Course." Rob's relief was almost palpable, even down a phone line. "Speak to you soon," he said cheerily and hung up.

Not even a Merry Christmas!

Ali put the phone down. So that was probably it

then. Nonetheless, she didn't have time to sulk. Quickly she put on some decent clothes and begged her father for a lift into town. He was only too happy to oblige. "Celia," he said, "I'm afraid I won't be able to empty and refill the dishwasher." Her mum sighed and muttered, but wished Ali good luck anyway.

SATURDAY night working behind the bar at The Sod and Shovel was quite a laugh really. A few faces from the previous night's party at Summer Homes looked familiar and, apparently also recognising her, congratulated her meaningfully on her stamina. Christ, was I that obviously drunk, thought Ali.

She'd rather been hoping she wouldn't be recognised. She wasn't sure how the firm would regard their 'associate' (as Wattsey described her to clients) working behind a bar. Well, they could go hang themselves she decided after a while. She hadn't signed any sort of exclusivity contract; or any contract at all in fact. The whole thing was completely informal and if they weren't prepared to pay her, she was a free agent. Yes, that was it, a free agent; in all respects. Rob didn't want a serious commitment either. Why should she beat herself up about it?

The other bar staff were nice. She got a break every two and a half hours and could sit in the kitchen and chat to the others on their breaks for fifteen minutes or so. There were quite a few like her who were there temporarily for the cash. In fact, between them, there was a range of talent.

There was Jessie trying to make it as an actress and, she said, because she'd been to drama school and was a professional, she shouldn't really even do any amateur dramatics to keep her hand in. The most she'd had recently was a bit part. Listening to her, Ali decided she maybe ought to count her blessings. The legal world was at least less restrictive than that.

Another high achiever with no actual job was Don, a chemistry PhD student. He'd have the doctorate soon and after that, well he might earn 20K per annum doing research if he was lucky.

Si would have liked to be a chef but couldn't find anyone to give him proper training. He hoped that by working in the S&S he'd be able to seize any opening that came up.

"Don't they just do snacks and stuff they re-heat?" asked Ali. She hoped he wouldn't be offended but it wasn't exactly haute cuisine that was served to the clientele, mostly suffering from varying degrees of inebriation. A large proportion of the food got stamped into the floor throughout the evening and must've caused a hell of a job for the cleaners in the morning.

"They're building a conservatory-cum-dining room and opening a proper restaurant soon," said Si. "So," he shrugged, "with any luck they'll get a decent chef in and need trainees."

"Ali," called Peter who was the bar manager that night, "your fifteen minutes is up and the bar's five deep. Can you come and serve again."

Later, mentally totting up what she would have earned that evening plus her share of tips, Ali realised that if paid work in the legal profession continued to elude her, and if the S&S kept her on after Christmas a couple of nights a week, and if she didn't die of exhaustion, she could probably afford to stay on at PWT for the time being. Which she was actually rather pleased about. The place had started to grow on her.

CHAPTER 14

ON MONDAY morning, Wattsey was cock-a-hoop for some reason. He called Ali into his room and, as usual, it looked like it had been turned over by a gang of burglars who had no idea what they were looking for.

Ali had come to realise that solicitors worked on the basis that out of sight meant out of mind, that is if they put a file away in the cabinet, they'd forget it needed more work doing on it or they were waiting for something to come in or whatever, and the necessary wouldn't get done. Hence, what with completed case files as well, all the fee earners' floors were always deep in files, to the extent that it was sometimes hard to get across the room without falling over them.

In fact, Wattsey dined out on the story of how the firm had once actually *been* burgled and when the police had seen his room, the constable had said: "Cor, they've given this one a right going over!" whereas in fact his room hadn't been touched!

Consequently, Ali picked her way carefully through the piles of files that were starting to tip over and sat down opposite Wattsey. Perhaps he was going to offer her a training contract. Or at least a proper job with pay and perks and whatnot.

But instead he said:

"Look sharp Ali. We've got a big job coming up. Darren Summers and his new partner bought the old leather factory and some adjoining land several years ago. At the time it seemed as though they'd develop it into industrial units, but they've decided on residential now and they're asking us to act for them. Hundreds of plots. And the factory buildings themselves to be converted into flats. It'll be very good experience for you, getting all the core documentation drafted et cetera. We'll have to have a session later about precisely what's going to be required."

Ali was thinking that if she knew anything about clients as

she'd come to know them, this new development company would want to pin them down to as low a price as possible per unit, regardless of the complications of the job.

She started to suggest that they offered an hourly rate to get the scheme going. It could take hundreds of man-hours. But Wattsey wasn't taking it in. His eyes were ringing up pound signs like a one-armed bandit and he shooed her out, saying again that they'd discuss the details later. He would be relying on her help and, again, what wonderful experience it'd be for her.

Back in The Privy, Ali found a note to ring Darren. It was his speeding case the next day. They hadn't managed to get it put back until after Christmas. She called him and tried to reassure him, told him she'd be there herself and thanked him for the bash on Friday. She'd enjoyed it, she said. Which was true.

She worked on a couple of briefs to counsel for Hugh for things he didn't want to do himself or was too busy to do.

Then she went for a lunchtime drink with Sam.

"So did you enjoy the party Friday?" said Ali, rooting about for information.

"Could have been better. Sorry I was such a grouch. I thought Darren might pay me a bit of attention but he, well he didn't ignore me, but I might as well have been just anyone."

Ali sighed. "It's probably for the best you know. Just think of the mess if you got into an affair with him. He seems quite a family man. He'd possibly lose his children and his home, not to mention the money side."

"I suppose so." Sam was silent. She shook her head. Ali sipped her drink and frowned at her friend.

Sam continued: "I'm not looking forward to Christmas. Do you know," she said, "I'd rather be pulling pints all Christmas like you than be at home walking on eggshells in case I do something to upset Den."

"Surely it's not that bad?"

"Yes it is. If he drinks. I'm dreading our family get-togethers. He'll be great while we're there and then when we're alone, he'll start. I just have to keep quiet. Anything I say'll be wrong."

"Well, I'm not working every night. Couldn't you come out with me one night at least."

"I could try to get away. OK, we'll keep in touch then."

To change the subject, Ali talked about Darren's case the next day. Sam was of course transfixed. Ali forbore to tell her about Darren's expression as he watched Sam leaving the party. It wasn't that she didn't want to help her friend out, but she couldn't be sure of her ground or the effect it might have if she said something. She could have got the wrong idea or it could all go horribly wrong. No, it was better to say nothing. So she didn't say anything.

"THE court will rise."

Ali stood up next to the young barrister Ken Warren who had put forward the plea in mitigation for Darren. Darren hadn't taken the stand. Normally in these high speeding cases, it was best for a defendant who pleaded guilty to take the oath and give evidence, but Darren hadn't wanted to. Ali wasn't sure why. He didn't seem the nervous type but, he said, he was well known in the area, he employed a lot of people, his reputation should speak for itself.

So Ken had gamely trotted out the story about the call from Sharon and Darren's mad rush to get home to his family. He'd spoken of Darren's spotless record. He'd given an account of Darren's rise from office boy to the owner of a multi-branch estate agency, his tireless work to provide employment and the best working conditions and to open new offices. There was more than a hint of further entrepreneurial activities to come and the difficulties which would be caused and the untold number of others who might suffer if Darren's means of getting about were to be restricted, though he said nothing specific about the intended development.

So that was it and the Bench was returning to hand down its sentence.

The chairman of the magistrates made a speech dwelling on

the death rate on the roads, emphasising that the court had to be seen not to condone excessive speeding.

Oh dear, here we go.

"But in view of Mr. Summers' excellent record, his huge input into the local economy and the mitigating circumstances of this case, we are not on this occasion going to order a disqualification."

Phew.

The Chairman had to have his say about any future breaches being harshly dealt with et cetera, et cetera. Then he handed out a huge fine and nine points on Darren's licence. The Chairman smiled at Darren and Ken, the clerk said a few words detailing the formalities and they were able to leave.

Outside, Ken was obviously delighted at the outcome and shook Darren's hand, nodded at Ali and then rushed off to drive back to his chambers. Ali and Darren watched him walk away. Darren was oddly subdued and unexpectedly asked Ali if she'd like a coffee. She was inclined to plead pressure of work, however Darren looked so serious that she agreed.

Oh no, she worried as they entered the nearest café on the walk back to Darren's office, I hope this isn't about Sam. What'll I say? By way of conversation as they took a table, Ali told Darren about her job at the Sod & Shovel over Christmas. Darren seemed surprised until Ali said she was only an intern at PWT. Darren frowned.

"It means I'm not paid. I just get the experience."

"Blimey the mean sods," said Darren. Ali was inclined privately to agree.

Darren brought their coffees over then, sitting opposite Ali, he looked at her earnestly and said:

"Ali you're a solicitor."

"No. No I'm not. I'm just a law–"

"Well near as dammit. You look and sound like a solicitor and I respect your opinion."

"Thanks." This didn't sound like a prelude to a discussion about Sam. Ali breathed a little more easily.

"What it is is that I'm worried about my kids. I'm worried

that Sharon's neglecting them."

And he told Ali what had really happened on the night he'd been pulled up for speeding.

Ali felt bound to say that lying to the police and putting up a bogus case in court was serious.

Darren shrugged. "Well, I can't help that. I'd do anything for my boys. They're more important than me and my standing with the law. They could suffer as much as me and Sharon by having our dirty linen aired in public. I've employed a nanny anyway so it's a bit better, but Sharon wouldn't hear of having one who lived-in, so I'm still really worried. What I wanted to ask is, if I split up with Sharon, what are my chances of getting custody of the kids? What do you think?"

"Darren, I'm really sorry. I've got very little experience of matrimonial cases at all. You'll have to come in and speak to Alison." However, she knew that Alison would only be able to give very standard advice and, even if she thought Darren would stand some chance of getting the children, if it came to a stand-up fight, it might not go in his favour. Solicitors rarely give very optimistic advice usually, not wanting to stoke up people's hopes just to bring about more disappointment later.

"Oh, God. Doing that makes it sound so formal. Like I'm definitely going to go through with this. It's a huge decision. I just don't know what to do." He looked forlornly at Ali. A good man who worked hard and just wanted a happy family life but saw it slipping away. All her previous preconceptions about him evaporated.

"I know what happens to dads when a couple split up," he said. "They sometimes never get to see the kids again."

"Darren, is it possible that Sharon might not object to your having the children. They seem to be a bit of a burden for her from what you say. You might not have to have a legal battle with her about it. She might be glad to let you take them if she knows she'll be able to see them regularly and if she isn't going to be short of money. Maybe if you broached the subject of a separation so she got used to that idea first, then you could bring in the issue of the kids."

"Maybe."

"But I shouldn't really be giving you personal advice. I'm not a counsellor. I'm not qualified to talk to you other than about the legal side of things and, as I say, I can't help much with that. Look, when I get back to the office, I'll see if I can get you an appointment with Alison soon. Are you free this afternoon?"

Darren said he was. He thanked Ali profusely for listening. They parted company and went back to their respective offices. Ali determined not to say anything about this to Sam. They'd have to get it together on their own. She was just relieved Sam was away today, having started her Christmas break early.

CHAPTER 15

APART from Darren's case, Ali rushed about doing completions for the two days before the Christmas break began. Remarkably, James phoned her on the Tuesday and invited her to a Boxing Day party at his house. No mention of her career though. Since she wasn't doing bar work Boxing Day she was able to say yes.

"Bring an overnight bag," said James artlessly.

"Right," said Ali, with an edge to her voice.

"No, I didn't mean – oh, what an oaf I am. It's just that everyone stays the night. The party goes on till the morning and then no one's in a fit state to go home."

After Ali had enquired as obliquely as she could about the mode of dress, they agreed that James would pick her up about 9 pm.

The next lunchtime, the day they broke up, the office had a little get-together and presents were handed out, paid for by the firm and suggested by the staff. Sandra arranged all this and it was apparently a long-standing tradition of the firm.

It hadn't escaped Ali's notice that members of staff had been trooping in to see Mr Watts one-by-one that morning to be told, so she found out, what bonuses they were to receive. They left with varying expressions of satisfaction or otherwise on their faces. There was no summons for Ali until last thing in the morning. When she went in, she was bowled over at being given a cheque for five hundred pounds. She gabbled her thanks and shoved it in her bag before it self-destructed.

When it came to Ali's present, she couldn't imagine what it could be. It was flat and uninteresting-looking in shape. She tore the paper off to find a plaque that said:

'THE PRIVY'

The sign had been produced using the same script Ali had used on her own hand-written sign. Ali felt like crying, it was so personal to her and obviously some thought must've gone into it. She assumed Sam had suggested it.

They all smiled at Ali. "It was Hugh's idea and he got it made specially," Alison said. You could have knocked Ali down with a feather.

"Oh. How thoughtful." Ali looked searchingly at Hugh, who acknowledged with a small bow. Something, like a tiny virtual arrow so it seemed, hit Ali just at the edge of her consciousness. She blinked. Then it glanced off and was gone.

After the present-giving was over, they all had some bubbly with sandwiches to mop it up. Sandra recorded a suitable Christmas message saying when the office was re-opening. Hugh told Ali that if she left the plaque, he'd put it on her office door over Christmas. And they all went home.

THE next day was Christmas Eve and Ali had to work at The S&S. Knackered wasn't the word for it by the end of the night.

On Christmas Day, the family went to Jan and Matt's house for Christmas lunch. They had a long lazy day and a walk before a late lunch. Afterwards, while the men cleared up and Ali's mum went to sleep during the Queen's Speech, Ali and Jan went through Jan's wardrobe for a suitable dress to wear the next day. She'd kind of started to suss that it was actually a ball she was going to, not just a regular party. She'd looked up the address on Google and it was a huge hall, and there was actually even a bit about the Boxing Day ball, a regular feature of the Christmas social calendar every year. James, it seemed, was an hereditary Honourable.

Jan possessed lots of lovely gowns she never wore since putting on an unshiftable stone after having the children. She and Ali were about the same height and Ali picked out three possibles to take home and try on again. One was low backed and flame red, another petrol blue and the third a brilliant sequinned jade gown slit up to the thigh on one side. Ali liked the flame red best.

She also selected some jewellery.

"So it's definitely over with Rob then?" said Jan.

"Looks like it. I expected I'd be upset but actually I'm quite relieved."

Jan wanted to know all about James in that case. Ali's lack of enthusiasm was disappointing.

"I don't know him really. I only met him at this office party last week. He said he'd see if his old man could help me get a training contract or some sort of job with a firm of solicitors. I never actually expected to hear from him again. He's nice enough. A bit plummy, a bit dense actually, on the surface anyway. We'll have to see."

She told Jan about the staying-the-night thing.

"Well, you never know," Jan said, "romance might blossom over the crenellations."

"Hey. If he takes me up onto the ramparts I might really start to worry. I very much doubt if there's any chance of romance. You know, they hunt and shoot and all that. It's not really my scene. All this hereditary wealth and thinking you're someone special just because of where you were born, it's all a bit sickening."

"Well, I know that's your philosophy. But we're all affected by our backgrounds. If you'd been brought up in the East End, say, you mayn't have gone off to get a law degree. I'm not saying anyone's better than anyone else, but people are bound to do the sorts of things their families do, by and large. It's not class. It's just life."

"Maybe, but I still can't see me blending in with members of the aristocracy. As far as I'm concerned it'll just be a bit of a laugh. And if I do see James again, I reckon that's all it'll be. Actually, if he starts to get remotely serious, I'll have to call it a day, contacts or no contacts in the legal world. I just don't really fancy him and I wouldn't want to hurt him."

Ali looked critically at her reflection in the red dress. Quite slim. Not short, yet not too tall. In and out in all the right places. Longish dark hair. Not too bad a face; slightly elfin.

I'll put on a bit of extra eye makeup and war paint tomorrow.

"You'll look stunning," said Jan. "You always do. You don't realise how lovely you are, little sister."

THE BALL had barely started by the time Ali and James

arrived at the Hall. James showed Ali to a room upstairs with her case. He said he'd come back in, what, twenty minutes to collect her and take her down again. Ali was relieved. The place was like a warren and she doubted she could have found her way on her own.

Back James duly came after almost exactly twenty minutes and knocked on the door. He, too, told her that she looked stunning. She'd chosen the flame red dress and jewellery to match. She didn't mind too much that he took her hand to lead her down. She was after all his date for that evening presumably, though her knowledge of the social niceties and nuances of that particular set was next to nothing. For all she knew, James would take her into the ballroom and then abandon her for the evening.

But he didn't. He introduced her to endless people including his parents and his sister and brothers who were charming though vague. There were hundreds of people there and everyone seemed to know each other and they all talked ten to the dozen about all the people they knew and what they were up to and who was going to what event. The girls were all fairly debby and the young men pretty much carbon copies of James.

Ali was relieved when the band struck up seriously and James asked her to dance. After dancing and a few more drinks, Ali loosened up and started to enjoy herself and stopped worrying about not knowing anyone. James was really sweet. He took her out onto a terrace at one point and kissed her softly and gently and Ali wondered if she might revise her previous certainty that there was nothing doing with James.

Somehow or other, as the evening wore on, both she and James got drunker and drunker and had to prop each other up on the dance floor. They were by no means the only ones and wherever they went they seemed to meet other couples staggering about not quite, but almost, legless.

James was the first to have to go to the bathroom. He recovered spectacularly quickly as he had at the Summers party. Ali didn't fare so well. When she returned from the loo, she told James she was going to have to go and lie down. He guided her up to her room and left saying he'd be back in a minute. Ali was too drunk to worry what he meant, but he came back in with a large washing up bowl and placed it strategically on the floor near her head.

"Just in case," he said cheerfully and off he went again.

After a room-spinning few minutes, she fell into a stupor.

Far too soon, she was awakened by a hammering at her door. The sun streamed through the mullioned window. She raised her head and then fell back with a blinding headache.

"'M'in," she managed to groan.

James bounced in with a cup of tea and some evil looking beverage he announced was an ace at getting rid of hangovers.

"You're missing breakfast," he said and brushed aside Ali's protestations that she'd have to change. She was still in the now-somewhat-crumpled ballgown.

"No need for that. Party's still in full swing."

Ali could only marvel at these people's constitutions and their capacity to enjoy themselves. Against expectations, she discovered that she was in fact ravenous and wolfed down an enormous full English breakfast.

"Second best hangover cure," laughed James.

Then he told her that he was going riding later and wanted to catch a bit of shut-eye beforehand,
so if she didn't mind too much, he'd take her home after breakfast. That was fine by Ali. She was working that evening and most of the rest of the week and needed to spend the day recovering, i.e. sleeping it off.

She couldn't be bothered to change out of the ballgown and therefore tottered up the drive to her house in full evening wear, clutching her overnight. Curtains twitched and her mother remarked on it and what people would think et cetera. Her dad just smiled and said he hoped she'd enjoyed herself. Five minutes later he took her a cup of tea in bed and she slept the rest of the day until she dragged herself up again to go and serve drinks to other people.

CHAPTER 16

WHILE the solicitors' firms were closed down for Christmas, Summer Homes remained open for business as usual, apart from the bank holidays.

Many of the staff had wanted to take days off over Christmas of course, so on the Tuesday morning when they re-opened, Darren was one of those manning the office, which was a change for him from the usual managerial duties nowadays, although he enjoyed it. A couple of part-timers turned up for the afternoon shift and Darren decided he'd go home midday and check up on things. He'd never done this before. He'd never previously realised it might be necessary.

And the nanny was off that week until Thursday. And then Friday too since Friday would be New Year's Day. He was finding this nanny business pretty expensive. The wages were far more than he'd ever imagined they might be and that was just for a nine-to-five, Monday-to-Friday nanny. He dreaded to think what it would cost if you actually wanted someone twenty-four-seven, which was the package kids came in.

He just hoped Sharon was coping. He had already broached the subject of separation with her after talking to Ali and Alison, and incredibly she had shrugged and said that would probably be for the best. He'd found it impossible to comprehend at first, but it was slowly starting to sink in that Sharon just didn't want to be married anymore and that maybe Ali had been right about her not wanting the children either.

And yet, what to do about it was the thing? He worked long unsocial hours. He could probably take a week or so off without the business collapsing, and of course did so to go on holiday, though that took a lot of advance planning and he was always in touch throughout.

If he had to suddenly down tools to accommodate a family emergency, that would be different. A few days at most would be all he could manage.

Darren drove home and let himself in. He could hear the TV

was on in the lounge and went in to find Perry and Larry playing by the gas fire which was on full blast.

He cuddled the boys as they ran to him offering him their toys to look at and importuning him for a game. "Where's Mum?" he asked. Upstairs, they said. So he picked them both up and carried them up with him. And found Sharon in bed asleep. He bent down to smell, but at least she didn't appear to have been drinking.

Sharon woke up slowly. Darren tried to control his temper in front of the children.

"Why weren't you downstairs with the boys? They were near the fire you know. How long have you been up here?"

"I was just having a nap," Sharon yawned as if it was the most natural thing in the world. "They don't want one after dinner anymore, but I bloody do."

"Sharon you can't leave two small children on their own like that. They could easily hurt themselves."

"Stop fussing. Perry's OK to look after them both."

"He's only six! They need their mother with them."

"I was reading them a story and I just couldn't keep my eyes open." And she yawned again.

"This can't go on you know Sharon. You know what we talked about just before Christmas."

Sharon just yawned again and turned over.

Darren took the children out of the room and downstairs. He called their regular babysitter and stayed with the kids until she arrived. Then went back upstairs to the bedroom and shut the door. He talked to Sharon for some time. She was reasonably attentive but avoided his eyes and shrugged when he asked her anything important. In particular, she raised no objections to his suggestion that he moved out with the kids and lived somewhere else for a time, so that Sharon could have some freedom. In fact her eyes lit up and she nodded.

"Right." Darren scratched the back of his neck and sat up straight. He had a lot to do in a few days.

He checked how long the babysitter could stay and told her

that Sharon wasn't well. Then jumped in the car and drove to the Colchester office. He went straight to the residential lettings department and asked to see details of reasonable fully furnished houses in Colchester currently available. There were a few possibles including, as luck would have it, a detached, modern, five-bedroomed house in a good area available for six months until the family returned to England. The previous tenants had left a couple of weeks ago and the place had been thoroughly cleaned from top to bottom. Darren looked at the photos and said he'd take it there and then.

"What, without seeing it?" said Laura in surprise.

"Have you seen it?" Darren asked her.

"Yes. It's lovely actually. I'd move in there tomorrow myself."

"Is it suitable for a family?"

"I should say so. It's got a nice enclosed back garden and cable TV and there's a primary school very nearby with a nursery section and–"

"Right I'll have it. Can you do me a favour and when you've sorted out the paperwork, could you shut up shop and pop out to – I don't know, wherever you think – and get anything we might need. Bedding, towels, some kitchen stuff. I'm moving in there with my kids. Two boys, six and three. Oh, and hopefully my mother or possibly both my mum and dad. I've got to make a few more calls. Take what you need out of the petty cash. If there's not enough I'll give you my debit card and the PIN so you can draw some more cash out. Can you meet me at the house in, say, two hours?"

Laura got cracking.

He called the agency to find out if they could supply a full-time live-in nanny at short notice and arranged someone to start next week. He cancelled the current Witham nanny who was only on a week-to-week booking. Then he called his mother and asked her if she could come and stay for a few days and told her what had happened. No question, she said.

Now for the difficult bit. Maybe. Darren went home and while Sharon looked on listlessly, he loaded the car up with what he could of the kids' clothes and toys and general paraphernalia, plus his own clothes, toiletries etc. It took less than forty-five minutes. He told Perry and Larry that he was taking them on a little holiday and to kiss Mum goodbye. They'd see her again soon and he'd come and get the rest of their stuff as soon as possible. Perry and Larry took this at face value and Sharon exhibited very little emotion. Consequently, Perry and Larry weren't traumatised or upset. It wasn't like he had to drag them away from their mother. They were excited, in fact, to be going away. Out for a McDonalds and maybe the cinema. And Grandma was coming too.

Darren wasn't stupid. He knew that seizing the initiative was the best thing. Give Sharon a few weeks or even days and she may be complaining bitterly and going to see a solicitor to try and get the children back. But now they were with him, it would be more difficult for her.

Had he done it the other way round and left the children with her and then tried to negotiate care and control of them, it would have been an uphill struggle, and proving she wasn't being a good mother might have been impossible. He had little illusion that if she really wanted to that she could pull herself together and present a picture of the perfect wronged wife and mother.

Whether it would last or not was another matter. As far as Darren was concerned, you didn't neglect your kids at all. Not even for a short time.

He had almost no time to think about his actual feelings for Sharon or regret the apparent failure of their marriage. He had to get on with the business of coping as a single dad for the time being.

That evening, after his mum had arrived and they had got the children to bed, he popped into The Sod & Shovel, where he thought Ali might be working, for a quick beer and to thank her for her suggestions which had been far more helpful than any stiff legal advice.

Ali was there looking composed and tired at the same time. Darren briefly told her about his new domestic arrangements and proffered his thanks. Ali was touched, saying she hoped it would work out. Darren could see she was busy and soon left.

THE next few days were hectic. Ali worked every night that week including New Year's Eve. One evening Hugh came in with Graham early on and they seemed in festive mood. It was admirable, in her opinion, that Hugh was standing by his friend socially as well as in a legal capacity and hadn't abandoned him. Ali served them and chatted to them. Graham bought the drinks and said bottoms up and they clinked glasses.

"Cheers mate," went Hugh in a cockney accent, "here's mud in your eye."

Blimey, they sound identical, thought Ali.

She watched them out of the corner of her eye while serving other customers and got the impression they might be talking about her. She smiled in their direction. They soon left, to go to some country club do they said. It was obviously a smart do because they were both wearing suits. They'd both looked really great. Tall, handsome, one fair-haired and blue-grey-eyed and the other dark haired and … actually she wasn't really sure what colour Graham's eyes were. Perhaps they, or either of them, would be getting off with someone this evening. For some reason the thought made Ali feel distinctly put out.

Finally on the Saturday, Ali had a day off. James had dutifully called her and asked her to go over for the shoot. Ali appreciated the effort and agreed to go though it was hardly her thing. She had to stay back with a group near the house because she simply couldn't bear to be anywhere near the action. It turned out she wasn't the only one. She got talking to Fiona, a girl who was apparently very keen on James's brother. Somehow, this girl had the impression that it was the same with her and James.

Ali didn't know what to say. She didn't want to show James up though nor did she want to create a false impression that could easily backfire if it got back to James. She didn't think James was that keen but you never knew how he'd react if he thought she was bearing a torch for him. She was therefore pleasant if non-committal until another girl in the group suddenly ran off crying.

"Oh, that's Maddie," Ali was told. "She's nuts about James but you've obviously stolen her thunder. He's not interested in her anyway. Well, not that you can tell."

"Er, does he know about Maddie?" Ali asked, not that she was at all bothered. She found these people insular and totally up their own arses. They just went on and on and on about themselves in loud foghorn voices.

"Don't know. Probably not. She hides it pretty well when he's about."

The shoot seemed to go on interminably. What did these people see in blasting poor creatures out of the sky that had been specially bred for the purpose, fed so that they hung about in a particular area and were then driven into the shooters' paths. It was hardly any form of sport at all.

Finally it ended and the 'guns' came back to the house for drinks and snacks and more rabbitting on about who was doing what with whom that they all knew and, Ali wouldn't be surprised, were distantly related to as well.

"Do they feed them after the shoots have finished?" Ali had to ask.

"Feed who?" James asked.

"The birds. The ones that survive."

"God, no. Course not."

"So what happens to them?"

"Well, they just have to fend for themselves. Like we all have to."

"Isn't that a bit irresponsible?"

"I haven't got a clue," said James, "but it's what happens and has done for centuries."

Ali decided to have a few drinks since it didn't look like there'd be the opportunity to get away any time soon. James was only too pleased to join her. He gave her a drunken tour of the house and once again they kissed under several bunches of mistletoe left hanging here and there. It wasn't horrible at all, but the earth didn't falter in its orbit, and James was obviously a gentleman who wouldn't try and take it to the next level without a bit of encouragement.

They sobered up while watching a film in the family sitting room with the family and others. Maddie looked stricken and Ali felt terribly guilty.

Several coffees later Ali was ready to be taken home and James to take her. As he dropped her off, Ali said that she'd enjoyed their dates and hoped they'd see each other in town.

"Oh, and, James, I don't know if anyone's told you, but word is that that girl Maddie is really very smitten with you." This was quite likely to put him off but since there was no future in it for her, and she thought he felt the same, she didn't want to leave it unsaid.

"You're kidding me. We've known each other since we were children."

"No. I don't know if it means anything to you. I thought I should just say."

"Well, thanks. No, I mean it. And I've enjoyed seeing you over Christmas too."

He gave a smile of brilliant white teeth and zoomed off back to the country pile.

CHAPTER 17

RETURNING to work at the end of the Christmas break was both good and bad. While Ali was pleased to get stuck into legal work again, she was also enjoying working at the S&S who had offered her bar work on Fridays and Saturdays. This was great from the financial angle, but would be exhausting on top of office work. And it meant no chance of socialising on Fridays and Saturdays.

Rob had never phoned so now she was boyfriendless and, while she didn't live for romance, it always made a nice icing on the cake of life in general. Not being able to go out on the razzle at weekends would limit the opportunities.

It was great to see all her colleagues. She and Sam hadn't got round to meeting up over the holiday and Ali got no chance to speak to her. Sam was noticeably pale and withdrawn and Ali made a mental note to get her alone at some point.

Ali started to look at the process of setting up a new housing estate. She had to familiarise herself with road-making agreements and sewer adoption agreements, planning requirements and simply the job of drawing up all the standard contracts, transfer deeds and leases, and replies to some standard enquiries that were going to be necessary. She was also preparing various indices for standard packs of information to go out to buyers' solicitors. Plans had already been drawn up and building was already starting even though the planning process wasn't finalised. How it went these days, it seemed. An environmental assessment had been carried out followed up by the necessary remediation. It was a funny word in Ali's opinion. Like a made-up word. There was tons of stuff to go through. It was likely to take weeks.

On Thursday morning Hugh spotted her at the bus stop and gave her a lift in. This didn't happen usually as he was generally much earlier.

"I know you're busy with the Leather Works development," he said to Ali, "but any chance you could do a bit of work for me this morning. Just seeing yet another drink-drive case and doing a brief. He's coming in at nine-thirty. Oh and a bit more stuff on Graham's case has come in. If you have a chance, maybe you could read it and tell me what you think."

"OK. Fine."

"Oh, and next week it's the Seaford case. I really was hoping you'd come and take notes. Do you think you can get away for it?"

"Wouldn't miss it for the world."

"Oh, good."

And then they chatted generally. Ali asked him how the country club do had gone and he replied that it was all right; just the usual thing, which told Ali nothing. So she continued:

"See any family or anything over Christmas?"

"No. They're in Australia. My sister and her husband went there several years ago and my mother couldn't stand not seeing her, especially after she had the baby. My dad was due to retire so they moved over there. I don't know if it's permanent but they seem to like it a lot."

Poor Uncle Hugh. All on his own for Christmas.

"I spent quite a bit of time over at Graham's," said Hugh. He always seemed to know what she was thinking. "We made quite a respectable Christmas lunch between us and had a few people round. I was having some stuff done on my cottage so it was rather a mess. What about you? I hope you didn't work too hard over Christmas."

"Not really. It was a bit frantic but I needed the cash."

And they were drawing into the car park, so that was the end of the conversation.

As Ali got out, Hugh's mobile sounded and he answered it. It wouldn't be polite just to march off into the office, so she waited for him outside the open car door. Hugh was saying:

"You're going to have to stop this. If you call again I won't answer or I'll just disconnect if it's you."

He listened again and then said: "Really. I don't think that's very likely do you. You know you don't – hang on..." And he leaned across to the open passenger door and told Ali this might take rather longer, he didn't mind if she went in without him. She nodded and walked off. Hugh's voice was raised but what he said was indistinct.

No doubt woman trouble again.

CHAPTER 18

ALI'S morning was spent dealing with the DUI client. The case was fairly straightforward and there was no way on earth he'd keep his licence. She used Darren's brief as a template and cribbed from it, adjusting as necessary given that Darren's case was merely speeding, not driving under the influence. She decided to brief Ken again.

As soon as she could, she went to Hugh's room and took the new stuff on Graham back to The Privy. Hugh was out. True to his word, Hugh had attached the posh new sign to the door. rom Hugh's desk.

There wasn't a lot more regarding Graham's case. A further statement had been taken from Angela to quiz her about the other unknown man's DNA and some more general information about what had happened during the day of the attack.

One sentence leapt out at Ali. Angela said that the only other visitor that day had been Hugh at about six-thirty in the evening. Ali supposed that wasn't really unexpected. They were both single and seemed to spend a lot of time together. He must have looked in on his way home from work.

Angela claimed that she hadn't had any man to visit her at the annexe in the weeks before the attack, much less gain admittance to her bedroom. The only explanation she could give for the unknown DNA was either that there was contamination from the coat or that it was there because the sheets and other washing were sent away to a laundry. Mrs. Allan wasn't expected to do all the laundry as well as clean the house and cook for Graham.

A short forensic report showed that tests on the coat were inconclusive as to whether the other DNA had come from the coat. It had been found on the coat but it might have been transferred to the coat from the bed. Indeed so might Graham's own DNA on the bed have originated from the coat.

There was information about the washing and how it was bagged up and labelled and collected by the laundry every other week and redelivered in purpose-made plastic bags.

Ali already knew that Hugh didn't plan to make anything of the unknown male DNA so far as Angela was concerned, feeling that it wouldn't help the case to try to impugn the morals of a young girl or question her credibility with nothing to back it up.

Ali wasn't sure whether it would be a realistic option to get DNA testing carried out on all the males in the probably floating probably foreign workforce of the laundry, which wasn't in any event local. Most likely not realistic, and she presumed they could refuse to take part in what would be a fishing expedition without a court order, but she'd talk to Hugh about it. Obviously the police had decided not to go down that route.

It looked as though Graham's defence would continue to allege that the alien DNA meant that someone else must have carried out the attack for reasons unknown. It might at least put doubt in the jury's minds to the extent that the case against Graham couldn't be proved beyond reasonable doubt. It wouldn't necessarily absolve Graham in the eyes of the public, but it might get him off.

SO IT was back to drafting the development documents for the rest of the afternoon.

Sam wasn't in the office, having phoned in sick. Ali tried calling and texting her and had to leave messages.

But as she was walking to the bus stop later, her mobile tinkled. It was a tearful, in fact almost hysterical Sam.

"Can you meet me at the pub Ali. I don't know what to do. Can you meet me?"

CHAPTER 19

ALI burst breathless into the Sod `n` Shovel, having run all the way. Peering around, she saw Sam huddled in a corner and hurried over. Sam didn't have a drink. She was wearing sunglasses and lifted them briefly to show Ali a large bruise on her left eye, which was rapidly swelling and closing.

Ali gasped. "What on earth's happened? Look, I'll get us both a drink then you can tell me."

Sam sobbed her way through an account of how awful Christmas had been. At first, Den was merely touchy. He drank a lot and became increasingly angry towards Sam no matter what she said. By yesterday evening, he was extremely drunk and had spent hours storming round the house, calling her a bitch over and over. She had cowered with the kids in their bedroom. Eventually, Den had gone to bed and flaked out.

He didn't go to work this morning, and Sam hadn't felt up to it either. She kept out of Den's way. But he started to drink again at lunchtime. Luckily the kids, still on their Christmas holiday, were out of the way. They were spending daytimes at the house of a friend who'd agreed to babysit until they went back to school next week.

About four in the afternoon, the ranting had started again. Sam decided it wasn't safe to stay in the house any longer. She had grabbed her bag, coat and car keys and was already halfway out of the door before Den heard and tried to stop her. In the process, he punched her in the eye. That was actually how she'd escaped, because he had to let go of her to aim the punch.

She drove to the friends' house and arranged for the children to stay the night, donning some sunglasses she kept in the car so that the children wouldn't see her eye. She told the friends' parents that on no account should they hand the children over to Den, although it wasn't likely he would come over in his present state.

"I'm supposed to collect them tomorrow morning. After

that, I just don't know what I'll do."

"We could maybe go for an injunction," said Ali.

"I don't know. I don't think I could go through that. I know what it's like. All the paperwork and the uncertainty. I'll just have to try and find somewhere to stay." A hunted, haunted, almost terrified look spread over her face at the thought of the disruption and her lack of options.

"Oh no," said Ali, noticing Darren walking in. He was bound to come over. In fact he didn't.

Sam had polished off her rum cocktail in record time.

"I need another," she said. "I'll pay."

"Don't worry. We can sort it out later."

Ali had no choice than to go to the bar. She ordered the drinks, positioning herself as far away from Darren as possible. Didn't work. Of course he smiled, saluted as was his habit, and came over to her anyway.

"How's tricks then?" he said very pleasantly and Ali smiled back. Fine, she said, and was the family settling in OK? Very well, he said. The new nanny was great and the children seemed very happy and, surprisingly, Sharon had taken the developments without a murmur. She hadn't tried to make any issues about the children and seemed to be getting on with her life now that she was a free agent again.

Ali must not have looked sufficiently interested and continually glanced over at Sam.

"Everything all right?" Darren asked and turned in Sam's direction himself. The forlorn cut of her shoulders said it all. Plus she was wearing dark glasses on a winter's day inside a pub.

"Come on. What's up?"

"I ... I don't know whether she'd want ... I'm not sure Darren..."

But he picked up his own drink, and Sam's, and marched over to their table before Ali could protest.

He sat down next to Sam who was sobbing quietly.

"Oh, Sam," he said, "what's the matter love?" He lifted up her dark glasses and gasped. "Oh no! What's happened to you?"

Sam muttered something which sounded like: "Ali'll tell you."

So Ali told him, including some background, ending that Sam didn't know where to spend the night and that Ali was about to phone her parents to see if Sam could come home with her.

"Oh, Sam," he said again, his voice breaking. "How could he?" He put his arm around her and she wept quietly into his shoulder, glasses off now, while he there-there'd her.

"Um, Sam," Darren said after a while, "I don't know if Ali's said anything, but I had to leave Sharon. And now I'm living in a house in Colchester with my sons. You're welcome to have the spare room."

Sam sat up straighter and aimed a look at Ali.

"No," she told Darren, "Ali hasn't mentioned that."

"I mean. If you want you can bring your children to mine. They're welcome to stay too. You know. As a stopgap until you get yourself sorted out."

"That's really kind. I think … actually I think I will. I'm not sure what I'll do long term but I'll sort something out."

"Long as you like, Sam. Do you think you should see a doctor. You might have concussion. Or a burst blood vessel or something."

"No, I don't want any fuss. It'll get better soon."

Ali watched the pair of them and their underlying body language. Open frank gazes into each other's eyes, knees crossed towards each other, unconscious mimicry of the other's actions. *It's going to happen*, thought Ali, *with or without my help.*

CHAPTER 20

JANUARY was pretty dull apart from the Seaford case when Ali was away for a week at the hearing with Hugh.

The drafting of documents on the Leather Works wasn't at all exciting. Preparing documents for a new development turned out to be extremely hard work though not desperately interesting, involving things rather than people. Ali visited the site a few times and marvelled at the speed of the construction work. The old Leather Works was a handsome Victorian building and the new flats within it were taking shape almost before one's eyes. They were going to be loft style apartments with high ceilings, large windows and bare brick walls. The grounds were to be landscaped into communal areas and car parks. Ali had seen the plans. Of course the grounds would be the last thing to be done.

She helped with the paperwork required to finance the development. Obviously Darren and his partner hadn't got the cash to finance the development outright. Many millions were involved. This too was not exactly boring and she had to take care, but it wasn't riveting either.

Hugh had a case on which she would have liked to spend more time, but the development was more important to the firm therefore she got stuck into it and, after the Seaford case ended, just gave Hugh a hand when she couldn't progress the development documents for some reason.

Hugh's case was a charge of an assault against a police officer. These sorts of cases came up from time to time. Someone carrying out either some innocent activity, or at the fringes of a possibly illegal activity, was man-handled and restrained by a police officer. In many cases, no offence had been committed and therefore there was no clear arrest and no caution so that effectively the person was themselves assaulted by the officer and subjected to false imprisonment.

In such a situation many people will allow themselves to be marched off to a waiting police car for a verbal dressing down, assuming that the police have the power to do that. However, a handful of people will resist. Often a tussle will then ensue, with the individual effectively forced to defend themselves and, in the process, causing some sort of injury, usually minor, to the officer.

The macho nature of the police then seemed to take over with an almost inevitable prosecution against the individual for assault, if the person wouldn't accept a bind-over, because it was 'one of our own' who'd been injured.

Maybe the hope was that the defendant would plead guilty or be frightened into accepting a bind-over later to get the case over and done with thereby breaking the defendant's spirit and making a claim or complaint against the police much less likely. Going through the full process of a defended prosecution was traumatic for most ordinary people and took a lot of courage, the case going on for months.

There would be publicity at every hearing, one's friends, relatives and colleagues would all know about it, not to mention the cost of being defended if one didn't qualify for legal aid. Furthermore, the outcome would be uncertain, because of course the police officer might actually be found, rightly or wrongly, to have been justified and acted reasonably.

Hugh's case concerned a twenty-year-old girl, Lynda Reece, who had been standing outside a night club in Colchester in the early hours of one Sunday morning having an altercation with another girl. Both of them had had quite a bit to drink. There was a totally unconnected fracas going on between some youths just along the pavement. When the police arrived principally to deal with the youths, Lynda was swearing at the other girl and telling her to piss off and stay away from her, Lynda's, boyfriend.

The argument abated after the police arrived, though Lynda still felt pretty worked up. One officer came over and said he'd heard the argument and asked politely for Lynda to come with him to his car and cool off, which she refused to do. He told her that shouting and swearing on the streets wasn't acceptable behaviour, but she still refused whereon he started to try to walk her to the car. She resisted. He gripped her arm tighter so that it hurt and Lynda, suspicious of the police and determined not to be put into a police car, went limp. On her account, her reasoning was that it would make the officer let her go. She also claimed it was an instinctive reaction to the violence apparently being used against her. To play dead.

But instead of releasing her, the officer began to drag her along the ground towards the car. She did the only thing she could to try to defend herself which was to bite the officer hard on his leg. Twice. Still, he didn't let go of her and punched her hard in the face to stop her from biting him. Then, he got her up against the side of the car, said he was arresting her for assaulting a police officer and cautioned her while applying handcuffs. The statement made by the officer later confirmed this account of what had happened.

Lynda was kept at the station overnight. The record showed that soon after arrival at the station she was examined by a doctor who considered that she might have a broken bone in her arm because her hand was so swollen. On balance, he decided there were no broken bones. This turned out to be correct. The doctor also shone a light in her eyes and looked her over for concussion and noted the bruising and swelling starting to form on her face and around one eye.

She was dealt with the next day, interviewed and given the opportunity to accept a caution. She had no convictions of any kind and wasn't prepared to have her record sullied. She didn't think she was at fault. She'd merely been having an argument with someone, no more than that, and was entitled to go about her business. The officer had assaulted her and illegally held her and she proposed to take the matter further when she had the opportunity.

She didn't get out of the police station until about four in the afternoon after being interviewed in the presence of a duty solicitor who implied it would be better for her to accept the caution and get it all over and done with and avoid being dragged through the courts for the next six months.

She refused, was charged and decided not to employ the duty solicitor. Her parents were paying for her defence. Hugh was convinced that the case would be thrown out and proposed to argue that there was no case to answer. That was if he couldn't get the prosecution to drop the charge altogether before trial and save Lynda the unpleasantness of going through a hearing.

Ali's thoughts strayed to the Reece case as she ploughed through some precedents for leases, looked at the various plans of the building and picked out the most appropriate clauses. It would all get checked by Wattsey later. Ali hoped she'd get a chance to assist with the Reece case at some point. It wouldn't come up for final hearing for another few months.

CHAPTER 21

IT TRANSPIRED that Baz *had* been planning a January bash. His wife was rich and they lived in a large house in the country where the party was to be held at the end of January. It was doubling as a Burns Night. Ali booked the Saturday night off work and visited Jan to pick out a suitable dress. A short one this time.

She recalled the conversation with Sam before Christmas. She wasn't going to be asking Rob as might have been the case previously. So presumably she would be going on her own.

Sam was inviting Darren to partner her, though their relationship was still platonic, much to Sam's disappointment. Tammy had a current young man she was taking along. Sandra was bringing her friend. Cathy and Amanda both had boyfriends who were partnering them. Lots of the others had husbands or wives to accompany them.

Oh dear. I can't ask James since he's involved with Maddie, thanks to me. I'm going to be a wallflower.

She said as much when the firm went out for a lunchtime drink on Wattsey's birthday a week before the party. "I'll take you if you like," said Paul.

"S'all right," said Hugh. "I'll be coming past your house. I'll pick you up."

And Paul couldn't really argue with that.

When the evening arrived, Ali took care getting ready. She'd found the most stunning petrol blue shoes several weeks before in the January sales and had chosen a short cocktail dress of her sister's to match. She supposed she'd better make an effort as she was going with a partner, or at least arriving with a partner.

She wasn't quite sure what the situation was. Whether it was a sort of date for the evening or just a lift from Hugh. Was she expected to stay with him all evening more or less or find her own entertainment when she got there? Oh well, since Paul had asked her, she could latch onto him if she was left on her own. Or maybe as the thing was principally to entertain the clients, they were expected to circulate.

Hugh arrived at Ali's house bang on time. Actually he arrived with Graham in Graham's car with a girl in the back who was presumably Graham's date. Ali slipped in the back next to the girl who was introduced as Tracey, someone from Graham's company.

On first arriving at Baz's home, the PWT crowd did get in a bit of a huddle, but gradually some of the corporate guests joined the group and some of the PWT people drifted away so it all became mixed up. Ali chatted to people she was introduced to and Hugh went off to talk to some business mogul Baz was keen to cultivate. There were a lot of people there. About eighty.

As an ice-breaker, Baz had organised a game that involved having the name of a famous person or character pinned to your back and then you had to ask people questions until you guessed who the person was. Paul came over and said he simply couldn't get his and had had several peculiar answers to the questions he'd asked. Ali looked; it was Bart Simpson. She wondered what hers was.

"Do I look anything like the person then?"

"Well, I supposed there might be a faint resemblance," Ali laughed.

"So which bit looks like this person?"

"The hair maybe?" Paul had spiky blond hair.

"Is it a movie star?"

"I don't think so, but I'm not sure if they've made a film of it yet. Might've been in a movie."

"So it must be someone in a TV show. Is it actually a real live person or a character then?"

"A character."

"How old is this character? Young, middle-aged, old?"

"Actually, fairly young I suppose."

"A child?"

"Yes."

"Oh great! Oddly, I don't as a rule often watch children's TV."

Ali didn't say anything.

"So perhaps it's not a child's programme. Do adults watch it?"

"Yes they do."

Paul frowned and said he was giving up for the time being. He bent to one side and looked at Ali's label.

"Oh. Sweet. I can see the resemblance." He looked at her appreciatively. "Oops. I'd better go. I promised Baz I'd help with the Haggi. Isn't that the plural of Haggis?" And he laughed and hurried away.

Ali decided she should be mingling and she walked over to Graham and Tracey. Graham was a client after all.

"Here she comes," said Graham, "the girl who walks on hallowed ground."

Ali wondered what he meant. Presumably he was talking about her celebrity. They examined each other's labels. Graham was Elvis Presley and Tracey was Miss Moneypenny. Quite a good one for Tracey actually, especially since Baz can't have known much about her. She looked the efficient PA type. They started trying to guess their celebrity names. Graham guessed his first.

"Pity I can't sing."

"Looking like a young elvis presley is enough, surely," said Tracey. "I think I can guess mine too."

She told them what she thought and she was right, but Ali just couldn't fathom hers.

"Athena?"

"No, not that."

"Er, Aphrodite? Persephone? Am I close?"

"No. I don't see the connection," said Graham.

"Well. Hallowed ground you said. I thought it might be a goddess."

"Oh, forget that. It was misleading."

"Oh well then. Is it … someone out of EastEnders or Coronation Street? Because if it is I'll never get it. I never watch them."

No, it wasn't. Yes, she was an actress but didn't do much acting. She was famous for being famous.

"Not Victoria Beckham? I'm not *that* thin! Oh, but she wasn't an actress of course." No it wasn't.

"Oh no. Not Katie Price!"

"No." Graham beckoned Hugh over. "Ali can't get her celebrity. You'll have to help."

"Well, I haven't got mine yet." Ali looked at his back. It was Mr. Spock. Unfortunately, she burst out laughing.

"Well, thanks a lot," he smiled.

Just then, a single, long, discordant note rent the air. Baz and Paul walked in slowly bearing an enormous tray with a huge steaming haggis, followed by a piper in full regalia. They placed the haggis reverently on a central table.

Everyone hushed and had their glasses charged with whisky. With a faltering Scottish-cum-Essex accent, Baz addressed the haggis with the tim'rous beastie poem after which glasses were raised and the shots downed in one. Ali, not a spirit drinker, found herself leaning on Hugh for support. She screwed up her face and shook her head.

"That was awful!"

"Come on. Let's get something to eat," he said and they went over to the buffet of haggis, neeps and tatties.

While they were eating, Ali sat with Tracey. Graham and Hugh sat nearby. Ali was dying to find out whether Tracey was the new girlfriend or what. She could hardly ask outright, and didn't think she could bring up the outstanding charge against him or his divorce. Instead she asked how long Tracey had worked for Graham.

"A few years. He's a really great boss. My husband works away a lot so I need to be doing something. It was really difficult to get a job when the kids started school, but Graham was willing to give me a chance."

Silly me, thought Ali. I'd got it so fixed in my mind that she was the new squeeze, I completely forgot to look and see if she was wearing a wedding ring.

Tracey went on: "Oh, you thought– No, it's not like that at all. Strictly business. I was only invited at the last moment. Graham was going to come along with Hugh but then Hugh wanted to bring someone, so Graham invited me to make up numbers. Er, I assumed the someone must be you."

"Oh no. No." Ali assured her. "It's not like that with Hugh and me either. He was just giving me a lift. That's all."

"Oh." Tracey eyed Ali rather doubtful, then shrugged and asked her about her job and career, and talked about her own job, children, husband. They both served themselves trifle, after which Ali excused herself and went off to the loo. While in there, she heard a Scottish band tuning up. That's right. Someone had said something about a ceilidh. She hoped it would be on a hard floor not carpet. In her high heels, a carpet would probably end in disaster for her.

As she re-entered the party room, she found Paul searching for her. "Come and make up an eight."

He took her into what he said was normally the large dining room. It had been cleared specially for the dance. She cast about for Hugh but he was already holding hands in another ring of eight people.

The caller was pretty good and Ali didn't manage to sabotage the dance. She even mastered stripping the willow without incident. After the first dance, she took her shoes off. She'd never last the evening otherwise.

By and by the groups became mixed up. Ali ended up with several different partners which seemed to be the object of the dances that had been chosen. Wattsey stood on her toes several times and a German businessman told her that he was a great fan of 'the English turnips' while staring pointedly at her elevated bosom protruding from the top of her cocktail dress. She ditched him as soon as she could.

Between dances, she gazed around again. Hugh was holding hands with his then partner, a pretty woman about his own age, and chatting to her in a friendly manner. He had his jacket off, his tie loosened and had rolled up his shirt sleeves. He could look quite charming sometimes. Actually, more than charming.

Sam had somehow contrived to stay with Darren and was looking up at him adoringly. Graham was partnering Amanda who was making the most of the opportunity to impress him with her wit and charisma, boyfriend forgotten for the moment. Ali's current partner she didn't know at all and tried to make general conversation with him. He offered the minimum response so she gave up. She looked over at Hugh again and, at the same time, he turned and looked at her. They both smiled faintly, then the dancing started again.

Ali didn't get to partner Hugh at all, but he came over while she was putting her shoes on and took her hand for Auld Lang Syne at the end of the evening. Afterwards, there was a last dance, a waltz.

"OK with that?" Hugh asked.

"More or less." She'd learned the basic steps at school. It was just one-two-three wasn't it?

"Well, follow my feet." And he put his arm round her waist and took her free hand and they made a passable turn or two round the crowded floor.

"You know, you're much prettier than your celebrity," he said at one point. Ali looked up at him in surprise. It wasn't at all the kind of thing she expected him to say. His eyes are beautiful, she thought. He had those lovely low straight eyebrows. To cover the moment, she said: "Well, you're much nicer than yours. Do you know who it is yet?"

"Yes," he said dryly. "Baz and Victor gave me some very obvious clues during the meal and then had a bloody good laugh. Do you know who yours is?"

"Not yet. I'd forgotten all about it."

Hugh let go of her hand and put both his arms round her back and fiddled with her label. It brought him much closer to her than the dance had done and Ali had to struggle to maintain her composure.

It must be the effect of being so close to a man after all this time.

She could feel the blood rushing to her extremities and rising to her cheeks. She hoped he hadn't felt her hand involuntarily squeeze his shoulder hard or felt her breathing quicken against his face as he bent over her to see what he was doing. What would he think of her? She turned her head quickly to face the other way.

He stepped back and handed her the label. 'Liz Hurley' it said.

"Oh. Could have been worse."

"Much worse," and his eyes met hers again. She had to look away quickly and find something mundane to say.

"Er, Hugh. If you want, I'll go into the office tomorrow and do some research on the Reece case." She'd said the first thing that had come into her head.

"Oh. Are you sure? You don't need to give up a Sunday. And how'll you get there?"

"It's all right. I'll cycle. I could do with the exercise and I'm so bogged down with this development, I'll enjoy doing something different."

"Well fine. That's really nice of you."

Then it was time to go. Ali piled into the back of Graham's car with Tracey and it wasn't long before she was being dropped off.

"See you then," she said and went in.

CHAPTER 22

ALI woke up early the next day to avoid seeing her mum, who was bound to fuss about Ali going into the office to work on a Sunday. She made sandwiches and filled a bottle of water, left a note and then set off. She'd been given an office key after Christmas.

After locking the door, she started up her PC. She could have done this at home really, but wouldn't have been able to stick at it and concentrate. There would have been too many distractions and she needed to be somewhere quiet. And the office was certainly quiet this Sunday following the party.

She went through the All England Law Reports and Halsbury's Laws of England online first for cases and narratives about detention without formal arrest, false imprisonment, trespass to the person and malicious prosecution. Then she looked at periodicals. She checked works on tort for anything up to date.

She printed off cases of interest.

She looked at authoritative works on the liability of public authorities and misfeasance in public office, assault, false imprisonment, malicious prosecution.

After eating her sandwiches, she made long lists and copious notes about cases and promising further reading. She decided she'd have to do more research another time.

She was thinking of packing up when her mobile started to vibrate in her pocket. She answered and it was Hugh checking whether she was still there and if so, as it would be getting dark soon, would she like a lift home. He was already in Colchester for something, so he said, and could be there in a few minutes and put her bike in the back of his car unless she'd walked in.

Ali wasn't sure. She felt uncomfortable about the previous evening and if he'd texted instead of calling she'd probably have made an excuse. On the phone, she felt she couldn't directly refuse so they agreed he'd text her when he was at the

116

car park.

Ali put all her notes and photocopies in order and, leaving them on her desk, she made her way out to the car park. Hugh was just turning in when she came out of the back entrance. She unlocked her bike and he more or less threw it into the back of his car. She quickly got into the car and slammed the door. It was freezing outside.

Hugh thanked her for doing the research and didn't say much else. She said she'd give him the notes and photocopies the next day after she'd been able to put them in better order. He merely nodded. She noticed he had a track suit and trainers on.

The silence was uncomfortable, so she said: "Good night last night."

"Yeah. Glad you enjoyed it. Actually do you fancy a hair of the dog." He nodded towards a pub that was coming up.

"Oh, well. OK. So long as it's not whisky. I can't stand the stuff." And she didn't want to end up shaking her head into his upper arm and grabbing as shed' done the previous evening.

She asked for a Crabbies ginger beer and Hugh had an orange juice. Ali looked askance at his drink and he said he'd gone back to Graham's after they'd dropped Tracey off. They'd had a bit of a session and he ended up staying the night. "I don't drink much normally. Oh God!" He rubbed his eyes. She realised now that he did look fairly fragile.

"I feel awful," he said. "I tried to go to the gym but it was no good. That's where I rang you from."

His eyelids were drooping and he looked as though he might fall asleep any second. He put his face in his hands.

"Er, do you think you should go home and go to bed. I always find nothing works but sleeping it off."

He parted two fingers and peered at her through the gap. He took a breath as though he was going to say something, but stopped and shook his head. "Yeah. Will soon."

To make conversation and hopefully make him laugh, Ali told him about 'the English turnips'. He did laugh, then said she needed looking after. "Sorry. That's sexist. I shouldn't have said that. It's just the state I'm in at the moment." And he lapsed into silent contemplation again.

"Thanks for the lift last night," Ali was having trouble finding anything to say. She couldn't get out of her mind what had happened last night when he put his arms round her to take her label off and the unexpected effect it had had on her. Though Hugh was hung over, he still looked devastating. The vulnerable look suited him.

She dug her nails into her palms and told herself severely to stop it. He was her boss and had never shown the slightest interest in her and she hadn't thought about him in any other context either. It was just that she was overwrought from lack of male companionship. This was no good. If she started fantasising about the first male that came anywhere near her, who knew what a fool she'd make of herself.

But Hugh was starting to say something. He was resting his chin on one hand and was looking at her over the hand in a rather maudlin way. He sniffed. "Ali, would you like to … do you want…"

"Yes?"

"Do you want … me to take you home now?"

"Yeah. Fine."

"Come on then." And he levered himself up and she followed him out. In the car park, she put her hand on his arm and asked him with concern: "Are you sure you're OK to drive, Hugh?"

"Yeah. Don't worry." And he patted her hand with his other hand and left it there. All sorts of messages seemed to be coming from the hand to Ali's overactive imagination and she started to feel … the only word for it was aroused, she had to admit to herself. Like last night.

She snatched her hand away and jumped in the passenger seat. Hugh climbed in and drove off competently enough and soon they were at her house.

They both got out and he helped her lift her bike out of the back. She looked at him and started to move to put her hand on his arm again. She changed it quickly to putting her hair behind her ear. "You will be OK won't you?"

"Sure I will. Thanks for worrying."

And off he went.

LATER, Ali checked her emails and opened a round robin from Paul. He'd been prowling around the night before taking photos and he had put them up for everyone to see. Some of them had cheeky little captions. Mainly they went chronologically through the evening but the first one was a picture of the large haggis with several little ones in a row behind it duckling fashion. The caption was: *Och, when you said you were going to grease my pan and give me a roasting, I didna think you meant that!*

Ali wondered if that set the tone for all of them.

There was one of Wattsey and wife. She was rubbing her feet. He was obviously getting a scolding and looked chastened. *The feet have it* said the caption.

The photo of Graham with Amanda determinedly getting his attention was labelled: *I could be so good for you!*

Among the unlabelled photos, was one of Hugh holding hands with the pretty woman between dances. Unexpectedly, Ali felt a bolt of unreasonable jealousy course through her and she had to tell herself for the umpteenth time to knock it off.

A hilarious photo of the German businessman leering at some woman's knockers bursting out of her dress was entitled: *Anne of Cleavage?*

Sam and Darren dancing, her head on his shoulder, was labelled: *Spring, SUMMER, Autumn, Winter.*

As she scrolled towards the final photos, she heaved a sigh of relief. The only photos of herself she'd seen so far were fairly innocuous but suddenly, bang, there on the screen was a picture of her and Hugh, his arms wrapped around her, she facing the camera, her hands round his neck and back and her head on his shoulder, eyes tight shut, lips parted, cheeks flushed. She zoomed into her face. Oh dear. She looked like she was … Oh, God, no. No. No!

The caption was: *Master and pupil!*

Luckily there were a couple of follow-ups which showed that Hugh had been removing her celebrity label and they were discussing it. Nonetheless, she was desperately embarrassed and her face burned scarlet. She could only hope most people wouldn't bother to scroll to the end or zoom in on other people's photos and would only be interested in pics of themselves. And, oh, she so hoped Hugh wouldn't see it. The email was timed late that morning, therefore he might have seen it before she met him later. Still, he hadn't said anything. So perhaps she was safe in that respect.

That night in bed, Ali had to fight off all sorts of erotic fantasies. I don't believe this, it's totally ridiculous, she told herself. But she'd had crushes on people before and that was all they were. They soon went away when nothing happened, so she told herself this would too. That is if it was a crush at all. Maybe she just needed to have sex with someone and that would sort her out.

Fat lot of opportunity for that, she thought.

CHAPTER 23

FOR A week or so after the Burns Night do and the Sunday drink, Ali kept completely out of Hugh's way. It seemed to do the trick and she stopped having lurid thoughts about having sex with him. She plonked the Reece research material on his desk when he wasn't there.

She did further research the following weekend and also put that on his desk in his absence.

When she did see Hugh, he acted no differently than normal, so she thought: *It's all your imagination, stupid.*

She decided she should do something with herself in the evenings, therefore she began calling, texting and messaging girls she'd been at school with who were still living around Colchester and got some sort of social life going again. She often saw Paul in the pubs and clubs she went to and he'd wink and come over and introduce her and her friends to his own friends.

She started to look for an activity of some sort. She quite liked painting, but only moderately. She considered amateur dramatics then rejected it as too time-consuming and too much of a commitment and you had to be really keen to want to do it.

She settled on cycling and joined a club. She had quite a good bike already. Cycling was convenient because the meetings and trips were often on Sundays which suited her schedule. When playing around on the internet, she read that cycle saddles often caused women to have decreased sexual sensation. Well, all to the good; it'd stop her having improper thoughts about the junior partner. Anyway, it would be bound to take a bit of time for significant insensitivity to kick in.

She persuaded Sam to come along with her, with the added incentive that cycling trips usually ended in pubs. She didn't tell Sam about the decreased sexual sensation. They had quite a lot of fun. Some of the guys were nice, but Sam only had eyes for Darren.

"Still no action?" asked Ali as they sipped their post-cycling drink.

"No. Nothing. But … I mean I am bothered, but on the other hand it's such a relief to be free of Den and living in a nice environment. I can wait a bit longer. Just not too much longer. Anyway. What about you? You must have someone in your sights. Surely."

"No, I'm enjoying single life and legal practice. Why should I bother?"

"Because you're bothered. I know you are."

"Well, I can't think of anyone. If you can, I'd be pleased to know about it."

"Come on, don't get stroppy. Isn't there *anyone* you've had the hots for recently?"

"No!" Ali lied.

"Ah. Raw nerve," said Sam, triumphantly.

"Look. Can you just drop it," said Ali. "I mean it."

"All right. All right." Sam put her hands up and they sat in silence until the cyclists all decided it was time to go home.

Thanks for re-opening that particular wound, thought Ali, staring at Sam's departing back.

ALI couldn't indefinitely avoid going into Hugh's room when he was there, and he wanted to talk to her about a shoplifting case. So on the Monday, she went in at his request and sat there looking rather sullen.

I bet he thinks it's the time of the month, thought Ali. Men always thought that. Couldn't be anything else, could it.

"Ali. Are you sure there's not something up?"

"No," she said through gritted teeth.

He looked at her curiously.

"Ali. This isn't like you," he smiled at her. "You know. I know I'm a partner and a bit older than you, but if there's something troubling you, you can talk to me about it."

Ali got up and walked out. As she shut the door she could see him shaking his head.

Women! he was no doubt thinking.

She took a look at the shoplifting file later and made an appointment to see the client when Hugh wasn't going to be in the office so she could use his room.

By way of a diversion, she decided to help her mother get ready for a little fund-raising show-cum-supper evening being put on by a women's group she belonged to, toraise funds for the local hospice. It was on for two nights. She even allowed herself to be talked into doing a turn during the evening. She had obtained from somewhere a very much abbreviated rather suggestive updated version of Pride and Prejudice in which the central characters ended up virtually naked. It had the potential to get the audience hanging on the edges of their seats, wondering what on earth was going to happen next, if in the right mood. She tried it out in front of her parents. Her dad laughed a lot though her mum was dubious.

"Isn't it rather rude?"

"You can't deprive them of that," said her dad. "It's hilarious."

"Do you really think so?" said Celia.

"I'm positive."

Ali sold tickets around the office. Most people wanted to come. Even Hugh. He said he'd bring along Graham. What with partners and others, she managed to sell twenty-two tickets for one of the nights and her mum was delighted.

The first night turned out to be a pretty good night. The audience were appreciative.

The second night, the PWT contingent were attending and Ali started to get nervous but by the time the show started she was ready to go. She wasn't used to standing in the limelight. In the event, she found she rather liked it. Anyway she didn't learn the lines thoroughly and had them in front of her in a book cover, therefore she didn't need to worry about forgetting them. She did all the characters' voices and accents and the more the audience responded, the better it was. She got lots of laughs and a huge round of applause when she came off.

Later she went to one of the PWT tables where Sam was sitting and had a glass of wine. Several people kissed her. Graham and Hugh came over and both kissed her on her cheek and congratulated her. When Hugh did so, she had to steel herself. She hoped no one noticed her flushed face though they didn't seem to. This has got to stop, she told herself. I can't cope with this. I'll have to find another job somewhere else. Of course, she knew she wouldn't. Not yet.

Standing in the car park later waiting for her dad to bring the car round, she had mixed feelings when Hugh came over. He said again how much he'd enjoyed the show and praised her performance. He told her that a few of them were going to go to Graham's. Did she want to come?

Ali tried to be pleasant, kicking herself for being tongue-tied.

"If you don't," Hugh said, "I might have to get very drunk again and have another terrible hangover tomorrow."

What's going on here? Is he coming onto me or what and do I want him to? Or am I imagining it because of my sex-starved state? Maybe I'm falling into the sad trap some women do of thinking any friendly man is interested in me. After all I've known Hugh a few months now. Perhaps he's just ready to be more friendly and that's it.

"I'm not sure how I'd get home afterwards."

"Well, I'll walk you home if necessary. It's not that far."

"Er. OK then. Shall I get my dad to drop me off?"

"No. Come with me." The words and his manner seemed to have a seductive quality about them.

This is just so silly, she told herself. I'm reading stuff into everything.

"I'll go and tell my dad then."

Accordingly, she ended up at Graham's house. Wattsey and wife were there, Baz and wife, Alison and her husband, and Amanda. Oh, so maybe Amanda had managed to inveigle her way into Graham's affections. Actually, it didn't look much like it. He was clearly trying to keep out of her way.

"She insisted on coming," Hugh whispered to Ali in the kitchen.

She stayed there for about an hour and a half and Hugh hung around her the whole time, though she wasn't sure if it was obvious to anyone else. And if it wasn't, why was she making something out of it inside her head. She didn't want any alcohol, so she made tea and Hugh took that rather than the beer and wine on offer.

She found his near presence incredibly affecting. He sat close by her on the sofa, their legs just touching. She couldn't look at him in case it showed on her face.

She just had to leave in the end. He fetched their coats and walked her back, as he'd said he would. For Hugh he was incredibly chatty. He went on and on about the different acts. Asked her where she'd got hers from. He'd never heard it before. She said that it was through a friend at university and it always went down well at small venues.

They stopped at her gate. And yet he didn't say goodbye. He just stood looking down at her. She tore her eyes away and said she'd better go in.

"Ali," he said, as she turned to leave.

"Yes?" she said turning back.

His eyes were so, so beautiful. "Sleep tight then."

She nodded and hurried to her door. He waited on the pavement until she was in the house. She raced upstairs to her room and squinted out of the window without turning the light on. He was walking back along the road with his shoulders hunched, hands in pockets and his head down. He turned round and looked back once.

CHAPTER 24

THE WINTER wore on into late February. Sam continued to live in Darren's house with her children and was feeling a lot better. The family jelled wonderfully and all got on well together but Sam said she was bursting for something to actually *happen* between Darren and her. Frustratingly, nothing did happen and Sam began to wonder if she'd lost her appeal.

"Well then," said Ali, "why don't you make the first move? He may be too cautious to do so. It's difficult for men. If they've misinterpreted the signals and take the plunge, well they could get into quite a bit of bother. Whereas for a girl … well, who's going to refuse? Know what I'm saying?"

Damn! I wasn't supposed to interfere.

The following Monday Sam came into the office looking as though she'd had the cream and gave Ali the thumbs up. Ali knew she'd get a blow-by-blow account later.

THE next day, in a rare departure from the normally frenetic urgent and immediate task of banging the work out come what may, Ali and Hugh were in his office reviewing some criminal files. Everything seemed back to normal with him. He was nice but rather distant and Ali was getting good at telling herself not to be so silly. Hugh advised Ali that the reviews would benefit her by giving her a better insight into the handling of criminal cases and he would value her input at the same time.

Darkness had fallen outside, but Ali was so absorbed in what they were doing that she hadn't noticed. Unconsciously, she had started to shiver and had turned pale as the heating had gone off some time ago. Eventually, even Hugh noticed and said that they could stop and try to do some more another time.

Ali was obviously disappointed and, unexpectedly, Hugh suggested taking the rest of the files back to his place and carrying on there. The next file related to an attempted murder which came up for trial in two months and Ali was really keen to examine that one in particular.

There was no one else in the office. Alison, the last to leave usually, had left already. Hugh set the alarm, locked up and they went out together to the deserted car park at the rear. As usual, his car was unlocked and Ali had to throw aside various sundry items of clothing and household effects.

They drove out along Bergholt Road towards Bures where Hugh lived somewhere about. On the way, he stopped at a convenience store and bought some sandwiches and, while he did so, Ali phoned home and said she'd be a tad late, not to bother with dinner. Some miles after the turn-off at Nayland, Hugh took a side road to the right and drove along a narrow country road. At some point it widened slightly and he parked up.

"Right, we have to walk from here," Hugh said.

Ali grabbed her bag and some of the files. Hugh took the rest and they left the car. A narrow track forked off from the road. 'Public footpath' a sign announced. No houses in sight.

Ali smiled in the moonlight. Did he live in a tent, or maybe a tree house?

"Come on then." Hugh gestured towards the footpath and, without locking the car, set out along the track. Ali trotted to keep up.

"Do you always leave your car unlocked, even out here?" she ventured.

"Well, the central locking's knackered. Anyway, nothing in it worth nicking. Even the car itself's hardly worth anything. I reckon if anyone tries to get into it, I'd rather they didn't have to smash the windows. Course I don't leave files in it. Ever."

"Well then, why don't you leave them a key too? It'd save it being hot-wired." She didn't really mean it. Hugh, however, appeared to take it at its face value and ignored any sarcasm.

"Worth considering. Except, I've only got one set and the house keys are on the same keyring," he said lightly. Then:

"As you'll have gathered, the house doesn't have a vehicular access. So it was a lot cheaper than it should have been."

He looked to their left. "I'm negotiating to purchase a strip of that field. But the farmer, never mind that he's a multi-millionaire who owns thousands of acres, all inherited, wants an arm and a leg for it. Tight bastard!"

Ali trudged behind him. I expect he'll sort it out eventually, she told herself.

No rain for a few weeks ensured that the path was dry, thank heavens. It was a bright, moonlit February night. Thankfully, she'd worn low-heeled shoes that day. They rounded a slight bend in the path. There on the left, in the moonlight, stood the prettiest cottage whose garden was bounded by a briar hedge. A picket gate was set into the hedge.

Hugh opened the gate and stood aside to let Ali pass through before him. They walked up the uneven gravel path to the front door. A traditional trellised porch framed the door, covered in dormant brown stems that would probably be covered in cascades of roses in the summer months. Ali's imagination was running riot, filling the garden with hollyhocks and night-scented stocks, sweet peas and foxgloves. The glass of mullioned windows reflected the moonlight unevenly back at them, and old, multi-coloured pantiles at odd angles clad the porch and roof.

The front door, however, was a horrid new uPVC thing as Hugh opened it.

"It was here when I bought the house. Very good at keeping the draughts out but it'll have to go," Hugh said, much to Ali's relief. It was sacrilege to disfigure this pretty cottage with such a hideous bright white plastic monstrosity.

Inside, Hugh turned the lights on. Ali noticed that the light switches were old-fashioned originals, although there were lines of new plaster up the walls. Presumably, the house, or part of it, had been re-wired. The hall was in need of more than a lick of paint but the house was quite warm and cosy.

"One thing the previous owner did get right was to put in a new oil-fired central heating system before he ran out of money." Hugh said. "I'll make some coffee. Or would you like a glass of wine? Or both maybe?"

"Actually both would be nice."

Ali settled down in the sitting room on the comfortable old sofa, the only seat in the room, and started to get the files back in order. She looked around. Like the hall, the room was clearly in need of redecoration for about the last fifty years at least. Actually, it looked like it needed replastering first. Hugh obviously had a job on his hands. She wandered towards the kitchen. If it was in the same state as the sitting room, how clean would the cups and plates be?

Not a problem, she discovered. Although there were dishes everywhere, the kitchen appeared to have been newly plastered and painted, with an antique dresser and free-standing real wood chests of drawers and cabinets, all newly waxed standing on the quarry tiles. Shelves and racks hung on the walls, instead of the usual mass-produced units. An Aga sat in a large old fireplace pumping out heat and a waxed table and chairs stood in the middle of the room.

A large wine rack filled one space and a huge silver fridge-freezer completed the look. An effortless mix of new and old, Ali opined, trying not to sound in her mind like a women's magazine. *I couldn't have put it all together any better myself.*

There was also an antique waxed pine bookcase crammed with books and magazines. On closer inspection, they were all law books!

Hugh reached for the only bottle in the huge rack and shut the fridge door on almost completely empty shelves.

Oh well. He obviously doesn't do much cooking!

"The kitchen's nice," said Ali.

"Yeah. I got it done over Christmas. Before that it was, well, you wouldn't want to be in here, let alone eat anything that came out of it."

The sandwiches and red wine went well together and the coffee rounded it off as they discussed at length the Desmond case. It was an awkward case, with subtle nuances making it difficult to know exactly how to defend it and difficult no doubt for the prosecution to know how exactly to proceed

129

themselves.

Desmond had driven to the flat of his estranged wife's new boyfriend, Andrews, intending to talk to him about the rights and wrongs of taking a wife away from the father of her children and whether he could actually cope with another man's kids. The new boyfriend had no children of his own and was several years younger than Desmond's wife.

Desmond thought his wife, Maggie, might come back to him if Andrews would back off. He also thought his children would suffer if subjected to a string of young largely uncommitted stepfathers such as Andrews. His wife wouldn't hand the children over to him and he stood scant chance of getting custody awarded to him, even though he was prepared to cut down his hours at work and his mother was more than willing to help him look after the children.

Andrews was watching football on the TV and hadn't wanted to stand at the door so Desmond walked in after him and put his case to Andrews. Andrews had barely listened and sat riveted to the TV. Exasperated, Desmond had walked to the TV and turned it off. Andrews was furious and sneered at Desmond:

"You're a useless husband and father. The kids just laugh about you. They were happier when you weren't there. Mags only ever wanted you in the first place for a quick exit away from her parents and that big family. They held her back and stopped her making a proper career for herself. And you did the same thing; saddling her with all the responsibility of a family and looking after yourself."

Desmond had protested that he was quite happy to give up his job or work part-time or whatever Maggie wanted. Andrews replied, oh yeah, so who'd pay the bills then?

"Hang on," said Desmond, "if she and the kids move in with you, then how is she going to get this wonderful career going unless *you* give up work and look after the kids and then in that case who's going to pay the bills?"

"Fuck you. You're just a loser with no answers. You'll never be any good to any woman."

At this point, Desmond had turned to go. Desmond's account was that Andrews, who had been drinking, had taunted him that he was a coward, he wouldn't even fight for his wife and family. Hugh read from Desmond's statement:

"'Andrews stood up and basically went for me. He was trying to stop me from leaving. He grabbed my arm and my clothes so that my shirt sleeve tore. I tried to shake him off he just hung on all the more. A few things got knocked to the floor and the bottle of beer Andrews had been drinking broke on the ceramic tiling, that was round the mantelpiece. That seemed to make Andrews really angry and he let go of me and picked up the broken bottle. He started waving it in my face.

"'With the other hand he was swinging punches. One punch landed on my jaw and I was worried he'd cut my face with the bottle. I just wanted to get away and so I punched him back. I didn't think it was that hard but I suppose it must have been. I just wanted to get out of there. I hit him on the left ear and he fell down. I saw blood pooling around his head as he was lying there. I realised I'd knocked him out. So I left and went back to my mum's house and phoned the police from there.'"

"I suppose being an ex-marine, he was used to hitting hard," said Ali.

Andrews might have died but he didn't; he recovered, although now, he was deaf in one ear, had minor brain damage and was no longer such a smart arse, and he was making a claim to the Criminal Injuries Compensation Authority.

Desmond's wife had gone back to him with the children and was attending college part-time to take GCSEs while Desmond worked part-time and they both looked after the children with the help of his mother while he was on bail awaiting trial.

The prosecution alleged that Desmond had gone to the flat with the intention of killing Andrews. Since the charge was unlikely to stick, there was an alternative charge of causing grievous bodily harm.

That was the case.

Hugh was going to defend it on the basis that Desmond was entitled to use reasonable force to prevent Andrews from holding him against his will, and that because of the broken bottle and the damage it could do plus Andrews' state of intoxication and growing anger, he had had to use sufficient force to disable Andrews before he came to serious harm himself. Also, the degree of harm Desmond had inflicted was unintentional. He hadn't meant to deafen him or knock him out completely, much less cause him brain damage. He had just wanted to disable him enough to be able to get out of the flat.

The court was only going to have Desmond's word as to what had happened and any forensic evidence plus the bruise on Desmond's jaw and his torn shirt. Andrews, when he came round, couldn't remember anything and was still in no fit state to give evidence.

"What about getting Desmond's wife to give evidence?" Ali suggested. "After all she's gone back to him hasn't she?"

"I think that could be a double-edged sword. The police did once get called out to a domestic at their house, though by all accounts it was Desmond's wife who was doing all the pushing and punching because she wanted him to leave but he wouldn't. Nevertheless no one likes to present themselves in that bad a light. Under cross- she might well be persuaded to say that Desmond was aggressive, that he'd hit her, and so on. And of course he may well have done. We don't know."

"OK, then what about work. Looks like he had a good record, been there eight years, been promoted. Surely the boss could put in a good word."

"We could think about it. But Desmond had some mental problems when he left the forces. A lot of them do, of course, after what they've been through. But if we open up the area of his work, it could backfire."

"Does he do any voluntary work or anything like that?"

"I don't know. But that'd be rather clutching at straws and that's more for mitigation anyway if he's convicted."

"Right. Well, if you want I'll go through the forensics tomorrow and see if I find anything that'd help. That's all I can suggest. Er, where's the loo?"

Hugh indicated a door off the hall. Ali switched the light on and entered what looked like a wartime set-up with an old overhead cistern and chain pull. The cistern was heavy with cobwebs. Ali nervously and quickly used the loo and pulled the chain. She went to pull up her knickers and tights when something large and black and hairy fell down onto her shoulder and ran down her arm. Ali let out a high-pitched scream and another and another, while she wrestled her knickers and tights on and fought with the large old key to get out.

Eventually she was free and hurtled out, cannoning into Hugh who looked down at her, his hands lightly resting on her arms, amusement and concern fighting to get the upper hand. Amusement won when he saw she was all right.

"What on earth's the matter?"

"It's not funny." Ali turned, panting, and pointed theatrically at the open toilet door. "It's en*or*mous. And black. It's the biggest one I've ever seen. And it crawled all *over* me. Oh." She tried not to sob. She was even unaffected by him touching her, so terrified was she of the spider.

"Right. Go back to the sitting room and I'll sort it out."

Ali hesitated. "You won't *kill* it, will you?"

"No. No. Of course not. How do you think it's survived this long?"

Ali returned to the sitting room as asked and huddled on the sofa, staring with renewed respect at the heavy old velvet curtains, imagining what might be lurking in their ample folds, not to mention under the sofa. She folded her legs up under her.

"There," said Hugh returning with an upturned pint glass in his hands with a beer mat underneath. He rested it on the mantelpiece and the captive creature ran circles round the beermat, when it wasn't rearing up the glass sides, fearsomely.

They went through another less riveting file for some minutes and Ali calmed down. Every so often she cast furtive glances at the mantelpiece and Hugh continued to faintly smile at her, as if to say: *Who'd have thought the determined career girl was frightened of spiders.*

Ali ignored him, but her heart obviously wasn't in it any longer, so Hugh proposed that they call it a day.

"It's nearly the ten o' clock news. D'you mind if we watch the headlines and then I'll take you home."

Ali concurred.

He turned on the TV. The tail end of a raunchy American drama was still showing and Hugh and Ali were treated to the sight of a couple preparing to screw each other over the end of an office desk. The man's hands were pulling down the woman's panties and her hands were expertly opening his zip. The closing scene left them going at it hammer and tongs.

Ali tried to appear indifferent. Hugh had a look of feigned derision. They automatically turned to each other, eyes meeting, for too long really. Ali couldn't tear her eyes away from Hugh's. Something seemed to slip, as though the physical universe had parted. Her vision went misty. Hugh's eyes softened almost imperceptibly and his face was flushed. Ali couldn't later say why she hadn't just backed off like she had before with Hugh. Pure lust she supposed. And the head of fantasies she'd built up around him. On an impulse she put one hand up to his face and kissed him full on the mouth.

Immediately she thought *this is a big mistake* but he didn't pull away. And when he took her head in his hands and his tongue started to explore her mouth, she knew he wasn't going to.

I can't believe this, she thought. Hugh kissing me like this. It wasn't like Hugh. He was normally so restrained. He wasn't rough or aggressive. Just very positive and assured. Not at all reticent. He didn't exactly tear her clothes off, but he started kissing her neck and ears and shoulders. His hands were soon kneading her breasts and feeling her body.

And any undressing move she made, he made a corresponding move, so that before long they were almost naked, horizontal on the old sofa. Insofar as she had any remaining rational thoughts, Ali was relieved that her underwear that day was reasonably new, though she couldn't say that she noticed what state his might have been in. She could already feel herself starting to come up to the boil and thought Hugh must be stretched pretty thin too, when he whispered into her hair:

"Oh Ali. You're so beautiful. Do you want to go upstairs?"

Ali stiffened and pulled away slightly. Her eyes widened in the bright light of the hundred watt incandescent bulb.

Hugh was mortified.

"I'm so sorry. I shouldn't have asked! I'll take you straight home. Come along–"

"No," yelped Ali, "but…" She glanced over at the mantelpiece and the glass with its contents which she'd secretly christened Alan, who seemed to have settled down for the night and accepted his lot.

"Oh. Right." Hugh let out a laugh that didn't make Ali feel any better.

"No. It's OK. The other room I've sorted out is my bedroom. It's been completely decorated and totally de-spidered." Hugh smiled at Ali then he shook his head and sighed. "That is if the spontaneity of the moment hasn't passed completely."

"Well, no. Actually it hasn't." She fought a wave of embarrassment. She hoped she wasn't being too obvious, too pushy even.

"How, er, fortunate. So…?"

Ali decided that false modesty would be a mistake.

"Fine then, up we go." *Or up you go.* Her attempt at sophistication took a dive as she had a Bridget Jones moment when she nearly fell over the coffee table as she stood up. Hugh caught her, kissed her neck and held her hand up the stairs which, it had to be said, were rather decked out with cobwebs overhead. Ali tried to ignore them.

The bedroom was as Hugh had said. In the light of the bedside table lamp, she took in white painted walls and more waxed pine before falling into the softest bed. No wonder Hugh always looked bright-eyed and bushy-tailed in the mornings. He must sleep like a baby.

Neither of them were very frivolous any more. Ali moaned

softly as Hugh took the rest of her clothes off and his own while kissing her again. All over. The things he did to her ear with his lips, teeth and tongue while making small sounds just drove her mad.

Before entering her, he looked down at her with those beautiful eyes and they held each other's eyes as he did it until she sought his mouth with hers. He was very gentle, very thorough. He'd acquired a condom at some point. Ali wasn't sure she'd have bothered the way she felt but it was good that he was responsible.

They both took their time. Ali felt she was being transported into paradise. All rational thought was gone. The physical surroundings disappeared and there was nothing but a hot, soft cloud around her. The fantasies weren't a patch on the real thing. Afterwards, they lay locked together for what seemed like ages, whispering each other's names and kissing. It was like a dam bursting and releasing a flood of pent-up emotion. Oh, and he smelled so nice.

Where did all this come from, thought Ali. Is it really possible to fall in love with someone just like that and without any prior warning? Or has it been lurking somewhere under the surface all the time? Not just stray spikes of lust but actual love?

Eventually, Ali felt she couldn't take any more and was going to start to cry, or actually tell him she loved him, so she tore herself away and went into the small en suite off the bedroom. Earlier, she'd just glimpsed gleaming white surfaces. Again the whole thing was beautifully done. Instead of a shower cubicle, there was a short ceramic slipper bath. The shower curtain was suspended from a cast iron ring above, itself suspended by chains from a hook in the ceiling. How novel.

Hugh, impeccably mannered it seemed in matters of the bedroom, waited for her to flush the chain before coming in himself. As she washed her hands with the sandalwood soap, he put his arms round her from behind and nibbled her ear.

"Oh, Hugh, that was just divine. I can't say how much."

"Yes it was divine. Unutterably exquisite. Just like you are." And he buried his face in her hair and hugged her tightly. Once again she had to try hard not to cry.

"These adorable shell-like ears'll never look the same again as they bend over my desk to get a file," he said. "Do you want to stay the night or shall I take you home?"

Ali hoped he'd ask.

"Stay the night please. I'll go and phone home. It's a nuisance but they'll worry."

When she came back he was in bed looking sleepy. And ravishing. As she got in he turned the light off and his arm folded round her and that was all she remembered.

CHAPTER 25

THE BRIGHT moonlight shone into the small bathroom through the window, no curtain or blind to hinders its ingress. Ali stood regarding herself in the mirror over the sink. Her hair was tangled and, to her mind, her face had a used, fallen look, appropriate to the hour or so's wonderful, steamy, unbridled sex the night before. She smiled a satisfied smile at the secret she now held. Hugh was a fucking ace in bed.

Hugh, her boss, that beautiful but controlled, closed person she so looked up to, about whom she'd fantasised for weeks, who was even now lying naked and sated, breathing softly and regularly in the bedroom next door, arm thrown over her side of the bed. The arm had tried to restrain her in its sleep as she'd slipped out from beneath it and had then pulled her pillow to its body and held that fast instead.

What, she wondered, would happen now. If it came to anything, what would he be like? Would he be kind and nice, loving and supportive? Or would he be casual and neglectful like Rob? Would he be distant and cold? He'd seemed quite the opposite last night. But that was sex. The strong desire to copulate and ultimately procreate could change everything while it lasted. She had no illusions about that.

Suddenly, his face swam into view in the mirror. In the blue light of the moon, the image seemed ethereal and foggy and for a second she wondered if she was dreaming on her feet. She hadn't heard anything. It was him, of course, behind her, looking at her reflection in the mirror in a predatory way, like a big animal. She was transfixed. He placed his hands lightly on her hips. His head dipped, his mouth opened and he bit and then sucked at her neck and breathed into her ear.

He raised his head and again his eyes met hers, while his hands moved up and down her body, kneading her breasts, down to her lower abdomen, massaging and stroking it, one hand briefly resting between her legs, cupping her mons veneris and squeezing, then moving on down her inner thighs with a featherlight touch.

"Ali," he said, "you drive me fucking crazy."

"Hugh." She turned around and they French kissed for at least a thousand years.

"Hugh," she said again, "Oh, Hugh," as his mouth touched her neck again biting and sucking at it and down under her armpit. His tongue and lips played sweet tunes with and around her nipples. Her fingers dug into his back and shoulders as he moved down her body licking and sucking at her, his tongue extending lightly into her crack before he kissed down her legs, licked and kissed her feet and bit lightly at her knees.

"Hugh, for God's sake fuck me," she said. He stood and reached into the cupboard next to the sink and handed her something.

"Here. You put it on."

She tore the small sachet with her teeth and worked the condom onto him. He was the biggest man she'd ever slept with.

"Oh, Ali, that's so nice," he breathed heavily, fondling her hair as she pulled harder to unwind the condom. "You'd better hurry," he smiled at her with his voice.

Then he stood over her, looking at her and gently pushing her tousled hair back from her face.

"Ali, you're so beautiful," he said, as he had last night.

"So are you, Hugh. You're perfect. You're divine."

He lowered his head and put his lips to her mouth. He didn't kiss her and his mouth didn't quite touch hers. He breathed heavily into her open mouth, saying her name over and over, looking up and down her face and into her eyes. She was overcome and started to cry silently.

"Oh, Hugh. Please. Please."

He lifted her up a few inches and pinned her body against the cupboard with his own. He was inside her so easily, so deftly. The size of him made it barely necessary to move at all. He had his eyes closed and his head thrown back in ecstasy. She rubbed her breasts against him and he moaned.

"Ali. Are you going to come soon? Are you?"

"Soon. Nearly." She put her hands on his buttocks and pulled him harder into her. She moved just a little and it set things off. A light started to glow deep inside her and became brighter and bigger and hotter. Involuntarily she went rigid for a few seconds, holding it in, concentrating it until she couldn't hold it any longer and it throbbed into her vagina, on and off and on and off. Without realising it she was crying out and so was he. The strong set of ring muscles made sure the message was effectively conveyed to Hugh and she could feel him pulsing strongly with a returning pale green iridescent light of his own.

When it was over, she said, "Hugh, will you come to bed and kiss me?"

"Of course sweetie. I'll be in in a minute. I've just got to get rid of this."

He kissed her to sleep. It was exquisite.

THE REST of the week went very slowly indeed. In the office Hugh was distant and rather stern, that is to say he acted normally. Ali marvelled at his self-control.

Naturally they'd had the obligatory sex the next morning when they woke up. Inevitable really. He woke up very early and related that normally he'd go for a run or to the gym, but *today* he'd make an exception. And he'd certainly done so exceptionally well.

Yet by the time they'd showered in the darling slipper bath and grabbed some toast, he'd sort of shut down again. And in the car, he'd said that of course they'd have to be discreet at the office. Ali had to work hard not to show how disappointed she was. But after all, she was a career girl she told herself. These things happened. She must act professionally, not like a silly schoolgirl.

Who was she kidding? She was besotted. She'd walk over glass shards for one touch of his hand, one nibble at her throat, one—

"It'd be embarrassing otherwise."

"Oh yes. Yes, of course," she readily agreed, hoping he couldn't read her mind like he always seemed to be able to do normally, in that uncanny way he had. Nor hear the catch in her throat.

Perhaps she was just being incredibly naïve. Perhaps Hugh was the 'Love you and leave you' type, only interested in a one-night stand. What was it she'd said to Sam so recently? *Whereas for a girl ... well who's going to refuse?*

"Good. Perhaps you can go over Desmond's forensics first thing when we get in as you suggested last night. Before you go off and help Alison. It is your day for Alison isn't it?"

Yes it was. It was her day to work under Alison, not to writhe ecstatically under Hugh.

She had to stop this, she told herself sharply, and for the rest of the journey she concentrated hard on what she could remember reading already of Desmond's forensics.

Hugh said nothing more and his expression remained closed.

CHAPTER 26

HUGH and Ali arriving at the office in the same car didn't attract any comment. After all she lived on his route into Colchester. He might've picked her up at the bus stop.

Ali shut herself in The Privy and scoured Desmond's forensics. The flat had been gone over, once it was realised that Andrews wasn't coming round straightaway and the police might have a homicide on their hands. He lived alone so no one else had access to the flat.

There was very little forensic evidence on the file. Apart from Andrews' blood on the floor and splatters of it on the wall, Desmond's prints had been found on the door, the TV and a small table near the door, fibres from his clothes had been found under Andrews' nails, fibres from Desmond's clothes had been found on Andrews' clothes and vice versa, and Andrews' prints and other unidentified prints had been found on the beer bottle. It was presumed that the unidentified prints were those of shopkeepers, warehouse workers et cetera. The fibres held no clues. No one was saying there hadn't been a tussle.

In addition, CCTV showed Desmond driving towards Andrews' building and driving away from it.

Ali sat and cogitated for some time and then went to Hugh's room after checking he was free. He smiled kindly and distantly. Ali felt a rush of anger that she brushed aside.

Somewhat coldly, she listed to him the points she'd come up with.

"It's not really a forensic point, but if the prosecution are claiming Desmond intended to murder Andrews, then he had the chance to finish him off before he left the flat but he didn't. You could use that."

"Yes, I'll get the point over of course. The counter-argument is that Desmond wouldn't be the first person to think better of his intended actions and change his mind when it came to it. Nor the first person to realise they were going to be caught and contacted the police. But at the actual time of the punch, he might have intended it to be fatal. Alternatively, Desmond might have thought Andrews actually *was* dead when he left."

"OK, then Desmond's prints weren't on the bottle at all. But if he'd wanted to kill Andrews, the perfect weapon was there and available and he obviously didn't handle the bottle and then wipe it because of the alien prints on it."

"Absolutely, but Desmond didn't need a knife or broken bottle or any weapon to do serious harm. He was quite capable of flooring him with just one punch apparently. Andrews might have used the bottle purely defensively against this much bigger stronger more competent man."

"All that's possibly true, but Desmond was in the flat a very short time. The CCTV evidence shows that. He had very little time to go round the flat, get invited in, get into an argument, have a fight and subtly rearrange things to make it look different. To make it look like he was someone who had turned up and was borne along by the circumstances. Basically the forensic evidence supports his account. It doesn't add up to a person who planned a serious attack."

"They're good points. But he could of course have thought up his account later based on what he thought the forensic evidence was likely to produce."

"Right then, finally, I checked the pattern of the fingerprints. Desmond's prints on the small table near the door were more akin to someone who had been backed up against the table, therefore acting *de*fensively rather than *o*ffensively. If he had cannoned off the table, you would have expected one hand or possibly both on the top of the table. But Desmond's prints showed he was gripping the table while facing away from it. His fingers were near the edge underneath the table top. I think it means he was backing away from this broken bottle."

"Good point."

"Well that's all I've got."

Hugh's private line rang and he answered it while swivelling his chair to face the window.

He listened for a few seconds, then said: "I told you I wasn't going to speak to you again. And that's what I meant. I'm not speaking to you. Goodbye." And he crashed the phone down.

It was a good job he couldn't see the filthy look on Ali's face as she stomped out of the office, slamming the door behind her.

THE day stretched uninvitingly ahead. Ali wasn't keen on matrimonial work. Having spent several weeks working on cases for Alison, she had already started to feel that one couple's excessive hatred for each other was much like another's. She secretly wanted to tell most of the people she saw to stop behaving like kids, to grow up and think about the harm they were doing to their children.

If anything, the ones who claimed to have just drifted apart, to be having a 'civilised' divorce and remained good friends were even more aggravating. Ali thought they could at least make some attempt to patch things up if only for the sake of the children. The marriage was going wrong anyway and no one else was involved they often claimed, or at least nothing had 'happened' until they were suitably and properly separated from the other party.

So, you couldn't possibly have channelled all that energy and effort into saving your marriage rather than using it to stoke up the next relationship. It was obvious that an old long-term relationship just couldn't conceivably compete on level terms with the excitement and sexual buzz of a new one.

Of course, she never said such things to the clients, however much she wanted to. Since a lot of them were private clients paying good money, they had to be pampered and indulged to some extent. It wouldn't have been appropriate to start mouthing off at legally-aided clients either, but paying customers could, to a slightly greater extent, expect their whims to be at least accorded some attention. You couldn't simply say to them that the public purse wouldn't pay for this or that outlandish course of action. You had to be a bit more subtle and suggest they might be wasting their money.

Nevertheless, even private clients had to be told that a judge would take a dim view of an application which was vexatious and whose only purpose was to get at the other party or which had no prospect of success at all; that they as solicitors had a duty not to bring such applications. Thanks goodness they could cite the Resolution Code of Practice and the various Guides to help persuade clients to be more reasonable.

One such client was sitting the opposite side of the desk from Ali right now. Charlotte Tippett, known as Sharl, a year or two younger than Ali, being funded and egged on by her *nouveau riche* parents, was adamant that her husband wasn't going to see the children.

"He's only saying he wants to see them to get at me. He weren't interested in them when we was tergevva."

Asked to expand, she said that the children were in bed when her husband got home from work and he only played with them at weekends. That he wouldn't be able to cope with the children on his own.

"How old are they?" Ali looked at the file. The children were aged eighteen months and three years.

"I imagine they would have been in bed by the time *most* people get home from work. You say he played with them at weekends though."

"Well, he minded them while I went out with me mates. He probably didn't, you know, like actually play with them."

"So, how much of the time did he spend with the children at weekends."

"Just when I went out. With me mates."

"Yes, so how often did you go out? Was it during the day or evenings?"

"Well," the client said defensively, "I `ad them all week. I'm entitled to a break aren't I?"

Ali rifled through the correspondence. "His Solicitors say you went out most weekends for periods ranging from a couple of hours to all day and at least one night most weekends."

"So, he looked after the kids 'cos he had to, not 'cos he actually wanted to. That don't make him a great dad."

"Well, it makes him look like a responsible one."

The client became aggressive. "What? Are you saying I'm *not* a responsible parent then?" And she came up with the trump card. The type of threat any nasty child would use if it couldn't get its own way. "I don't 'ave to use this firm of solicitors you know. I'm only here 'cos my dad says Mr Trimble's a great bloke at the company stuff. If I say I'm getting crap service, then my dad'll take his business elsewhere."

Ali tried to calm the girl down although she felt no sympathy for her whatsoever so far. She suspected that Alison felt the same and that was why Ali was seeing her instead. Ali didn't directly answer the girl's initial question.

"Your husband has never made any allegations about your fitness as a mother. That's not what the dispute is about as I understand it. The children are with you and no one's challenging that. We're just talking about your husband being given the opportunity to see them and, moreover, them being able to see their father."

The client grunted and her face resolved into a heavy sulk.

"If their dad is a good dad, then do you agree that they'll benefit from seeing him."

"But he ain't. He don't care."

"Is there anything at all you like about him?"

"No. He's a total wanker."

"Does he have any friends?"

"Course he does. Loads of 'em."

"So other people like him and think he's OK but you don't."

"I suppose."

"So other people, people who like him, may think he's a good dad."

"Well they might."

"Obviously you and he don't get on, do you?"

"Not now, no."

"But just because the two of you have fallen out, are you saying that that automatically makes him a horrible person and a bad father?"

"Well no."

"So others might think he's a reasonable father."

"Maybe. But it's not them's got to hand the kids over to him."

"OK, perhaps your parents could help with that. You're living with them at the moment, aren't you. Maybe for the time being you could be somewhere else when he comes to collect the children."

"Gawd. Are you kidding? My mum and dad 'ate him. It's them that … They don't like him anyway."

"So why's that?"

"Well, he's posher 'an them. They don't like it. 'Specially me dad."

Ali declined to ask for more detail. So far as she knew, Charlotte's father was in the scrap business. Anyway it was irrelevant just how much further up the social scale this husband was than these parents who seemed to be prepared to help wreck their daughter's marriage over some petty sense of inferiority.

"Do you think you ever had a good marriage?" she asked instead.

"Well. It was OK to begin with. Yeah. It was good," Charlotte said wistfully.

"So what do you think went wrong?"

"I s'pose I was a bit young to settle down and have kids. Actually, you probably guessed I was already pregnant when we got married."

Ali had indeed already done the basic maths.

"So what went wrong?" she asked again.

"Our son Jason cried all night for almost the whole of the first year. I asked my mum and dad if they'd have him for a weekend or two but they wouldn't. I was just exhausted. Then Kyra came along and she was just the same. We rowed a lot. My mates was going out having a good time so my mum says, let Pete look after them. Pete said let them, me mum and dad that is, have the kids and we'll go out together but me mum and dad wouldn't. We were short of money. I just couldn't cope any more. So I took the kids and went home to

147

my parents."

"I'm surprised they agreed. I mean they didn't want to help with babysitting and so on."

"They were pleased I'd left him."

So, these well-off parents wouldn't help with a bit of babysitting and yet readily agreed, apparently, to having their daughter and two small children living with them full-time. They were also seemingly prepared to finance a potentially contentious and expensive divorce but wouldn't give their daughter a bit of financial help towards keeping her marriage together.

"Can I ask, Charlotte, whether you still have feelings for Pete?"

Charlotte's face crumpled and she started to cry. Ali suddenly felt sorry for this young girl who was being manipulated by her parents into doing what they wanted, regardless of whether it was the best thing for her or not. Ali wanted to go round the desk and put her arm round Charlotte it would probably be unprofessional to do so.

"Charlotte. You don't have to go ahead with this divorce if you don't really want to. At least not immediately. There's really no hurry at all. You can give yourself as much time as you need to decide properly. In the meantime you could see Pete sometimes with the children and just let things take their course until you're both ready to make a proper decision."

"Me mum and dad'd be furious," Charlotte sobbed.

"It's your life Charlotte, not theirs. And they don't have to know do they? You could take the children out somewhere and meet Pete for an hour or so at the weekend. I could try to fix it up with Pete's Solicitors. I could call them now if you want."

Charlotte looked up uncertainly, hanky at her nose. She said nothing, and neither did Ali. She certainly wasn't going to put more pressure on this vulnerable girl.

"Yes," Charlotte said at last. "Can you ring them?"

Ali did so and they managed to get Pete on his mobile and made an arrangement for that Saturday afternoon in a park. Charlotte said her dad would be going to watch

Colchester play and her mother always went clothes shopping on Saturday afternoons.

Charlotte bit her lip and asked that no one at PWT told her dad. Of course, not said Ali. Charlotte's case was entirely confidential and Charlotte went off happier than when she'd come into the office, saying she'd let Ali know next week how it'd gone.

Ali just hoped she'd done the right thing. She made a vague note about the interview and told Alison not much progress had been made.

CHAPTER 27

In the clefts of the rock, In the secret places of the stairs
(The Song of Solomon 2)

BY the end of the week, Ali couldn't believe she'd actually slept with Hugh. It seemed a couple of centuries ago. She had to pinch herself to know she wasn't dreaming the whole thing. The bathroom encounter had happened on another planet, in another galaxy.

Friday came and, though she was due to work both nights at the S&S, Ali hoped so much that Hugh would say something. Perhaps an invite to see a film, dinner somewhere. Or just have a coffee together. She'd cheerfully have phoned in sick and foregone the precious income.

But all Hugh said, when he saw her leaving the office with her bar gear to change into, was: "Don't work too hard."

Blessedly, Friday night was so busy that, for once, Ali had no time to dwell on the pleasures of the flesh. She didn't finish until 2 am and luckily was given a lift home with the manager to spare her father dragging himself out of bed. On the drive home, she toyed with idea of going into the office the next day as she knew Hugh often worked Saturday mornings. In the event, she slept until nearly midday.

"Mum! Why didn't you wake me up?" she said crossly.

"You're wearing yourself out," was her mother's reply. "Anyway you're doing an early shift today aren't you? You'll be off again soon. Those skinflint solicitors certainly don't deserve to have you going into the office on Saturdays as well. They're working you ragged and not a penny to show for it. Your father's very unhappy about it. If it goes on much longer, I think he'll march in there and *say* something." And on and on and on.

"Well that's filled in half an hour nicely," said Ali huffily. "I'll barely have time to shower and change now."

She was starting at 4 pm and finishing at elevenish. Again it was busy. The tips were good and Ali thought she might even be able to afford that strapless number she had her eye on for Jan and Matt's sixth anniversary bash.

At ten-thirty-five, she was winding down when she saw a figure at the end of the bar nursing a Coke. Ali had barely if ever seen Hugh out of a suit and had to double take. He hadn't shaved, his hair was tousled and he looked younger and utterly gorgeous in very tight jeans and a slim fitting shirt.

Ali finished serving her customer and went over. They gazed at each other. Her heart missed a beat and she couldn't tear her eyes away. Her mouth went dry and she moistened her top lip slowly with her tongue. She didn't mean it to be provocative though perhaps it came over that way.

"Will you come home with me?" he said.

Ali blushed all over and had to fight off a wave of lust. To hide it, she gave a silly saccharine smile and said in a rather high voice:

"Oh. How nice. Thank you very much."

"Hmm," said Hugh, his expression amused.

"I'd better go and phone my dad or he'll be turning out soon."

And she tottered off on legs of jelly to where they hung their outdoor clothes and rifled through her coat pocket for her mobile. Her mother answered sleepily and when Ali said she didn't need a lift and would probably stay the night at a friend's, her mother said:

"Is it a young man?"

"Oh well, er, it's er…"

"You will be careful won't you, Ali? Goodnight dear." And her mother put the phone down.

"The car's in the car park at the front. I'll go and wait for you," said Hugh.

It was another ten minutes before Ali slipped in beside Hugh. He was listening to the news and moved off as soon as she had strapped up.

Neither of them said anything. Hugh seemed to be giving off waves of electricity. At least that's how it felt. Ali was physically uncomfortable, hot and breathless and like a balloon about to burst. She touched his left hand and he let her take it off the steering wheel, draw it to her mouth and kiss it. He stopped the car and, taking her in his arms, he kissed her passionately.

"Oh, Ali," he said. "I've missed you so."

Ali could say nothing at all.

It seemed a lifetime before they arrived at the public footpath. He put his arm around her and she managed to control herself until they were inside the house. He kissed her hands, undid her blouse and kissed and licked the tops of her breasts showing above her bra while running his hands up and down her body and through her hair.

"We should go upstairs," he said, thinking about the spiders, so they did.

Before long she was begging him to enter her. And he kept on kissing her. Most men didn't do that. It was intoxicating. And he didn't go in for all that enthusiastic thrusting either that men seemed to think would transport a woman to another plane. He was firm and gentle. Ali wound her legs around his and they moved perfectly together. He kissed her all the time with his tongue deep in her mouth. Just like last time it went on for a long time. She'd had no idea before that orgasms could be so frequently and easily come by or so knee-tremblingly volcanic. She wondered briefly how Hugh did it for so long but who could care.

Afterwards he kissed her gently all over until she fell sleep, sighing deeply.

IF possible, the next morning was even better. Ali felt dizzy from it, and yet strangely dissatisfied and unsettled, as though, having experienced such heights, she was never going to be able to get enough of it. She couldn't keep her hands off him.

When he left the bed to go to the loo or get them a cup of tea, she felt as though a large part of her had been wrenched away. She wanted to run after him and attach herself to him to be complete again. What was she going to do when she went home that night? She literally choked at the thought of it.

"You all right?" said Hugh when he came back with their second cup of tea.

"Yes," she said rolling her eyes and breathing hard into the pillow so he couldn't see her face.

"What do you want to do today?"

Ali had had to laugh.

"We could go to a pub somewhere and get lunch or go for a bracing walk. The public footpath has some wonderful views further along. Why are you laughing?"

She studied his kind concerned face and wanted to take it in her hands and kiss it forever. She wanted to tell him she loved him to distraction, that she was bereft when he wasn't within a few inches of her. She wanted to crawl right inside his body and be absorbed into him.

"Now why are you looking so sad?"

Ali pulled herself together. "A walk sounds lovely."

She couldn't eat any breakfast. Her stomach was churning. Sick of love, wasn't that what The Song said. *Stay me with flagons, comfort me with apples, for I am sick of love.*

The walk was delightful. With her arm through his, Ali just about managed.

Hugh cooked them something stir-fried for lunch. And afterwards, amazingly, they went back to bed. And then he took her home. Ali asked to be dropped some way from her home. She didn't want any invites in for coffee and a thinly veiled grilling.

Before she got out of the car, she asked the second most important question that had been troubling her on the journey back.

"So. No names, no pack-drill again this week?"

"I think it's for the best. For the time being."

So, no updating of her Facebook page then to tell the world that Ali and Hugh were an item. No twitters with veiled references to their activities. No instant messaging all her friends and associates about his exceptionally wonderful qualities.

He looked at Ali. "You know what dreadful gossips they are in the office, some of them. Those girls!" He shook his head. "I don't want you being subjected to smirks and innuendo."

"Right," said Ali, who would willingly have swapped the cloying silence about their relationship for a bit of harmless nudging and winking. "But I don't care about that."

"Well, I do. I don't want you to lose respect. And as for me. It would make me look somewhat predatory don't you think. Having a steamy relationship with a junior *unpaid* member of the firm." He smiled. "And you could hardly go about telling everyone you had seduced me."

Ali didn't say anything.

"Let's just give it a little while shall we and see what happens."

"Right," she said again and got out of the car. "See you tomorrow."

The first question had been when she was going to see him again, as in *see* him. But she didn't want to appear too limpet-like.

And, as soon as she was in the house, she raced up to her room and stayed there.

CHAPTER 28

MONDAYS are usually dull and miserable. This one was actually bright and warm and Ali made a pact with herself to turn over a new leaf and concentrate on her career. PWT knew she wanted a training contract and so allowed her to spend any free time on the internet looking for possible openings and sending out hopeful CVs. First thing Monday morning wasn't the best time to look for new stuff but she tried anyway.

There were a few possibilities. She now had about four months' experience so it wasn't almost nothing anymore.

A large firm in Chelmsford, Lakes, were looking for paralegals with a view to possible training contracts, so she filled in the online application form and uploaded her CV. Might lead to something.

There were similar situations on the website of a smaller more specialised firm in Cambridge. They were big in civil rights. Unlikely she'd get one but she had to try. In the unlikely event she was successful, it would be a bit of a hike to Cambridge every day. Maybe her parents would help her out to get a small car and she could do a travel-share. It would cost an arm and a leg by train and take hours.

Tammy had had a regular stream of calls that morning which she fielded or put through as necessary. It wasn't an especially busy morning, however the steady rhythm was suddenly interrupted by a commotion in reception.

Ali peered round her door and could just see part of the waiting area. A plump, balding, small man in an expensively cut suit was demanding to see Baz. No, he didn't care if Baz was booked up weeks ahead. He had to see him now. Yes, it was important. It wouldn't take long. He was a big client of the firm. And blah blah blah.

Tammy relented and said she'd buzz Mr Trimble.

"Mr Wright isn't it?"

The name sounded familiar to Ali; she wasn't sure why.

Before Tammy could pick up the phone, Baz waddled into

reception. He'd obviously heard the row but hadn't associated it with himself. Usually it was those pesky matrimonial clients who made a fuss, and sometimes the conveyancing ones who Wattsey wouldn't speak to. Not usually the criminal ones. They were often banged up and unable to sully the office with their actual persons. And definitely not the commercial clients who were stuck in their offices and shops and factories and the like getting on with the honest business of making loads and loads of money.

Similarly built just not quite so fat as Mr Wright, Baz greeted the man and shook his hand.

"Hello Dave. What a surprise to see you here. Come in. Come in."

And he ushered the man off to his office from whence issued a great deal of cantankerous speech that sounded like accusations followed, by restrained responses. It went on for about fifteen minutes and then Mr Wright left.

Two minutes later Ali was asked by Tammy to go to Baz's office.

Ali smiled. This was an unexpected development. Perhaps she was going to get a crash course in company takeovers or mergers.

"You can wipe that smirk off your face." Baz was a bit East End himself. It seemed to go with the territory.

Ali imagined he must be joking and her smile turned to a knowing look. She assumed the client was looking for something impossible or at least improbable and that Baz was going to challenge her to perform some minor miracle for the firm. She hoped she'd be able to produce the required rabbit from the hat if she was tenacious enough. God knew she needed something difficult to work on to divert her.

Instead, Baz let forth a string of invective that would have impressed the average barrow boy.

Ali was stunned and said nothing throughout. When he'd finished, she said as bravely as possible that she had no idea what he was talking about, that she had no contractual relationship with this firm and that if he carried on she'd walk out, but that it would do the firm no credit to intimidate unpaid interns such as herself with threats and abuse.

The word 'abuse' seemed to calm Baz down. It obviously rang bells and summoned demons from somewhere or other.

Baz breathed in deeply. "Ali," he said, "there's no place in this firm for lightweights."

"Yes. And?"

"We're not running a charity. Or a counselling service. We're running a business."

"That's what I assumed when I joined the firm."

"So why has Dave Wright's daughter gone back to her husband then?"

Ali still didn't get it and shook her head.

"What's her name? Some silly name, Shilly or Shally or something!"

The penny dropped. "Do you mean Charlotte Tippett, AKA Sharl?"

"Yes, that was it. Apparently she saw you last week and, hey presto, a lucrative divorce case has suddenly turned into a reconciliation. Her father's furious. Hates the little twat, the husband, and says this firm has turned his daughter against her parents. He's been a bloody good client and now we'll probably lose him! What have you got to say about that?"

"I think you're overreacting. The parents are likely to come round and hopefully see that what's happened is the best thing for Charlotte and the children."

"Yeah, and Colchester might get into the Premier League. Look, I've acted for Dave Wright for quite a few years now and he doesn't strike me as the forgive-and-forget type. And what about the divorce costs? Like it's not difficult enough already for us to make a shekel or two. Of course I realise *you* don't have to worry about the money coming in. But partners have to keep the bucks rolling in."

"Fat lot of good it would do me if I were to be worried solely about money!"

"Come again?"

"I said no contractual relationship. *I'm not being paid.*"

"OK, but why persuade some stupid girl to go back to her husband. It's nothing to *do* with us. It's just cash straight out the window!" Baz was working himself up again.

"We're not here to preach to these people. If they want to wreck their lives, that's *their* business. It's totally unprofessional to talk to people about reconciliation."

"I'd have to beg to differ actually. How long is it since you did any serious matrimonial work?"

"That's beside the point. At the end of the day, if we can't make money, we close. Comprende?

"My mastery of economics is of course very basic but what I do understand is that if you can persuade people with reasonably high levels of qualifications to work full-time for nothing for extended periods, then surely you're quids in aren't you? Kapish?"

"Look, the point is that we're here first and foremost to make money," said Baz. "If we can't do that we're finished. Obviously, we maintain high principles, don't do anything illegal and we uphold the law and abide by the rules et cetera, but if some silly slip of a girl leaves her husband and wants to get divorced and wants to pay us a lot of money to fight over the dad having access to the children, it's not up to us to dissuade her."

"Principles! You talk about principles! What about the children? What if it were *your* children who were going to grow up without the opportunity to have a proper relationship with their father?"

Suddenly the door opened and a voice said:

"Baz isn't that hot on principles are you, Baz? Where the money comes from is secondary, isn't that right?"

It was Hugh sounding calm but authoritative. He walked in, shut the door and stood towering over Baz. Though he was the junior partner, he had such an air about him that pushing him around wasn't really an option.

Baz spluttered. "This is a completely different case to … that other thing!"

Hugh ignored the remark.

"And bullying unpaid assistants ought to be beneath us."

"Ha! You heard. She was giving as good as she got."

"Actually, I don't listen at keyholes," said Hugh, "I'd have to take your word for that. But whatever. I'm sure Ali did what she thought was right. Perhaps I'd better take it over from here."

Baz looked deflated.

"Come on Ali. I'll come back to you, Baz."

Ali followed him out turning and giving a small shrug at Baz.

They went to Hugh's room and Hugh smiled at Ali.

"You did very well in there. You should make an excellent advocate. And I wasn't listening at the keyhole. Everyone could hear all over the office. I thought I'd better come and intervene."

"So what are you going to tell Baz?"

"Don't worry, I'll sort Baz out. I suggest we leave it a few weeks to see how things turn out. As you said, the parents may come round. You can maybe try and find out from the girl what's happening after a week or so if she doesn't contact you."

And Hugh was already looking at the file on his desk again. Ali turned and left after a few seconds and went back to The Privy. She sighed to herself. The weekend's blissful events felt light years away.

CHAPTER 29

TUESDAY Hugh was out all day at court. Desolate at his absence, Ali accepted an invite from Sam for a lunchtime drink.

Sam wasted no time on preliminaries.

"Come on. What's wrong?"

"Sorry, not with you."

"Look. You're all over the place. There's clearly something up. You're so preoccupied it's not true. It's not Rob again is it?"

"God, no."

"So is it that surveyor James you saw at Christmas?"

Ali sighed. "No. No."

"Well, it must be someone."

"No it's not. Why should it be anyone? I'm just tired from working so hard in the office and then at the weekends at the pub."

"That's not ordinary fatigue. I know the after-effects of a good shag when I see them. Come on. Spill. I won't give up."

Ali was so bursting to tell someone. "You won't say anything will you. Not to anyone at all?"

"Of course not. I'm the soul of discretion."

"What about Darren?"

"So is he."

"That's not what I meant."

"You don't expect me to keep anything from him do you. We're like this." And she held up both hands fingers crossed. "He's totally the sweetest, kindest man I've ever met."

"You really won't say anything will you? Not either of you, though I'm not convinced of the reason for all this secrecy but it's what he wants."

"Who wants?"

"It's Hugh."

"What? Who, I mean? I don't believe you."

"Well it is."

"But how? When?"

So Ali told her.

"It's … I've never had a relationship like this. I can't explain it. OK the secrecy makes it a bit special. But it's not that really. I can't cope when he's not around. It's like an obsession. I can't really cope when he is there. I just want to…"

"Yes? What?"

"To be honest, I can't keep my hands off him. It sounds awful and it is rather. I'm all charged up all the time. It just doesn't ever stop. It's like a disease." She put her head in her hands. "Perhaps I should get myself lobotomised or something. Perhaps have my gonads removed. I don't know," she ended forlornly.

"Steady on. I can't believe it. I've been with the firm for four years. I'd only just started when Hugh arrived and you know, we all thought, wow, who's *this* the Gods have sent down to Earth to tempt us. He would've been about twenty-five or something. Actually, now I think about it, there was some sort of difficulty over girlfriends to begin with. I'm not sure what. It was a partner thing. But not for long."

"Oh," Ali said, frowning at her friend. "Well, come on. Tell me some more."

"Nothing really. He never took any notice of any of us. He wasn't rude or anything and as far as I know he's never got in a temper with anyone. He was just remote and totally cool about everything. And he insisted on becoming a partner straight away. He'd already got something of a reputation for criminal stuff and I suppose he wasn't prepared to be treated like the assistant solicitor who the partners could push around.

"Anyway, what is it he does exactly? To provoke such, er, feelings?"

"I don't know. It's just him. And … well, I suppose it's the sex too. It's just spectacular. It just goes on and on."

"You mean like tantric sex?" Sam's eyes were wide.

"No. Well maybe. Him not me. He's just amazing."

"Oh. Sweet. You lucky thing," Sam looked bemused. "Who'd have thought it. Mr Iceberg himself. Though I suppose that figures. Supreme self-control, yeah?"

"I don't know about lucky. I'm torn to shreds most of the

time."

"Goodness girl. Enjoy it while it's going I say. You dog!" And she smiled broadly and nudged Ali hard. "Wow."

Ali found that the revelation made her feel no better.

"ALI. Mr Watts has been looking for you," said Tammy the next morning, as Ali emerged from the kitchen with her life-saving first coffee of the day.

Ali walked expectantly into Wattsey's room and could immediately see that something was up. He was purple in the face and fuming over a piece of paper in front of him. He thrust it at her.

"What do you think of this, then? The cheek of it."

Ali leaned over and peered at the sheet of paper, an email apparently from one of his clients forwarding an email to the client from some estate agents. It wasn't that obvious from the communications exactly what was going on, though it looked as though the client was saying that she still wanted Wattsey to act for her if her house sale went ahead.

Ali had heard of the client, a rich woman whose house was selling for something like three million pounds, and she knew that some problem had come up with the title or something though, unusually, Wattsey hadn't asked her to look into it.

She read on. The agent's email went round the houses about the buyer 'seeing sense' and ended by the observation '…I note you want to keep your solicitor on for now…'

"Keep me on! The cheek of it. As though–"

"What's actually happened?" Ali cut in, hoping to calm him down.

"Well," he said with more composure, "the client said she wasn't going ahead with her buyers and in effect she hadn't liked my handling of the matter. And she sacked me. Of course she's quite entitled to do that and I'm not complaining about that. Not really. I'd given her advice about the best course to follow but she preferred to take advice from her estate agent, would you believe. Bloody overbearing idiot suggesting all sorts of totally unrealistic solutions. Wouldn't have worked.

But would she listen to me? Oh no. She–"

Wattsey's voice was rising again. Hysteria wasn't far off and his colour was warming up.

"Oh well, she says she wants you to carry on acting for her. So that's all right isn't it?"

"All right! Look at what the bloody agent says." He poked repeatedly at the email on the desk between them. "Cheeky sod! '…I note you want to keep your solicitor on for now…'." He mimicked an upper-class-twit voice. Ali knew who the agent was. She'd come across him. A buffoon who thought he knew everything.

"As though," Wattsey exclaimed, "I'm a scullery maid who's been at the silver and is being let off. Keep me on indeed! *I* didn't do anything wrong. Just exercised a bit of professionalism and honesty if you please. I'm not prepared to be taken on and cast off at will. And then taken on again. No. I'm going to email the client and say she cancelled the contract and I'm not prepared to revive it. No I am not. And that's final." He hesitated. "Er. What do you think, Ali?"

"How much was the fee going to be?"

Wattsey's face fell several feet.

"Three and a half grand," he pouted lugubriously.

"Would you like me to take it over?"

"Well. I don't know," he whined and paused. At length he raised his eyes to her, rather dog-like and submissive. "I suppose you could. Would you?"

"Of course. Do you want to give the file to me?"

He smiled at last, picked it off the floor next to his chair and handed it over.

"Ali, you're an angel. I'll take you out to lunch later this week. Oh, by the way, I've got to go out now. Can you do these completions for me?" And he placed a large pile of more heavy files in her arms.

SHE was just about finished with the completion preparations and had got some out of the way already when Hugh came in about eleven-thirty. He put his head round The Privy door. "Can you pop in a sec."

Ali went to his room and shut the door.

"We've got another high-speeding case I'd rather not do. Story seems a bit fishy. Can you see the punter and take a statement and then go through it with me. No big hurry. The hearing's not till next month." And he held the file out to her. He was standing near the window behind his desk so she had to walk by the side of the desk to get it. When she went to take it, he didn't let it go.

"You've told Samantha haven't you?" When Ali didn't answer he said, "I know you have. It's the way she looked at me when I walked through reception. Like I was some sort of rare specimen at a zoo. God knows what you said to her!" He passed his free hand over his forehead and eyes.

Ali moved closer to him. "I couldn't help it," she said biting her lip with her head down. She thought he'd be angry. Instead he ran his hand through her hair. That was it. Ali lost it. She put her arms round his neck and pressed her body to his. He moaned softly and tried to pull away but Ali moved her hands further down to his buttocks and pulled him urgently to her. She felt her loins tighten. She knew what that meant but couldn't help herself and she moved against him. It just happened. Her breathing got faster and seconds later she shuddered and gave a small cry.

Hugh cleared his throat and whispered in her ear: "Ali. You really are a very, *very* naughty girl. I ought to take you out and spank you hard."

"I know. It won't happen again." Ali said into his chest. She was scarlet. She felt like a bad puppy that had done something disgusting and smelly in the corner.

"Well, let's not be too hasty. Perhaps just not in the office, hey? Look you'd better hoppit back to The Privy before anything else happens."

Ali took the file and walked as steadily as she could towards the door. As she opened it, Hugh said: "I think there's likely to be an outside appointment later Ali. I'll tell Sheila. We'd need to leave about twelve-forty-five. It might take several hours."

"Fine," said Ali.

She returned to The Privy and made more phone calls.

About twelve-fifteen Hugh buzzed her and said that the appointment had been brought forward. Could she be ready in five minutes. So she dumped the files and notes she'd made on Sandra who huffed and blew but got on with it.

In the car, Ali felt some sort of apology was due or at least that something should be said.

"It must be a terrible burden to you."

"Sorry. What must?"

"Me."

"Oh yes. It's awful. A beautiful woman who wants to have sex with me all the time. I can't imagine how I'll cope."

Ali sighed. She wanted to thump him.

He looked over. "Or we could always stop off at a chemist and get you some bromide."

It was slightly humiliating to be the butt of his amusement, however gentle, about something so personal. She felt ashamed at wanting to be his sex slave and him knowing it. It must have shown.

"I didn't mean it." Hugh took one hand off the steering wheel and held her hand and kissed it occasionally. When he had to drop it to change gear, Ali massaged his left leg going higher up but never too high. Hugh half closed his eyes.

"Ali you'll have to stop or we'll get arrested. We're nearly there. Oh, Ali." Her heart turned over when he said it like that. He looked at her briefly with soft eyes. He picked up her hand again and kissed it.

LATER when he was doing that thing he did afterwards which was to kiss her all over to calm her down that only worked if he didn't nibble or bite or lick at all, he said: "It's not that easy for me either you know, being in the office with you all day and knowing how gorgeous you are under those black suits you wear."

"Charcoal grey."

"Whatever. Ali, don't be grumpy. Don't you think we're

lucky. To have found someone that we're each so compatible with. It doesn't happen to everyone. It's never happened to me before. I mean, I've never had a relationship that was so powerful."

"But you can control it. Not show it. I find it so difficult." And she turned away.

"Ali." He put his arm round her. "I just think … I just think it hasn't been that long to lose it completely. Come here." And she turned around again and he hugged her tight. When he put his hand under her chin and tipped her face up, there were tears running down it. "Oh, Ali, darling."

"I'm sorry. I can't help it. I'm overwhelmed. All the time."

"All right. Why not just enjoy it. Just think how awful it could have been. If that semi-pornographic American programme hadn't been on the TV that night when you first came round, you'd never have made inappropriate advances to me and we'd never have found out how very compatible we are would we?"

Ali chuckled through the tears. "Well, you have to give some credit to Alan as well. I hope he's OK."

"That's better. Actually, I think a change of name might be in order. He appears to be nursing a large brood of little ones. You'd just love it in that shed."

Ali shuddered.

"Hugh, will you come to my sister's anniversary party with me in a few weeks' time after Easter."

"OK."

"Oh really? Brilliant! I'd hate it if you weren't with me. Sam's going to be there with Darren but since, you know, she knows, it doesn't really matter. Jan and Matt got to know Darren when they bought their house. That was a few years ago before he opened loads of branches."

"I'm sure it'll be heaps of fun."

"Actually, there's something I never told you about Darren. I suppose I should have, but it sort of slipped my mind. I've been meaning to say."

He carried on kissing her.

"You know his speeding offence," she continued, "well, you remember the explanation he gave, that his wife thought there was an intruder at his house so that's why he rushed home. Actually, that wasn't exactly true."

"Oh, God. So what did happen?"

"His wife called him to say she was off to her mother's nearby. He had to get home quickly because the children were being left on their own."

"OK. So what's wrong with that?"

"It's just that he didn't tell me this until later, and in court the magistrates got the story about the intruder but it was a lie. Darren said he wasn't prepared to have his dirty linen washed in public so he struck to the intruder story. Turned out she was neglecting the children, which is why he left her and brought them to live in Colchester with him."

"I see." He sighed. "There's bugger-all we can do about it now. Thanks for telling me though."

"Oh, good. I thought you might be cross."

Ali ran her fingers through Hugh's golden hair wondering whether to raise another concern. "And Hugh," she went on, "something else has been bothering me rather a lot. Who's that woman who phones you sometimes?"

"You've lost me."

"At the office. I've heard the tail ends usually of conversations. She calls you on your private line or your mobile and it sounds like she's trying to – I don't know – it sounds like she wants to see you and you're putting her off or something. It sounds as though she's very determined from your side of the conversation."

"Sorry. I still don't know what you're talking about."

"Er, you get rather cross. No actually very cross and put the phone down on her." She turned large, worried eyes on Hugh.

"Are you sure it's a woman? I don't have any women phoning me. At least not about anything but work."

"I don't know then."

Hugh pursed his lips, frowning. "It might be Don Grimsby. He's a local villain I won't act for anymore. He's just too vicious. Actually, he's a psychopath."

"Really?"

"Yes, he is. I'm sure he's murdered people. And God knows where his cash comes from. You know, to pay us. I was seriously worried we might get done for money laundering. Some of the other partners were none too happy. Cutting off a stream of income. But I couldn't help that. There's very little he does that's legit."

"Oh, so when you and Baz were talking about money and principles on Monday, it was about him."

"That's right. Yes. Anyway this guy's called me from time to time trying to persuade me to act for him again. I got him off some charges and I know a great deal about him. He keeps reminding me about solicitors-client privilege. Of course he couches it in less formal language, shall we say, but that's what he means, and he's right. I can't start shooting my mouth off about him."

"Didn't you tell the other partners what you know? They'd understand then, wouldn't they?"

"Christ no. I couldn't trust them not to open their mouths either by mistake or possibly deliberately. I wonder about them sometimes. One of them might be stupid enough to think it'd make an entertaining dinner party story, and the next thing, we'd find the office had been burned to the ground. No way can I involve them."

Ali swallowed. It sounded almost too extreme. Hugh hadn't finished yet.

"He wanted to pay me vast sums of money. If I'd been fool enough to accept, that would have been it. I'd never have got rid of him. He keeps threatening me now."

"Hugh. Aren't you worried? What sorts of threats?"

"Oh, all sorts. Says he's got mates with IT skills and he'll make it look as though I did accept money from him. Or he'll get some cash planted on me. And other vague things, like he'll make sure something unpleasant happens to me. He's got lots of ways of making my life uncomfortable. He'll show me the next time and so on. Nothing specific."

"The next time! What does he mean by that?"

"Ali, darling, I haven't a clue."

Darling!

"I assume you haven't told the police, from what you've just said."

"I can't. And I've got very little hard evidence. I mean of what I think he's done. I could tape the calls. But I just don't see the police jumping around for what would sound like vague intimidation. If it did go anywhere, there'd be publicity. I'd feel like an idiot. No, it's a non-starter."

"Hugh, it sounds like you're actually in danger though."

"Don't worry about me. I used to box at Southend and at Oxford. I could probably look after myself in most situations. I've just ignored it. I expect it'll all evaporate in the end. Anyway, he hasn't called for some time and it looks like he might soon get banged up for something serious."

"But, Hugh. You live all the way out here on your own," Ali said wretchedly. If all this was true, anything could happen. She hoped he was exaggerating. He hadn't sounded terribly worried, added to which, some months had gone by and nothing bad had happened yet.

"Hmm. We could soon do something about that. Why don't you come and stay a few more nights a week. It'd kill two birds with one stone. Provide me with a protectress and help with your excessive libido."

Ali's face turned crimson and she buried her face in the pillow. "You're making fun of me again," she said, her voice muffled.

"Well, that's only because I adore you so much. You're everything. The sun and the moon and the sky and the stars. Beautiful, sexy, smart and funny."

"That's so sweet. You're everything too. Everything to me."

And it was a while longer before they left his house and drove back to the office.

CHAPTER 30

ALI sat in one of the courts at Chelmsford Crown Court taking notes on Desmond's case which had nearly finished. It was just before Easter and she had especially wanted to be there given the significance of the Desmond case to her relationship with Hugh.

Hugh was finishing his address to the jury by telling them that they couldn't find Desmond guilty if they had any doubt about his having intended to kill or seriously harm Andrews. If they thought that there was any merit at all in Desmond's argument that he was just trying to get away from the serious damage a bottle in the face could do to him, then they had to acquit him.

Hugh had already been through Ali's suggested point about the fingerprint pattern on the small table near the door both during the forensic scientist's evidence and Desmond's evidence and earlier during his address to the jury. He'd also mentioned the shortness of the time available to Desmond to arrange things to make it merely look as though he had been defending himself as the prosecution had suggested as one possible scenario.

Hugh sat down and the jury retired. Ali went outside into the corridor. Hugh came out but spoke to the prosecuting barrister and hardly gave Ali a glance. Since this was par for the course, Ali didn't mind too much. She walked over and chatted to them as well.

Sooner than they thought, the jury returned. Asked to give their verdict, they found Desmond "Not guilty" on both counts.

Desmond's wife burst into tears and he went over and hugged her. Hugh collected up his papers and Desmond said thanks and he didn't want any statements to the press waiting outside. He'd decided to wait inside for a time, have a coffee and leave later when the press might have dispersed or found someone else to prey on.

Ali and Hugh slipped out of a side door and were soon on the A12 back to Colchester to enjoy their Easter break.

Easter came early that year, barely into April. Ali and Hugh had arranged that she should stay over. He had another case coming up in the Crown Court soon and needed to spend time on it. Ali managed to get the whole Easter off from working at the S&S. There were lots of students home from university and plenty of spare labour.

To occupy herself when Hugh was working, Ali had decided to do some redecorating at the cottage. She'd been tapping the walls and had decided that most of them could get away without complete replastering if the dull-sounding bits were removed and filled. The previous weekend they had visited a DIY store at Ipswich to get what she needed. Not the Colchester branch of course. They might have bumped into someone from PWT!

On the Wednesday evening before the holiday, Hugh brushed down the cobwebs and de-spidered the hall, stairs and landing and the small downstairs toilet. The de-spidering was a bit of a nightmare, trying to get them all into jars without injury or without them disappearing under skirting boards. Ali hid away in the bedroom upstairs until the jars had been emptied outside. After it was all finished, it looked better already.

She hope that over the four days of Easter, she could get the loose plaster raked out, the holes filled and dried and the lining paper hung; probably no more than that. Painting would have to wait.

And she absolutely loved it. Hugh came and watched sometimes and at turns shook his head at her enthusiasm and encouraged her efforts. He steadied the ladder when needed and of course laid hands on her. When she got covered in dust and detritus, he took her upstairs and showered her down. Then he went off and came back with a couple of packs of stuff. One of them was face masks. The other turned out to be forensic suits.

"These should help," he said.

"Where on earth did you get them from?"

"The masks were left behind by the bods who did the kitchen and bedroom. My mum got me the suits when she found out I was doing criminal work. She thought I'd be turning up at scenes of crime all the time. I hadn't the heart to tell her it doesn't happen that way."

"I suppose whoever assaulted Angela must've worn something like that."

"I imagine so. You can get them at any safety suppliers. But it's difficult not to leave any evidence at all."

They both left it there and Ali donned a suit and mask and they did the trick.

The four days were blissful. On Easter Sunday, Hugh took Ali to a little pub near Bures for a meal and then they walked by the river. Every so often when there were no other walkers about, Hugh stopped and backed her up against a tree and kissed her and rubbed his whole clothed body against hers and, well, Ali wasn't accountable for her response.

And their nights together were just something else. Ali had had to go on the pill. There was a danger that otherwise they'd get through every condom in Essex and, horror of horrors, they might have to abstain. She'd wondered if the hormones or just the psychological element of more or less total safety would affect the love-making.

Not so. If anything, the complete freedom and skin contact made it even better if such were possible. They often woke during the night already kissing and wrapped in each other's arms saying each other's names. She wished he'd tell her he loved her and she had a hard time not saying it to him, but all rational thought was usually swept away pretty quickly.

"I'm glad you didn't become a doctor," said Ali, "looking at all those women's bits all the time. It would be just awful."

"How do you know about the doctor thing?"

"Sheila mentioned once about your degree in medicine. Why didn't you carry on with that?"

"We'd done debating at school and at university and I liked that and I got interested in the law. I did some forensic science as well and decided I'd rather get involved in criminal law.

Anyway it could have been much worse than just examining women's genitalia. We might not have met at all if I'd become a doctor! That would've been tragic wouldn't it?"

"Oh. Unbearable!"

"We were meant to be together you know. Obviously I didn't become a doctor so that I could meet you."

"Oh, Hugh. That's the nicest thing you've said to me."

CHAPTER 31

ALL too soon, it was Tuesday morning. Most of the wall-papering had been completed. They'd also chosen a parchment white Farrow & Ball matt emulsion for the walls and a matching oil-based paint for the woodwork. Ali was dying to get on with the painting. The old toilet was a work of art in itself when cleaned up and they merely fitted a new wooden seat and a shiny brass chain.

Going into the office, which always used to be such a thrill, was something of a let-down these days after staying with Hugh. If only she could have proudly paraded her and Hugh's attachment, that might have made it better. Instead, all she could do was fret and hanker after the next time they'd be together.

Ali was working for Alison, drafting a statement regarding a financial relief application from some notes taken last week. And she was due to see Graham and take instructions from him that afternoon about his divorce and finances which was going to be interesting.

She had lots of interruptions though. The form had become that if anyone troublesome or a bit difficult called, they'd usually be put through to Ali.

Accordingly she ended up speaking to Ms Bates, a frequent caller, who ran a small dog breeding enterprise and had a pregnant Peruvian hairless bitch called Peaches. A hairless dog; it sounded disgusting. Ms Bates was moving house and worrying constantly whether the completion date would conflict with the dog giving birth. And the expected date of confinement was getting nearer and nearer with exchange of contracts expected any day and parties in the chain talking about moving on the very date Peaches was expected to whelp. And she just couldn't move while the dog was giving birth.

Ali rolled her eyes. Her sister Jan had had to move house the day before she gave birth to their son and hadn't made as much fuss as this.

Women seem to manage all right, she was tempted to say, but didn't.

"Couldn't you send her somewhere now," Ali suggested, "then she wouldn't have to be unsettled again."

"No, it's too close. She'd just lose them. I don't think I'm going to be able to move now until a few weeks after she's actually had them."

"You do know don't you that your sellers are desperate to move before the start of the school summer term so their children can start their new school."

"Well, it won't kill them not to will it? Not like the pups!"

"Right," said Ali, glad that Ms Bates couldn't see her expression. "And the other thing is that someone further up the chain has a mortgage offer that runs out in about ten days. I just think if you insist on delaying things the whole chain will fall through. I wonder, er, you know why you decided to move house at all while this was going on."

"At the beginning, the agents said it would be through in six weeks. And that was three months ago."

"Unfortunately, as you know, those same agents sent your buyers to a firm of production line conveyancers who are now holding everything up until they can get the case signed off by a 'team leader' who's away at the moment. It's likely the agents have received a referral fee from the conveyancers. If they did receive a fee and haven't disclosed that to you, you may be able to refuse to pay their commission."

"Look I can't be bothered about that at the moment. You'll have to tell the chain I can't move now until the end of April at least. I've got to go now." And she hung up.

Ali sent an email to the buyers' conveyancer and the sellers' solicitors and thought: Well when they both come back saying no, the clients'll have to sort it out direct because it's impossible.

She was just getting stuck into the matrimonial statement again when Tammy buzzed her.

"Sorry Ali but no one else'll take this call. Can you? It's something to do with horses."

Ali sighed and said she would.

"So how can I help you?" Ali said pleasantly.

"Er, about a year or two ago I bought a field from the farmer next door for my horses and now the council are saying I've got to make an application for change of use from agricultural to leisure/amenity."

"Did we act for you when you bought the land?"

"No. I do usually use you but it seemed so simple I went to some internet conveyancers. It was really cheap and it was all through in a couple of weeks."

"Did they know what you wanted the land for?"

"I'm not sure. I don't think so."

"Did they ask?"

"No. Anyway, the council are saying that the planning won't necessarily be granted."

"I assume you'll make an application anyway."

"Yes, but what I want to know is: what will I do with the horses if the planning application is refused?"

This floored Ali. What a stupid, stupid question.

"What are you thinking? That you might be able to make some sort of claim against the conveyancers?"

"Well, what do you think?"

"It's impossible to say. One would need to know a lot more about the case, see the conveyancers' terms and conditions. They may have excluded liability for advice about the use of the land, planning issues, other things. Their conditions may say that they were only responsible to get the land adequately transferred to you and registered in your name and nothing else. That might not wash for a solicitor. But it might for a conveyancer."

"So what do I do?"

"I can send you our terms of business and hourly rates if you like and you can decide if you want to take it any further and get a more considered opinion what your options and prospects are."

"That's not very helpful."

"Sorry. I can't give you any definitive opinion on the phone.

It wouldn't be—"

But the woman had hung up. And Ali hadn't even taken her name, though she knew Tammy kept a log of callers' names. No one would get past her without proffering a name and return phone number, even if it was Jane Marple St Mary Mead 123.

Ali ploughed on with the matrimonial statement, printed it off and handed it to Alison to check and by that time it was nearly lunchtime.

Tammy called her and said Graham Spellings was on the phone for her. She didn't know why. She put him through and Graham said he was in town already and since they had a meeting at two fifteen, would she like to go for a quick drink and a bite with him. Ali was charmed and diverted from her usual obsession and said yes immediately. She went off to meet Graham in The George.

"How are you bearing up?" she asked Graham after they sat down. He insisted on buying the snacks and drinks and Ali tucked in.

"I'm not too bad," said Graham. "I've got used to it now. In fact I'm more or less resigned to getting convicted and probably going down."

"No. You can't think like that. Hugh's convinced…" she stopped herself from saying he was convinced Graham hadn't done it. Of course he was. They were best friends for, like, forever. "He's right behind you. He'll do the very best he can for you. I mean I keep thinking. Is there anything else we haven't covered? You know, anyone else who might want to get at you?"

"No one that I know of."

"Do you mind talking about it, the case I mean because I'll shut up if you don't want me to."

"No, that's OK. It's all pretty unreal. But I've got to assume I might go down and make plans for the business to be looked after. Lots of people depend on it for jobs you know. I can't just disappear one day which is what would happen if I get put inside and expect it to all keep ticking over without me. And

I'd be worried to death. So I'm making the appropriate arrangements."

"Yes, of course. So, going back to what we were talking about, have you ever, say, double-crossed anyone in business?"

"Ali it's not like that. I've certainly not done anything illegal. I've taken opportunities others could have taken. I've beaten other companies in getting contracts. Of course I have. That's the essence of business. It's unthinkable that any business opponents would set me up with the kind of trouble I've got now. Unthinkable. It's the sort of thing only a hardened criminal would do. Or someone with a warped mind."

"OK, if not a business opponent, then what about your personal life."

"As I told everyone at the police interview, I haven't got a personal life."

"No, I meant in the past. Have you ever nicked another man's girlfriend for example? It wouldn't be the first time in history if you had. It appears to be rife in Colchester anyway from my short experience of matrimonial work."

"No. That's not my thing." He hesitated. "I mean..." He frowned.

"Yes?"

"It's completely irrelevant. I'm not even going to dignify it with an airing."

"I'm intrigued now, Graham. Even if it's got nothing to do with anything, you'll have to tell me."

"There was someone once. But it's ridiculous to associate it with this charge against me."

"OK, then just tell me as a friend. It can't hurt."

"I hope not."

"So tell me."

"What it is is that when Hugh went to university, he was engaged to a girl. I suppose he's told you," then seeing her face, "oh, perhaps not. They'd been going out together since they were *sixteen* for God's sake and everyone thought it would be a good idea if they got engaged before he went away. I'm not sure Hugh himself did but he buckled under and did it. Anyway, when he was away, I started to see her. She was a girl we'd both been friends with for years and it just happened. Even before the first Christmas holiday. Honestly Ali, he wasn't bothered at all. He liked Oxford and he wanted to be free to date girls there."

"So Hugh's been engaged to someone?" Ali sounded stunned.

"Look Ali I know about you and Hugh. He's told me. He's my oldest friend. We've known each other since we were babies. We grew up in the same street. I know just about everything there is to know about him and I know you don't need to bother about the fact that he was once engaged. Either from the point of view of my current predicament or your relationship with him."

Ali sat silently looking at her drink. *Engaged! Sixteen! No wonder he was such a genius in bed. He must've had years more practice than her.*

"I know Hugh's rather, I suppose, a private person," Graham carried on. "And he doesn't necessarily conform to peoples' assumptions about the way we should all behave. But it doesn't mean anything. Thing is. His family are just about as different to him as they could be. I mean they're nice but they're not at all intellectual. When he passed the eleven-plus, it was something really special. No one in our street passed the eleven-plus. No one on our estate for that matter. You know he's really clever. He got the highest marks for the eleven-plus that year in the whole of Essex. He could have gone to any of the better grammar schools in Essex like say the Colchester one but they were too far away so he went to one of the Southend ones. And it wasn't that easy for him."

Ali scrutinised Graham, the best friend of her boyfriend who knew just about everything there was to know about Hugh, and she knew so little. She might as well let him continue and find out what he was prepared to tell her.

"That was when he became contained. I think he had to. In order to cope. The other boys mostly came from middle class families. Their boys had gone to private schools or received an enormous amount of tutoring. Hugh didn't have those advantages. His parents were supportive but they couldn't help him fit in. He had to work that out for himself. So he went – I don't know – he started to be sort of watchful. He couldn't relax. His accent changed. And he felt all the time he had to do his very best. I noticed all this but it never affected our friendship."

Ali just listened, glued to her seat.

"He got the highest points for A-levels in the whole country that year. He's not just anyone Ali. I'm not saying he's a genius or anything but he's much much brighter than most of us. You know he's got a PhD in forensic science or something. He's entitled to call himself 'Dr Sutherland' but he doesn't."

Graham looked at her.

"I don't know why I'm telling you all this. Hugh wouldn't thank me. In fact he'd be furious probably. Anyway, him and Debbie wouldn't have lasted."

Her questioning to Graham was largely forgotten in the wake of his revelations about Hugh. Whether he might have upset anyone enough for them to have tried to mess up his life by fitting him up for an attempted rape seemed of less interest.

"What's she doing now?" Ali asked.

"She was a hairdresser for some years. Now I believe she's married with a number of children."

"More fool her then," said Ali and smiled.

"Good. I'm glad you think that way. I wouldn't want him to be hurt."

Ali's eyes widened, her expression wry. "Hugh can't have told you everything about us. If you think I might hurt, as in leave, Hugh, well ... I suppose the planets might stop in their orbits, but..."

She spread her hands.

The rest of her food had grown cold. And she was supposed to be the professional here. She thanked Graham for lunch and suggested they get themselves back to the office for his interview proper.

CHAPTER 32

"HUGH about?" asked Graham when they got back to the office.

"No. I'm not sure where he is."

Ali could hardly continually ask Sheila for updates on his location or sneak into his office every five minutes to take surreptitious looks at his diary.

The interview took all afternoon. Petunia wanted the house, the horses (of course), half Graham's business assets and two thirds of his other assets, notwithstanding that there was a pre-nup and they'd only been married for three years, that they had no children, and regardless of the fact that she was now shacked up with a rich banker.

Ali wasn't sufficiently qualified to give advice on her prospects but it seemed pretty excessive. At least she was able to go through the laborious task of taking Graham through each sordid allegation Petunia had raised and each argument for her needing such an excessive settlement.

Basically the business wasn't up for grabs. It was a continually evolving, expanding entity. Every advance financed another advance and so on. There was no spare capacity. No spare meat that could be pared off for a greedy, estranged wife or anyone else. It was so complicated that Ali had to suggest another appointment with Graham to go through all the points.

Petunia alleged that she was coerced into signing the pre-nup, going into detail about his aggressive behaviour and the circumstances surrounding the signing of the pre-nup. She alleged she'd had miscarriages during the marriage and forewent lucrative modelling contracts to concentrate on the pregnancies. Graham denied it all and there didn't seem to be any independent evidence. As to Graham's alleged philandering, the allegations Petunia made were almost laughable.

"I'm just thankful we didn't actually have any children,"

Graham said. "Poor little buggers would have been dragged through all this. How awful!"

Ali saw him out of the office and he agreed to phone for another appointment.

After seeing and speaking to Graham, Ali felt more buoyant. The possibility that she might be able to hurt Hugh! Unthinkable. But if somebody else thought it, perhaps her stock with Hugh was higher than she'd imagined. And so she poked her nose round Sam's door as she went back to The Privy to collect her things to go home.

"Good Easter?"

"Yeah. You?"

"Brilliant." Sam must have detected something worth knowing because Ali could almost see her antennae re-adjusting to the appropriate frequency and Sam said the words Ali had been hoping for:

"How about a post-oestrous drink at the you know where? Darren's picked up the kids today so I'm free for … ooh … I don't know … two hours maybe ... three, tops."

"Lovely," said Ali.

"SO, the big, bad wolf didn't eat Little Red Riding Hood *all* up over Easter, then?"

"No," said Ali, "I've survived. It could have been worse. But it wasn't!"

"Well, come on. What did you *do*?"

"I spent most of the time decorating."

"What? That's not what I came to hear!"

"Actually, there was the odd interlude of, you know, unbridled passion. Oh, Sam. It was heavenly. I don't have the vocabulary to describe it. Sorry. It's beyond ordinary words. I'd have to☐"

"OK. Cut the crap. I do know what rampant sex is like. What I want to know is: has he declared undying love yet or what?"

"Sadly, no," sighed Ali.

"Oh. How disappointing."

"Yes. I've had adoration. We were meant to be together. I'm *everything*. But no actual declaration of love. No."

"Oh. How disappointing!" Sam said again. "Still, it's a jolly good start though. So, er, has your previous problem got any better? Your, you know, obsession with *it*?"

"Not really. It's just as bad. Even thinking about it now," she sighed. "And I've got to wait until tomorrow."

"You could always go and have therapy for sex addiction you know. Both of you if necessary."

"Don't you start. He's always teasing me about it. That's quite enough."

"Sounds sweet."

"Maybe. Er, I have found out a lot more about him. You mustn't tell a soul but…"

And she related Graham's account of Hugh's background regarding romantic matters.

"Oh. Engaged! Who would have thought it!"

"You know. I've been having some dark thoughts that are, well, a bit disturbing. I don't suppose there's anything in it, but…"

"Sound a little unpleasant."

"Yes, it would be. It's just … Hugh is so secretive and closed. It's difficult not to think all sorts of things. It's fine when I'm with him. Other times, though, when he's ignoring me in the office, it's really horrible and my imagination goes off the scale."

"Such as?"

"OK, what about this? It'll seem ridiculous, but hear me out." Ali was a little tipsy by this time.

Sam nodded seriously, in an equally half-cut fashion.

"OK," she said again, "what it is is that on the day of Angela's assault at Graham's place, you know, Hugh had been there that day. Earlier on in that day. Then he only goes and produces to me some forensic suits he had about his house of a sort that must have been used by Angela's attacker to avoid fibres, DNA and all that being left all over her bed." She explained why Hugh said he had them and that, yes, she had actually worn them to decorate and, yes, they had worked but still…

Oh, and Hugh sometimes received phone calls which sounded as though they were from a woman pestering him. He'd told her it was an ex-criminal client, but the story was pretty far-fetched...

And, aha, this was the thing, Graham had taken Hugh's teenage fiancée away from him after he'd gone off to Oxford!

"I'm sorry," said Sam, "I'm not sure what I'm supposed to be concluding from all this."

"Well, the theory is, and it's just a theory," said Ali in a slightly slurred voice, "that Hugh was so cut up about the fiancée thing that he staged the attempted rape!" Ali sat back triumphantly.

"Sorry. Er, have I heard you right? You think Hugh set up what looked like an attempted rape of a girl because his friend took away his fiancée ten years previously? Is that it?"

"Pretty much. It's just a theory mind."

"Ali. You're barking. Hugh wouldn't do such a thing in a million years."

"Yes, but he's so secretive. And he's obviously had lots of contact with all sorts of criminals. Maybe he's jealous of Graham for being so rich. He doesn't tell me anything about himself or what he's thinking. Last year he gave me, sort of, pointed looks when we discussed Graham's case. He took me to the pub one lunchtime and, I don't know, it just seemed the way he looked at me so intently. Like he wanted to know what I thought about Graham's case because he wondered if I thought it was him. Which of course I didn't – at that time."

"So you don't think a more obvious explanation for his interest in you was … his interest in you?"

"It didn't seem like it. Oh, and he put on an Essex accent once, and do you know what, he sounded *just* like Graham. It was unbelievable."

"Don't be ridiculous. If you got Darren to do it, he'd probably sound just the same. In fact, that's what he *does* sound like."

"Do you really think so?"

"I'm positive."

"Oh."

"And apart from that he adores you apparently, you were meant to be together. For a bloke, those *are* declarations of undying love. Don't push him. It'll come."

"Maybe."

"Ali. Don't let your imagination run away with you because he's a bit remote at times. Not others apparently." And she nudged Ali in that way that made everything make sense.

Then misery set in again.

"At least you're going home to Darren tonight. I've no idea where Hugh is at the moment."

"Yes, you do now," came a voice from behind.

"Can I offer either of you a lift home. Or anywhere else?" Hugh nodded to Sam and smiled, bending over Ali's chair and kissing her.

CHAPTER 33

ALI WAS WALKING ON air. She was going to spend the whole of the forthcoming weekend with Hugh *and* was going to her sister's party with him the next day.

The Friday morning brought a minor surprise. Ali was walking past reception when Baz bustled through importantly and ushered a man back to his room.

"Who was that?" she asked Tammy.

"Dave Wright, come to see Baz about a new yard somewhere."

Interesting. Ali filed it away and when, later that morning, she met Baz in the kitchen she said it didn't look as though the firm had lost his clientele after all.

"No, that's true, Ali," he said.

"So? It wasn't all bad then."

"Not at all."

Ali offered him a pleasant smile and he relented.

"All right. He's pleased about his daughter and the marriage and – I can't believe this – you won't either – he's offered the son-in-law a job and a share in the business. They're going to expand! People never cease to amaze me!" And, gripping his coffee mug, he walked off shaking his head.

Ali spent the Friday lunchtime and early afternoon prowling around the town to find a suitable dress, only to settle fairly easily on the dusky pink sparkly strapless number she'd had her eye on for weeks. Shoes were a different matter though and required considerable attention to detail, tryings-on and strutting about to make sure the final article was high enough to make her look streamlined but not so high as to reduce her mobility to a shuffle. She eventually chose a pair of slingbacks the same colour as the dress.

It took longer than she'd expected. The narrow pedestrian ways were so picturesque and lovely to amble through slowly and lulled her into forgetting she was in a hurry. She even took a break for far longer than she should have at an outside table for a coffee and a fancy cake, an almost unheard of luxury for a weekday. She wasn't the only one. The atmosphere was continental as, say, in Paris, where people seemed to ignore the weather and take refreshments in the open regardless of the cold.

At one of the shops she bumped into Trish, the avid lady she and Hugh had met at the Pink Elephant during the lunchtime drink all those months ago. Trish was buying shoes for a golf club do and made a beeline for Ali, re-introducing herself in case Ali had forgotten who she was. Which she had rather.

"So how are you and Hugh getting on? You certainly looked like a couple with possibilities."

Perhaps she wasn't as daft as she seemed. She must've seen something I didn't at the time.

Trish prattled on. "I'm completely out of touch. I've been staying with my friend in Florida since New Year's. Honestly, I've had a wonderful time. My you should see the young men out there. 'Toned' doesn't do it justice. And the parties! Well, they certainly know how to enjoy themselves over there."

Ali tuned out after a few minutes as Trish droned away. She'd had a lot of practice with her mum.

"What do you think of these? You don't think they're too young for me, do you?" Ali gazed at the impossible creation Trish was forcing her left foot into. Before she could make any useful comment, Trish was off again.

"Of course," she was saying, "when I read about it in the papers, I knew Hugh would be the first person Graham would call, so I wasn't surprised."

"Sorry, what was that?"

"Last year. I was on the way to Stansted late in the evening to get an early flight the next day to visit my sister in Newcastle-upon-Tyne for a couple of days for her birthday. I always fly there now. It's the only way to travel. Of course I'd set out two hours earlier but I'd forgotten my contact lenses. Couldn't go anywhere without them so although I'd booked a hotel for the night near the airport I had to come

187

back, didn't I. You know I live in Bakers Lane too, don't you. Very handy for the golf club. That taxi driver took advantage though. He charged me a small fortune."

Ali began to daydream again, listening with only half an ear.

"Of course the weather was awful and he had to put on snow chains so I do understand really but still. I didn't think at the time and Graham wasn't charged straight away but now I keep thinking it was a bit odd really. If someone's arrested, they generally call their solicitor to the police station don't they, not to their house. Or at least they do in films. So what do you think I should do? Do you think I should mention it to the police? That poor man's awaiting trial. It must be awful for him. Should I? You're a solicitor. You'll know about these things."

"Actually I'm not. But yeah I suppose if you've got any more information you should tell the police. They need to know everything." Ali was eyeing up some sheer tights and thinking about going to Boots to buy more of her favourite perfume.

"Yes. You're quite right. I know it was Hugh's car because I know his number. And I know it was about half past ten because we'd been all the way to Stansted and back and I'd even nearly booked into the airport hotel before I realised I'd forgotten my contacts. And I know what date it was because of course it was my sister's birthday the next day and I've checked since and it was definitely the date the assault was supposed to have happened. I'll pop in about it on Monday. Too much to do before then."

All this made a vague, imprecise impression on Ali. It sort of started to sink in somewhat later what Trish appeared to be saying but she dismissed it as ridiculous and when she did think about it at all seriously, she reasoned that, given her relationship with Hugh, she'd better not get involved. You never knew how things would turn out. To be found later to have tried to persuade a possible witness to withhold evidence could backfire horribly. It might detrimentally affect Graham's chances. No, it was best to forget it and leave things to take their course.

CHAPTER 34

ALI and Hugh drove straight to his cottage after leaving the office. She passed a day happily messing about at the cottage on Saturday while Hugh worked. She was bringing on some cottage garden flower seedlings to plant out later and digging over borders ready for them.

It was a lovely day and about half-past-two Hugh took himself off for a run while Ali gardened on in a T shirt and shorts. He was soon back and leaned against the gate, getting his breath back as he watched her for a time. She was trying to decide what to do next, what would look best where.

After a time, he sauntered over to her and, without saying anything, took her hand, kissed the inside of her wrist and licked and lightly bit all the way up her arm, especially the inner elbow and forced his tongue inside the short sleeve of her T shirt. She was breathing hard by now. Hugh went down on his knees.

Is he going to propose?

But he did the same thing to her legs as he had to her arms, biting her knees quite hard round the knee caps and putting his tongue inside the legs of her brief shorts.

"Hugh. Please!" she moaned with her hands on his shoulders.

He pushed her down onto the grass, got on top of her and moved against her while French kissing her. She arched her back. He was enormous through his thin running shorts. They were still both fully clothed. Her cries rang out across the softly undulating Essex countryside. He watched her face as she came, finding it wildly sexy and strengthening even more his bonding with her. He knew she liked to watch him too, to see him, so she told him, so vulnerable and abandoned when he was normally ultra-controlled.

Her eyes opened into his. She rolled him onto his back, pulled his running shorts down at the front and finished him off in her mouth. They both lay back on the grass gazing up at the duck-egg-blue sky with soft, billowy clouds drifting slowly over.

"Hmm. Yum," she said, laughing. It seemed a travesty that she couldn't tell him she loved him. "Hugh, I do so adore you," she said instead.

"I can't kiss you," he said, pulling a face.

"You must. I won't be happy if you don't."

"Oh, all right then. Just this once." There was no kiss though. Suddenly, a large, black, panting shape appeared beside them. The Labrador's wet nose went unerringly for their crotches. They both noticed the dull humming sound at the same time and, turning their heads sideways, saw a large crowd of middle-aged and older people peering over the hedge at them from the public footpath, talking in low voices.

"Oh great!" he said, "It's one of the walking groups. I've read about them in the parish mag." He pulled her to her feet, shooed the dog, gave the group a wave and took her inside.

Indoors, she wrapped Jan and Matt's present, an antique vase. Then, before dressing for the evening, she soaked slowly for an hour in the slipper bath, with occasional interventions from Hugh.

He seemed to get ready in about five minute flat. He used the same bath water as Ali, claiming the water felt nicer as she'd been in it. They walked to the end of the footpath where they were meeting their taxi. Ali wore an old, artificial-fur coat, a charity shop find. The sunny day had transformed into a frosty night. The coat was a blessing as they waited in the dark.

"You do think the taxi'll find us don't you," she started to fuss, however a minute or so later they saw from a distance the lights turn down the road and soon they were snuggling up in the back of the heated car.

They arrived about on time and stood around with others for a time making small talk and trying not to drink too much too early. Matt and Hugh appeared to know each other quite well, so Ali went off to find Jan or Sam or someone.

Jan and Matt had a marquee in their garden decked out

with strobe lights and huge speakers for dancing later. The marquee was attached to the French windows by a canvas corridor. Plates of finger-food sat on every surface.

Ali nodded to herself. Very well organised.

Everyone else seemed to be in the kitchen.

"So that's 'Ali's young man'," Jan was saying to Sam when Ali sidled up behind them. "It's a big secret in the family, so I'm obviously intrigued."

"It's not exactly front page news in the office either," replied Sam. "Oh, you don't know then. The guy's Hugh Sutherland, Colchester's most eligible male. At least in the legal world. He's a partner in PWT."

"Oh," Jan said as though some penny had dropped. "The one I keep reading about in the local press. He gets rogues off all sorts of charges. Oh," she said again.

Ali coughed from behind. They both turned round guiltily.

Ali hugged Jan. "You did it then. Reached six years. What an achievement!"

"The happiest six years of my life," said Jan.

Then Ali hugged Sam.

Sam and Jan raised their eyebrows at each other.

"S'all right. I didn't hear all that much," said Ali. "*But* it's a good job Mum and Dad are off on that cruise or I'd face the grilling of the century tomorrow."

"Poor Mum. She's dying to know," said Jan. "Well, he's quite a catch. I've got to hand it to you, Ali."

Ali realised, hearing these hackneyed clichés, that Jan was already slightly tipsy. And, Ali thought, why not. It's her night.

Ali felt a light hand on her waist. She hadn't noticed Hugh coming into the kitchen. She introduced him as 'my date'. No one was fooled by this. What else could she say though; she didn't want to make a big thing of it in front of Hugh. He smiled and said how well organised the party was and he'd look forward to coming to their twelfth anniversary party.

Please God I hope so, thought Ali.

Then he asked Ali if she wanted to dance and Ali realised that the disco had started.

"See you later," said Ali. Out of the corner of her eye, she saw Jan and Sam give each other exaggerated nudges and winks.

"And you wonder why I want to keep it under wraps," Hugh whispered. Right in her ear where it always had the most effect.

Hugh turned out to be quite a good dancer. Or at least between them, they moved rather well. With most blokes she would have gyrated around and only got together for any really smoochy numbers but Hugh put his arm round her waist and took her other hand and she found that they almost always anticipated each other's moves. Actually, she thought after a time, it's him. He's the one who knows what's going on.

There was plenty of opportunity to smooch. Most of the stuff Matt had lined up was seventies or eighties or nineties. Ali wasn't too familiar with music from those decades apart from rock music, but there was a lot of really sexy stuff and she melted into Hugh's arms when the opportunity arose.

He took her outside every so often and they walked hand in hand around the rest of the garden. Ali was tempted to think that he was keeping her away from people and said as much at one point.

"I just want to be alone with you. And you know what people are like. They always want to pigeonhole you or fit you into their version of things and know all about you. Or worst of all, they want you to do what they expect you to do."

"Well if you feel that way, why don't you just disappear and go and live in Thailand or somewhere."

He laughed and said: "Pretending for a moment that that's a serious question, I like things as they are. My job, practising law, friends. I just don't want to live other people's lives. And then of course there's you." And he gave her a long lingering kiss.

Lots of police were attending, as of course there would be. Ali recognised DI Hunter who'd conducted Graham's interview. He greeted Hugh and Ali and smiled knowingly. Ali felt relieved that she hadn't tried to interfere with whatever

Trish decided to do. He and Hugh seemed to know each other socially and Ali left them chatting while she sauntered off to powder the proverbial nose.

She took a short cut through the utility room where she happened across Jan and Matt. They were in a clinch up against the central heating boiler and Jan had one foot raised, rubbing Matt's leg with hers. He was telling her to spread 'em and she was asking him if she had the right to remain horny. Ali laughed and they did too and she walked on through.

"So how did you become such a good dancer?" Ali asked Hugh later on.

"I went to a few salsa classes with a girlfriend at Oxford, but you're just a natural." Ali totally hated that girlfriend.

He took her in his arms and said quietly: "There's never been anyone like you,` Ali. And there never will be."

She put her head on his shoulder. "Nor you. Oh Hugh. I could stay frozen with you like this forever. I want to be with you for always."

And quite involuntarily their lips found each other's and they kissed as unobtrusively as they could, or so they thought, while the music swirled around them until eventually there was a huge crash of cymbals and Matt announced that the fireworks would be in five minutes.

Outside they found Jan. "I thought the fireworks weren't going to be until midnight and it's only eleven-thirty," said Ali.

"Well, it was either that or a bucket of freezing cold water!" her sister replied.

Ali gave an embarrassed giggle. Hugh put his arm around her and said: "Well, you shouldn't have such a beautiful, desirable sister."

JAN sighed and shook her head. She just hoped it wouldn't all go pear-shaped for some reason as these extra-steamy love affairs sometimes did. She hadn't realised her sister was in so deep. She decided to find Sam when the fireworks were over.

She tracked her down taking a breather in the sitting room with Darren. "You couldn't come and help me with some cocktails could you, Sam?" And together they repaired to the kitchen.

"I was wondering, Sam," she said as they squeezed oranges, sliced lemons and speared cherries with cocktail sticks, "do you think it's serious with Ali and Hugh?"

"On one level I suppose it is."

"You mean carnal. Yeah, I kind of got that. But what about, you know, deeper feelings?"

"I'm not sure. They're obviously besotted with one another by the looks of things. It's only been a couple of months or so. I know it's not much longer for me and Darren. But we've got kids. We can't afford to mess around or make a mistake a second time. Hugh and Ali. I'm not sure."

"I'm just worried she might get hurt. Why doesn't he want anyone to know about them? I hope he's not just using her."

"I expect he just doesn't want the whole office gossiping about them. You can see what they're like together. If they let it slip a bit in the office, they'd be in for quite a bit of ribbing. Especially Ali. There'd probably even be jealousy and snide whisperings about favouritism. Hugh'd probably be all right because he's a partner. And he's just so reserved usually."

"Yes, except none of that means he isn't using her. Isn't he friends with that businessman Graham Spellings? The tabloids make him out to be a bit of a lad, apart from the fact he's been charged with molesting some girl. Perhaps they're two of a kind."

"Yeah. No. It doesn't actually look like any of that tabloid stuff's actually true. There's nothing Graham can do about it. It'd just draw more attention to it. And the assault he's obviously defending. But I can't say any more about that."

"No. Course. I understand. What about Hugh though?"

"Er, he's pretty serious most of the time. As far as I know he hasn't had any girlfriend in the four years he's been with the firm which is pretty amazing when you think about it. He's not exactly Mr Ugly. At the beginning, there was some trouble or other about a girl or girls. I told Ali that. Anyway, that was three or four years ago. I think he was attracted to Ali from the

195

outset, when she first came to the firm. I wouldn't think he's a flighty sort, or unreliable. And, well, if they hit it off in the sack, that's at least halfway there isn't it?"

"I hope so. Right, do you want to taste a few of these before we take them in. Make sure they're not *too* strong!"

BACK on the dance floor, Ali caught Sam glancing at her and Hugh as they alternately danced and smooched. A conflab was definitely in order. She told Hugh she must go and powder her nose again and walked out straight past Sam. Shortly, Sam followed her and got her in the upstairs bathroom.

"You know I wouldn't have believed it if I hadn't seen it with my own eyes. He's totally besotted with you. The way you move together when you're dancing. You're like a pair of gloves. That thing you said about … you know. I can believe it. Wow. And that *kiss*. It's the sexiest thing I've seen including on TV and in films. I nearly dragged Darren out to the car by his hair for a good seeing-to. It's a wonder you didn't start off an orgy and find copulating couples all over the floor when you eventually came round."

"Well, it's not all below the navel you know. Some of it's cerebral."

"*I* saw him whispering sweet nothings into your ear," Sam was swaying about, leaning on the sink for support. "Or was it lewd, unrepeatable suggestions?"

"Maybe. Maybe not. Not everyone's minds are sunk in their nether regions."

"No. Just yours and Hugh's."

"Actually," said Ali, "we *will* have to be going fairly soon. I'm working tomorrow night and Hugh's got a case to prepare. Anyway. I suppose you and Darren won't be going home later to shell peas together for tomorrow's dinner."

"Well possibly not. I dare say we'll grab an hour or two to ourselves. But it is more difficult with children you know," Sam said. "Oh to be young and fancy-free again!"

Darren suddenly appeared behind her.

"If peas are going to get in the way, we'll have to adopt

196

other less demanding vegetables." And he folded his arms around Sam, kissed her hair and looked at her very lovingly. Perhaps people see Hugh looking that way at me. But, Ali thought, perhaps prophetically, I must remember, Hugh is a tad more complicated than Darren.

Hugh was suddenly there too. "Our taxi's here," he said.

This was a surprise to Ali who didn't know that a taxi had been ordered for them.

"Matt's been prowling around," said Hugh. "He obviously doesn't want DUI cases resulting from his party to turn up in the next few weeks' court lists."

"Well done him," said Ali and leaned conspicuously on Hugh while he bore her away downstairs.

They kissed and more all the way home in the back of the taxi. Oh dear! Full sex was starting to be unnecessary. The taxi driver didn't seem to mind and Hugh gave him a large tip.

"I think I got him off a speeding charge a few years ago, actually," Hugh said as the taxi drove away.

"DID you enjoy yourself?" Ali asked Hugh later. For once they hadn't gone straight to bed and were watching a late film in front of the fire.

"I was with you, so of course I did."

"You can be quite a creep when you want to. I enjoyed it anyway." She kissed him. "And you were there."

"Let's go to bed. And make the most of what's left of the weekend."

A small shiver passed through Ali. She couldn't have said why. After all they had their whole lives left together. Didn't they?

CHAPTER 35

HUGH dropped Ali off at the S&S early Sunday evening and then collected her later and took her home, as in home, afterwards to re-charge her batteries (not to mention his). Normally her dad would have collected her but the parents were away. Ed was at a friend's.

A night or two away from Hugh wasn't too bad. In fact it fuelled her insatiable desire for him. Normally she would be with him again from the Wednesday night onwards so it wasn't too long and she looked forward to it intensely.

On Monday Hugh was expected in late in the morning after a hearing in Chelmsford. By three-thirty in the afternoon he still hadn't shown up at the office. Sheila hadn't been able to get hold of him and the court couldn't give her any information. Ali had to go out to see an older client who lived in a nearby housing estate to talk about a Lasting Power of Attorney. She went on foot, leaving by the back entrance, and took a short cut through the car park.

She was delighted therefore to see Hugh's car turn into the car park and park in his usual place.

She couldn't of course run into his arms or anything similar but she smiled broadly at him as he got out of his car. He ignored her.

"Hugh. Hello."

He turned round and his face was like stone. Ali's heart stopped.

"Hugh. What's wrong?"

"How *could* you, Ali?"

"What? What do you mean?"

"I've just spent the last few hours at the nick. '*Helping the police with their enquiries'.* In other words I was as near as damn it *arrested.*"

"But why?"

"Well, apparently Trish says she saw my car driving down Graham's drive the night his stable girl was assaulted and at about the same time it happened. I had to go and have my *DNA* taken for *elimination* purposes. So I'm now on their records."

"Oh. Yes. I saw her in town. She said something about it."

"So why didn't you say anything to me? I spoke to her when I got out of the nick and she said *you* said she should tell the police. Why on earth did you do that? Why didn't you speak to me?"

"I wasn't really listening to her. Not at the time. We were in a shoe shop and it was surreal really. And afterwards I just thought … I don't know what I thought actually. I was trying–"

"So did you tell her to go to the police or not?"

"Er, she said should she. So I thought I shouldn't interfere."

"Well, thanks a lot, Ali. Thank you so much for the vote of confidence."

This was all very well, but Ali wasn't in the wrong that she could see. She became a little rattled herself. "OK then. If I had told you about it, what would you have said then? Let's suppress evidence? Let's coerce Trish into keeping quiet?"

"I'd have *said* that we should have a bloody good laugh about it! Trish is a complete air head. Oh! Didn't you realise? She doesn't know what bloody day it is. And I would have reminded her as politely as possible that she might be mistaken! Have you any idea what this would do for my reputation if it got out? Being questioned about an *attempted bloody rape*?"

Hugh was shouting at her in a way she'd never heard before. He looked furious in a way that she'd never seen before.

Ali looked over at the back of the office and at least five pairs of eyes were peering at them with huge interest out of Wattsey's window, Wattsey himself included. Wattsey saw Ali look over. He gave an exaggerated shrug and walked away. Another face took his place.

"OK, if you care so much about your bloody privacy and what the rest of the firm think about us," Ali said, "then I suggest you keep your voice down."

"What?"

"FYI, most of the office are glued to that window."

"Fuck them!" Hugh shouted. Ali gasped.

"Hugh. Try to keep some perspective about this. Try and be reasonable."

"*Reasonable*?" He cast about him as though the answer might lie in one of the parked cars or in one of the adjoining offices. "I might even have to stop acting for Graham now."

"Really?"

"Yes, really," he snapped back. "Look, I saw the way you looked at that forensic suit at the cottage. And I know you questioned Graham about my engagement and whether I resented him taking her away from me."

"What?"

"He told me. Honestly he did me a favour. We were pushed into it by our parents. We were far too young. I was at Oxford and it would never have worked. Do you really think I've stewed over that for nearly ten years and set Graham up for an assault charge to get back at him? Do you *really* think I could go into a girl's apartment and scare her half to death and try to rape her to get back at a mate for something that happened donkey's years ago? How could you, Ali?" he repeated.

"Well then, that was weeks ago when I saw Graham. Why didn't *you* speak to *me* after you'd seen him? Why keep it to yourself if it bothered you? You didn't give any indication there was anything wrong. Oh, but of course you don't show emotion do you? It doesn't go with the image does it? Mr Cool couldn't possibly lose it and let down his defences for a few minutes to sort out a misunderstanding. He couldn't possibly–"

"Do give it a rest, Ali," Hugh said icily.

Ali moved towards him. "Hugh," she almost pleaded. As she approached him he put his hands up and backed away from her.

"Don't think you can get round me that way."

"Hugh, of course I don't think you had anything to do with Angela's assault. But, d'you know, even if you had, it wouldn't actually matter to me. It wouldn't make me feel any–"

"Oh. That's so comforting! My girlfriend doesn't care if I'm an attempted rapist!"

"I didn't mean that! Stop twisting everything. Hugh, this isn't like you at all. Please say we can meet later and talk about this."

"No. It's over!"

"What?"

"You heard. We're finished. I couldn't be with you anymore knowing you think that about me."

"Hugh," Ali was aghast, "You can't mean that. You can't."

"Just see if I can't."

"Please, Hugh!"

Ali stood there, unable to take it in. Everything went quiet. Time appeared to stand still. All she could hear was the throb of her heartbeat in her ears. She swallowed hard.

"Hugh, I can't live without you," she said softly staring into the far distance.

He paused for a moment and appeared uncertain. Then his expression closed down. "I'm sure you'll manage." And he stalked off to the office.

Ali didn't make it to the appointment with the client who wanted a Lasting Power of Attorney. Instead she walked straight home, crawled into her bed fully clothed and lay there. There was no one at home. Her parents were still on their cruise for a couple more weeks and Ed was at his friend's for the duration. Ali didn't get out of bed apart from going to the loo and getting glasses of water. She didn't cry, she just lay there.

The telephone rang many times but she ignored it. If the doorbell rang she ignored that. On the Thursday afternoon, the front door opened and she heard Jan, who had a key, call up the stairs whether she was all right. Ali didn't answer. She registered talking below, followed by footsteps coming up the stairs.

Jan and Sam came into her room and over to her bed. Ali didn't react.

"Ali," said Jan and took Ali in her arms. "Oh, Ali," she said, tears streaming down her face. "Ali, say something. What's he *done* to you?"

Sam came round the other side and sat on the bed and put her arm round Ali. "We're all missing you," she said. Ali remained curled up staring into space.

Jan's and Sam's eyes met over Ali's foetal form. Now they were here, they couldn't leave her on her own but neither could either of them stay with her for long. They both had kids and jobs and homes to run.

"Come home with me, Ali," said Jan. There was no reaction.

Sam excused herself and left the room. She went downstairs and telephoned PWT. She spoke to Mr Watts. She said it didn't look as though Ali would be returning to work that week.

"Is she very upset?" he said.

"More than."

"Right. Well, I'll come round shortly though I'm not sure what good I can do."

Sam let him in and he followed her upstairs.

When he saw Ali his eyes filled with tears. He sat on her bed and put an avuncular hand on her shoulder. Ali's bottom lip started to tremble.

"Ali," he said, "I'm so sorry this has happened to you. You're a clever girl. You must try to get over it. Hugh Sutherland's a … unique person. But you're such a lovely girl. Someone else will come along. I know they will."

The tears started to fall. His bluff kindness did it for Ali and she let Wattsey take her in his arms while she sobbed her heart out. No one tried to stop her. It was clearly what she needed.

"I can't come back," she said eventually.

"Well, leave it a little longer before you make a decision," said Wattsey. "I'd miss you certainly very much. I know it'll be difficult for you but think about it first. It'd probably do you good."

Many more tears were shed before he left saying he'd keep in touch. Jan thanked him profusely for his help. Without him she wasn't sure Ali wouldn't have gone into some sort of catatonic state long-term.

Ali wasn't beyond realising that Wattsey's finality on the subject of her and Hugh must mean that Hugh wasn't prepared to reconsider. Men didn't talk much about that sort of thing but she imagined words must have been said. Knowing Hugh, he'd make short shrift of any attempts to interfere.

Jan managed to sort things out so that she could stay the night and Ali got up for the first time since Monday and mooched about for the evening. She found her office suits and other clothes on the sofa. Jan said quietly that Sam had found them at work in what she called The Privy. Ali couldn't bear it. She took a couple of sleeping pills Jan was able to give her and went to bed.

The next two evenings she was due to work at the S&S and she decided she'd show up however awful she felt. They were bad nights and she got through them like a zombie.

The following day on her own at home she played the haunting "I'm So Afraid" by Fleetwood Mac's Lindsey Buckingham, the slow version with the long guitar solo. She set the CD player to repeat it over and over again and gave herself over to its tormented power and extreme emotional message. She felt ecstatic with pain and anguish and ranged about the house wailing out loud, pleading with the gods to reunite her with her other half or sobbing in a gut-wrenching fashion. After five hours of this she felt some small part of the hurt had been exorcised.

She couldn't go on like this. She was either going to fade away and die or else make some sort of effort, and sheer common sense dictated that she would get over it eventually. Everybody did.

CHAPTER 36

By night on my bed I sought him whom my soul loveth; I sought him, but I found him not.

(The Song of Solomon 3)

BUT apparently not Ali, so it turned out. She put a brave face on things and tried not to show what was going on inside. If Hugh could do it, so could she.

It wasn't easy. Inside she was a mass of pain. Previously with Hugh it'd been so exquisite it had been almost painful. Now the pain itself was almost exquisite. It tore through her and washed about her. There was no escape from it. She pondered the mystery of time and space, how one second could separate two such different sets of circumstances, how it was now impossible to recover the before part. It would never return again.

If only one could rearrange the molecules, atoms, subatomic particles back into the order they had been before, occupying the same time and space they had occupied before. If only she could tap into the forces of the universe to do that. She supposed that must be why some people believe in God, because they needed to believe that more than the here and now, the physical present, are possible. If she'd thought it would have been any comfort to her, she'd have tried it herself. But she knew it wouldn't be.

The only thing that seemed to help was not to eat. It gave her a sense of having control over at least something.

Outwardly she was able to appear reasonably composed. She was well aware that people mostly didn't like displays of extreme emotion and didn't know how to cope with them in everyday life. She didn't want to lose friends and what sympathy she had. Therefore, she learned to turn up the sides of her mouth as though in a semi-smile and behave normally. It worked a dream on most people.

Going back to the office on the Monday turned out to be

much easier than expected.

"Tha'd a girl," said Wattsey.

She kept out of Hugh's way and he hers apparently and she never saw him drive past her at the bus stop again. And she stopped spending time with him at work, though inevitably she saw him and they were merely polite to each other and that was that.

But she stepped up her efforts to find alternative employment. After a couple of weeks, she called James again to see if 'the old man' could pull any strings. They met for a lunchtime drink. James kissed her on the cheek and said she looked stunning as ever though, he frowned slightly at her, somewhat tragic. He told her it suited her.

James drank several beers and Ali stuck to orange juice. She couldn't trust alcohol to pass her lips, what with her low calorie intake and need for total control.

James asked what jobs she'd applied for and she gave him a list. The Cambridge civil rights firm still had vacancies. That was her favourite and it would get her as far from Hugh as she could be without moving away entirely. James promised to see if any strings could be pulled.

"So how's your love life?" said James.

"Oh. You know. Slings and arrows," replied Ali.

"Too bad," said James. "Well, me, I've actually got some good news. Your hot tip about Maddie struck gold for me. For both of us. We're quite a couple now. Early days of course but from little acorns et cetera. Actually, incredibly, it turns out we're distantly related."

"You don't say!" And they both laughed.

At least James doesn't take himself too seriously. Why can't everyone be like that. Uncomplicated and transparent. But of course Hugh wasn't everyone, or she'd wouldn't have fallen in love with him.

James walked her back to her office and kissed her again on her cheek. He put his hand up to someone as he left and, turning, Ali saw that it was Hugh walking a little way behind. He appeared inscrutable as usual but still, he was staring hard at Ali and James.

Stuff him. Thought Ali. I hope he does think James and I are an item.

ABOUT a month later, Hugh came to see Ali in The Privy.

"I've had a call from the nick. They said there's been some new developments about Graham's case so I've got to go and see what's up." He was still acting for Graham after all. "I couldn't get hold of Graham. Since you've taken such an interest in his case," he said pointedly, "I thought you might like to come with me. And take some notes if you wouldn't mind."

"Oh. Yes, of course I will."

They didn't talk on the way to the station. Ali couldn't think of anything to say and Hugh stared straight ahead giving nothing away. They had to wait quite a time before anyone saw them. Hugh had his briefcase with him. He pulled out a file and scrutinised the contents in earnest. Ali thumbed through some magazines, trying to avoid the articles about bedroom issues and romantic problems.

Eventually DI Hunter put his face round the door and asked if they'd follow him to an interview room.

Might it have been DI Hunter who'd interviewed Hugh about Trish's allegation? It would be impossible to raise it with Hugh later.

It was all quite informal. Hugh and DI Hunter called each other by their first names, so it was 'Hugh' and 'Andrew'. If he noticed the change in Hugh's and Ali's demeanour towards one another, Andrew gave no sign of it.

"Well, it's good news for your client," said DI Hunter. "You'll recall that we found some evidence of another man in Angela Cadman's annexe but couldn't get a DNA match on it. However, we recently arrested a man in connection with a number of other incidents and a match came up with the DNA in Ms Cadman's flat. He's someone we've had in our sights for years but never been able to get anywhere near before. The man has admitted that it was him who carried out the assault and he's asked for the offence to be taken into consideration with a number of other offences."

"So who is this man and why did he bother with such an out of the way place for an attempted assault."

"I must ask you to keep this to yourselves but his name is Symonds. He's thought to be associated with Don Grimsby. You used to act for him, Hugh, but I believe you don't any longer. Symonds won't admit to any connection with Grimsby and says he was 'casing' the place at the time with a view to a possible later burglary. He's vague about the detail. He doesn't account for the coat. Says it must have been there already. He doesn't admit to taking your car, just says he took a four wheel drive vehicle he found parked unlocked in the countryside but can't remember where. Says he didn't want his own vehicle to be recorded visiting the premises.

"We can only speculate why he really did it. One of our theories was that it was intended as some sort of frightener for you, maybe to encourage you to keep quiet about whatever you know about Grimsby. You came and answered some questions recently after there was a report that your car was seen entering Graham's drive the same night as the assault at about the right time. We dismissed it at the time, the witness didn't appear very reliable, but one possibility is that your car was taken to make it appear you had carried out the assault. You said you never locked your car and left it on the road. Criminals have skeleton keys for all sorts of makes and models of cars so they wouldn't have had to hot-wire it. I think you know Graham very well and he may have left his coat in your car. You do have quite a lot of bits and pieces in your car although you said you were moving home at the time. It's possible that the coat was taken assuming it was yours and left in Ms Cadman's flat."

He let this sink in. Then he continued. "Obviously they didn't anticipate that the CCTV would be off. They assumed there'd be a record of your car visiting the premises that night at that time. Ms Cadman thought she recognised Graham's voice but one man's London-accented deep voice can probably sound much like another's especially when it's pitch black and the girl was terrified."

Hugh glanced briefly at Ali who looked steadfastly down at her note-taking.

"We've spoken to Angela. She also doesn't recognise Symonds when shown a photograph of him. She says it was common knowledge she wanted to be a model. The people who organised the attack could have found out fairly easily."

Andrew continued: "They may also have found out that Graham was expected to be out that night. But of course he wasn't, and the snow absorbed the sound and covered up all the tracks. Can I ask you, Hugh, whether you've received any threats from Don Grimsby or anyone on his behalf?"

"He phoned me a few times to try to persuade me to act for him again. Yes, he was rather threatening but I ignored him. Then I heard he was likely to go down for a conspiracy to murder."

"No. I don't think that's going to happen. Between you and me," said Andrew, "the charge is very likely to have to be dropped."

"Oh, that's a pity, to put it mildly. Anyway, I did have a visit from a couple of knuckle draggers when I was at the gym one time. I don't know how they got in because they're not members. They just said the sort of stuff you might expect. They didn't mention Grimsby, just said I should remember what's good for me, I wouldn't want to wake up at the bottom of the Colne one night, I'd better learn to be discreet, and something about me having been lucky and I wouldn't be so lucky next time. I suppose now they must've meant the assault. Perhaps they thought I knew it was intended for me."

DI Hunter produced a photograph.

"Would this have been one of the men who came to visit you at the gym?"

"Actually, yes. That was one of them."

"That's Symonds. Do you want to press charges for threatening behaviour or taking your car?"

"No. I don't think so."

"It would have been sensible to have told us about these threats. It might have pointed us in the right direction and have avoided further unpleasantness for your friend Graham."

"Come off it," said Hugh. "This is the most outlandish thing I've come across in years and probably you too. I didn't connect the threats in any way with Graham's charge. Why would I? Why would you have either? I wouldn't have been able to identify this Symonds to you because he hadn't been arrested at that time. For heaven's sake, you didn't even seriously connect it to me when a witness came along saying they'd seen my car in Graham's drive on the night and at the time it happened. Get real. You wouldn't have provided me with any significant protection. And as far as I'm concerned, I do criminal work and I have to take the rough with the smooth. Thanks, but I'm not being made a scapegoat for this mess."

"Right. Obviously it'll be a while before Symonds gets dealt with so you'll have to keep all this to yourselves. However, we're withdrawing the charges against Graham. We'll get the paperwork done as soon as possible. I'll let you know."

"I knew Graham didn't do it. I just never dreamed it was all about me really."

Andrew shook their hands and, as they walked out, he said to Hugh: "You know it might be more sensible to lock your car. But I said that to you before. As to leaving all that stuff in it, well I suppose it's your prerogative but it could be a fire hazard or attract interest in the wrong quarters."

"Message received," said Hugh and they walked out and climbed into the (unlocked) car.

"What a mess," said Hugh as they were driving away.

"Well, it wasn't your fault. They'd have got into the car even if it had been locked. And if they hadn't been able to set up that apparent assault, they'd have done something else. Perhaps something worse."

"It's my fault it involved Graham though. His coat in my unlocked car and so on. Poor sod's been through the hoop and for nothing. And we can't even let the full story out because Symonds hasn't been dealt with yet and there's no evidence that it was anything to do with Grimsby trying to get at me. If we say anything openly, he's not above dragging me through a defamation action. So Graham still won't really be able to clear his name. No smoke without fire is what people'll think."

"You didn't tell me you'd been threatened by a couple of thugs," said Ali.

"I didn't want to worry you at the time. Anyway nothing's come of it has it. The whole thing's farcical if you think about it. A totally bungled attempt to blacken my name. Kind of like an Ealing comedy. No wonder they gave up."

"Well, at least no one got injured."

"We'll have to refund Graham's legal fees. It was nothing to do with him at all. The partners won't be pleased. I'll have to pay him back myself. I don't mind doing that, it's just not a good result." Hugh looked very downhearted.

"Still, overall it's good news isn't it? Graham probably won't be bothered so much why the charge is being dropped, just that it *is* being dropped. There's a pub coming up. Do you fancy popping in for a drink to celebrate?" She crossed her fingers.

"No. No thanks, Ali. I'd better get back to the office and start sorting out this mess."

Ali turned away and swallowed hard. She fought down the strong wave of nausea and panic that seemed to characterise the desperation she always felt when any thoughts she ever allowed herself to have about a reconciliation had to be swept back behind her carefully constructed veil of normality. She wondered if Hugh's composure in her presence was just an act as well. It didn't look like it.

Oh well, she'd had *some* good news earlier. James's father and a partner in the civil rights Cambridge firm had turned out to be on the board of trustees of the same charity. James's dad had put in a word and incredibly Ali, having been to an interview a couple of weeks previously, had been offered one of the paralegal jobs. As soon as she was back in the office, she'd have to prepare a letter of resignation. With no contract she could leave at any time but wanted to give them reasonable notice.

She stared forlornly out of the passenger window. At least she'd tried. She watched the people going about their business, getting on with their lives and thought: *I'll just have to try somehow to get on with mine.*

A few days later Ali sat at home with her family and watched a news item featuring Hugh and Graham on the steps of the court after the charge had been formally withdrawn. Hugh made a short statement:

"Mr Spellings is of course very much relieved that this charge is not proceeding. He has always vociferously protested his innocence. The police are following another line of enquiry in connection with the incident. I can't give any further details about that. My client now wishes to put the whole thing behind him and get on with his life and concentrate on his business interests. It is hoped that the media will allow him the breathing space to do so."

And despite the sea of microphones and the barrage of questions directed at them, they walked away quickly to a waiting car.

Ali sat and bled inside and when her parents started asking questions about Hugh, she pleaded a headache and went upstairs to her room.

BEFORE she knew it, it was Ali's last day at PWT. She had no idea if anything was planned but put on one of her better suits nonetheless. The day was bright, clear and warm. A beautiful June day. She worked a normal morning, that is to say she broke her neck trying to get completions done and documents drafted and telephone calls answered.

About twelve-forty-five, Wattsey summoned everyone into reception and said they were closing for a couple of hours to take Ali out for lunch. Ali tried not to show how touched she was.

Everyone came. Even Hugh. He sat with Sheila and sipped a small lager. Ali on the other hand was persuaded by all and sundry to break her no alcohol rule fairly spectacularly.

They were in a Spanish restaurant where a section had been

set aside for them and Wattsey ordered tons of tapas and carafes of wine.

Ali became tremendously emotional and she wasn't the only one. By the time pudding was served, at least half the company had their hankies out and there were shouts of "Speech, speech."

Ali rose unsteadily to her feet with Wattsey's hanky in her hand and did her best.

"I've so enjoyed my eight months with PWT. I never thought it would be as long as this to begin with but I've learned so much from all of you and the experience gained has been invaluable."

There were surreptitious glances by many members of staff at Hugh which he ignored and Ali didn't notice.

"I can't thank you all enough. I shall miss you all *so* much. I hope you'll miss me a little bit too. I shall definitely keep in touch." And she blew her nose hard as everyone cheered.

Wattsey then rose and said his few words, emphasising what a pleasure it had been to have such a bright star working in their office, how cheerful but conscientious she'd always been, that he for one didn't know what he was going to do without her but he wanted her to develop the successful career she deserved. And would they all raise their glasses to the prettiest intern any law firm had ever taken on.

OK, it was sexist but very, very well meant.

He then presented her with an envelope which he said was in recognition of the firm's appreciation for her huge efforts over the months. Ali opened it and inside was a cheque for fifteen hundred pounds. She gasped and gabbled her thanks. She could pay her dad back now for the little car he'd bought her.

It turned out everyone had individual gifts for her. She tore open package after package. Favourite perfume, tights, lace underwear, earrings.

At last Hugh gave her his. It was a small flat rectangular package. Ali knew what it was instantly before she opened it. But she had to open it. It was of course The Privy sign.

"I took it down just after everyone left the office. I thought you'd want to take it with you."

Everyone had gone quiet. Hugh gazed looked down at her in that heart-stopping, entrail-melting way he used to. Ali held the sign to her, bit her bottom lip and closed her eyes. She swallowed and her breathing became laboured. She felt faint and started to sway.

Wattsey took her arm. "Come on Ali. It's time to go." He stared angrily at Hugh who sighed and looked away. He doesn't care, thought Ali.

Ali was shaking and her head was spinning and not from the alcohol. Wattsey and Sam led her away out of the restaurant and back to the office.

She went through her drawers and put all her presents in bags. Wattsey said she could and probably should leave early. She agreed and he called for a taxi. She went round and said goodbye to everyone. Hugh wasn't in his room and she didn't see him again.

CHAPTER 37

STARTING A new job was nerve-wracking. Ali was desperately nervous on her first day at the new firm. Her father wouldn't hear of her paying him back for the car, hence she'd splurged on some expensive new suits, blouses and shoes for the new job with some of her unexpected leaving bonus. At least she looked presentable even if she was shaking like a leaf inside.

She set off very early, or so she thought, but wasn't prepared for the traffic in Cambridge. The congestion was epic. It took her well over an hour to get anywhere near the office from the outskirts of Cambridge. She was late as a result and resolved to try the park and ride the next day. They seemed to have dedicated bus lanes.

The new firm were much more structured than PWT. She wasn't left sitting about wondering what to do. There was a proper induction procedure. She had a session with the HR person and was given a contract of employment to take away and read. It was just to cover her probationary period.

She was told in detail what her training would consist of and she was shown where copies of the office manuals were kept and asked to read certain ones as a minimum within the next two weeks. She was shown the room in which she would work with a number of other trainee paralegals and she was allocated her own desk. She had a talk about office safety and procedures in the event of fire and other accidents or emergencies.

And by this time it was lunchtime. She hadn't brought any sandwiches, so she took herself off for a wander round the city centre and bought and forced down a small bean salad, trying to fend off the feelings of loneliness and unfamiliarity.

HUGH sat at home moping. Badly. He'd had to leave the office early because he couldn't concentrate on anything. His beautiful lover had left and he would probably never see her again. Hugh was under no illusion that she would visit the firm. He knew she wouldn't. Some other man would fall in love with her and she with him. Perhaps she was dating James already. He didn't think she was fickle or shallow but he did think she'd need someone to love her and that he'd have lost her forever when that happened.

He was starting to feel terrible anguish. Much worse than at the beginning. To begin with he'd been buoyed up and carried along by his anger. And his horror at having to remain in a police station, having to give a DNA sample and answer questions more or less against his will. Or at least it wasn't something he'd sought out or had any control over. The system was going to relentlessly process him and spit him out. He realised properly and for the first time what Lynda Reece must have felt like. And Graham. And countless other people he'd acted for. Complete loss of any control over your own destiny. He'd been substantially traumatised by it. It was like a mental castration.

The horror of the police interview and the anger he'd felt about what Ali apparently thought he was capable of kept him going for a month or so.

And he got a certain cruel pleasure out of hurting her, knowing she was hurt, looking as though he didn't care. He knew he shouldn't have given her The Privy sign in public as he had but hadn't actually imagined she'd nearly faint over it. He really had wanted to upset her and that was too bad he now realised. Much too cruel. Another reason why she'd probably never come back to him even if he was willing to ask. Which he wasn't.

But at least while he could see her most days at the office, it gave him some sense of comfort even though she wasn't his any longer. Seeing her daily was an almost tangible relief to him even if he couldn't touch her. That had certainly had to be enough for him during those long months when he'd yearned for her at a distance, not prepared to start anything with her. The hassle he'd had in the past over one or two relationships that had got completely out of control and become very unpleasant led to him positively avoiding romantic entanglements.

That was until that evening at his house when she had so wonderfully and incredibly shown him that she wanted him too.

He supposed that she wouldn't have understood what he meant by saying he adored her. She'd have wanted a declaration of love. But would it have made any difference anyway in the long run? Probably not.

And while he was seeing her every day, he could dupe himself into imagining that they were back to their old days together and that in a few days' time she'd come and stay with him and he could lose himself in her.

He'd been undone by the effect on him of their first night together. It was too much. It made him feel too vulnerable and his first instinct was not to see her again and he'd more or less decided not to. But he hadn't been able to stay away. The next weekend on the Saturday night after the first time, he'd wrestled with himself all day whether to go and find her or not. In the end he'd had to go and seek her out.

As the older more responsible one, he had tried to exercise some restraint, at least on the surface. But it hadn't worked any better for him than it had for her; he was just better at not showing how he felt. It was always there. The desperate unrequited need for her when they weren't alone together. The urgent insistent longing that couldn't be satisfied and now never would.

What had sunk in that second night with her was that he had to keep her. She had to be his. He would try to remain cool, but he wouldn't lose sight of that essential objective. At least that's what he'd thought.

So how had it gone so horribly wrong?

This awful feeling was gripping him, it was gut-wrenching, really hurting like a physical injury. He'd never felt anything like it before. He didn't know what to do.

It would seem simple to anyone else. Just go and get her back. But he didn't think he could stand what she had apparently thought he was capable of doing and it had taken a revelation about Graham's case to convince her otherwise. Didn't she know very well that he wasn't violent or weird? She should never have thought that about him at all. Ever. She should have trusted him. If he were to get close to her again, he might want to start punishing and hurting her and that would be a very sick relationship. Doubly horrible after something that had been so sweet.

And now she was gone forever and he'd never be able to hold her again.

He put his head in his hands and stayed like that for nearly an hour. Then he started to thumb listlessly through some post. He looked with disinterest through the parish magazine and one item caught his eye. The parish council had been asked to review the routes taken by the walking groups as to their suitability following a perturbing incident in April. Some house owners had conducted unsuitable outdoor activities which a group of walkers had witnessed in full.

Well they had had an obvious solution open to them, which they signally hadn't taken.

Luckily no children were in the group but easily could have been. The clerk to the council had been asked to write to the owner and complain and express the council's hope that there would be no repetition.

You can count on that.

He read it again.

In other circumstances it would have been risible. He'd have shown it to Ali and they would have derived an enormous amount of fun from it. But she wasn't here and wasn't going to be ever again. What was he to do?

Only the nearly-empty bottle of brandy promised to dull his misery.

SAM was missing Ali too. She missed their lunchtime conflabs and drunken evening sessions. Ali didn't get back from Cambridge until about eight in the evening and then was tired and had to go to bed early in order to get up early the next day. Sam and Darren between them had four children to cope with. They didn't have a nanny any longer, wanting the privacy to work on their relationship.

But they too felt the strain of late nights; getting four children ready for bed, homework, bathing them, reading to them and staying with them until they went to sleep, being woken up in the night sometimes, then the busy morning routine every day. They loved every second of it, but it really was tiring.

And there were the kids' various activities. They involved a lot of running around.

They had some daily help with the house, washing, cleaning and the like, but they wanted to look after the kids themselves, apart from the odd weekend away together when his or her mother came to stay.

Sam reckoned whatever the work of looking after four children, she'd never been so happy in her life. On the rare occasions she did see Ali, she had to try hard not to rub it in.

Infrequently, Ali left work early and they met as before at the S&S. She had to admit Ali looked pretty good on the surface, slim, new makeup, smarter clothes. And Ali laughed and joked about her new place of work and the people there and some of the cases. Nevertheless, Sam knew it was just superficial. There was a kind of brittle cynical edge to Ali's chatter. Sam was sad to see her going that way.

"What else have I got?" Ali said. "He didn't want me anymore. I've got to harden up a bit."

Sam didn't tell Ali that Hugh sometimes, quite often in fact, looked a bit rough. Not untidy or dishevelled, just very tired, as though he hadn't slept well and sometimes like he had a hangover. She didn't think any good could come of telling Ali. Ali was too proud to go and beg to be taken back and if Hugh wanted to ask presumably he would. And he didn't.

Therefore, what was the point in telling Ali that Hugh appeared to be suffering too. It wasn't going to lead anywhere. Anyway, his behaviour generally was more or less as before, giving nothing away, doing his job well, getting clients off various charges, attracting new business. He didn't come out for any lunchtime drinks any longer if it was someone's birthday, but who was she to decide that Hugh was pining. He might not have been. And Ali was trying to get over it. It was best not to interfere. Darren thought so too.

CHAPTER 38

TIME wore on. The Cambridge job was wonderful, all she'd ever previously wanted out of life. Ali threw herself into it and spent all her free time researching, and printing and taking home articles to read as well as logging into the firm's accounts with various legal publishers to consume chapter after chapter of text on anything to do with civil rights.

Although she'd promised to visit PWT, she found it impossible. It would have been too evocative of those few precious weeks she'd had with Hugh and how desperately, exquisitely alive she'd felt. It was like another lifetime. She kept in touch with some members of the firm, in particular Sam, Amanda sometimes and, amazingly, with Wattsey. If he ever had any family do's, he invited Ali. She'd got into the habit of calling him Wattsey. She just couldn't think of him as Victor and he didn't seem to mind.

When she and Sam were both free, they went on shopping trips and, of course, girls' nights out when the opportunity arose. Sam could see the old sparkle start to come back although Ali was still painfully thin. "It's my way of coping," said Ali, "if I didn't do this, I think I'd still go to pieces. Anyway it's not healthy to overeat."

Sam would sigh and drop the subject.

Ali carried on with the cycling and it improved her mood a little.

She'd been asked out several times by a trainee solicitor at work. He was a great guy, quite plummy like James but really, really bright. They'd had a couple of lunchtime drinks together and he seemed to know intuitively that she'd had a romantic upset of some sort and not to be too pushy about wanting a date. His name was Phil and he had similar mannerisms to Hugh and looked at her in the same way.

But there the resemblance ended. He was dark, cheerful and very outgoing, classy though not at all reserved. Ali didn't want to disappoint either him or herself by accepting and then having it turn out that she couldn't cope or that he wasn't any sort of substitute for Hugh.

He was very easy-going, but any bloke would be a touch pissed off if a girl burst into tears the first time he kissed her. She didn't want another break with a work colleague, messy or otherwise. So she said she'd come back to him about it and that was where they were at.

Truth to tell, she wasn't sure she was ready to relinquish her broken heart quite yet. She was still capable of wallowing in a deep mire of regrets about Hugh when she was on her own, revelling in recollections of all their times together, their totally brilliant sex life and just him and everything about him. What if she fell head over heels in love with Phil straight away? After all she'd been astounded when it happened with Hugh after just one dance together and later one night together. She didn't want to be that fickle.

She told Sam who advised caution. Definitely.

THE weeks went by. Hugh knew he had to get on with things. He couldn't just let everything fall apart. He tried to throw himself into his work. He was good at hiding his feelings and could just about shove his bleeding heart into a corner of his mind so it wasn't at least written all over his face.

He tried not to walk past The Privy. The name seemed to have stuck. Though on occasions, after everyone else had left the office, he'd go into The Privy and think about Ali. He fancied he could still smell the perfume she wore and see the imprint of her beautiful bum on the soft seat of her chair. No one had moved anything. It was like a shrine. If anyone did start to rearrange the small room, he wondered if he'd try to stop them. They'd think he was a headcase.

The letter from the parish clerk arrived. Initially he tore it up then he regretted it and taped it back together. He kept it in his bedside table with the parish magazine. In loving memory. He penned a polite non-committal reply.

Sitting at home sometimes, he really did think seriously about driving to the nearest quiet beach and walking into the sea, especially late at night after a few brandies. He wondered how Ali felt. He experienced sudden urges to contact her but the longer time went by, the more he felt he'd blown it. She probably wouldn't take him back and he couldn't stand to feel any worse than he did already.

He spent hours and hours and hours, week after week after week sitting at home thinking all these things and getting nowhere at all. What should he do?

There was nothing he could do. He decided one Friday evening to take a walk; follow in the footsteps of the daft group who'd stood and gawped at him and Ali getting over-friendly in the garden. The fresh air and exercise might help a little, help him to fight off the worst of his misery. He donned boots and outer clothing and left by the picket gate leading onto the public footpath.

Dusk was falling, the birds were no longer singing and a peace had settled on the surrounding countryside. It was a time of day he usually loved. Lost in thought, he took no notice of the rustle of undergrowth in the copse on the other side of the footpath.

THE young doctor was fussing over Hugh after the police officer had left. Hugh had felt perfectly capable of giving a statement to the police but Dr Stuart had thought otherwise and Hugh had had to be pretty forceful. Not that there was a great deal he could tell the uniformed sergeant.

He'd walked nearly a mile before the two thugs had jumped him and near darkness had fallen by then, not to mention the closing in of the vegetation each side of the footpath which was overdue for a trim. He should bring it up with the parish council, was his wry observation to himself.

So he didn't see much of them as he ducked to avoid the blows until his instincts kicked in and he fought back, obviously far harder than they'd expected. Unfortunately, this had the effect of spurring them on and eventually, between them and using some sort of blunt instrument, they'd scored a knock-out blow.

Quite honestly, if a dog-walker hadn't happened on him, he might have lain there for much longer, coming round intermittently and being unable to get to his feet.

There was nothing to connect the attack with Grimsby. Nothing was said by the attackers. Certainly neither of them *was* Grimsby. They must have run off after realising he was unconscious. Perhaps they thought he was dead. It had been a hard blow to the head and the stitches itched like hell.

Bruises were emerging all over his body and there wasn't anywhere left which didn't protest keenly every time he moved an inch or two.

He had no doubt that Grimsby was responsible and had to hope that the attack was a one-off; that Grimsby would feel he'd got the message over and that such assaults wouldn't become a regular feature of his life. As he'd said to Andrew Hunter, he did criminal work and had to take the rough with the smooth.

He knew he was being an awkward patient but he just couldn't stand it any longer. And Ali hadn't come to visit him. Someone would be bound to have told her he was in hospital.

The pretty doctor was worse than his mother. "Mr Sutherland, just settle down and get some rest. We'll see about discharging you tomorrow."

"Fuck this," he said under his breath. He'd suffered worse in the boxing ring and lived to tell the tale. "I'm getting out of here," he told her. "No, I am. You can't keep me here against my will. Thank you for all you've done, but would you please sort out the discharge forms and then I'll leave."

Once she had indulged in a fit of huffing, moved away and left the ward, he picked up his phone from the bedside cabinet, and called his mother in Australia. He said nothing about his injuries and told her he was coming over as soon as he could get a flight and sort things out at work.

"ALI. Where've you been? I've been trying to get hold of you all weekend and most of today."

"Sorry. I left my mobile at work all weekend. And the

battery was flat so I had to borrow someone's charger, and–"

"Ali, stop, listen. Hugh was found unconscious near his house late Friday evening. He's–"

"What? He's not…is he…hurt? What happened?"

"He's in hospital. I'm not sure how bad it is. He had to have stitches to his head and a scan. He was badly beaten up by a couple of thugs, but he doesn't know who. They wanted to keep him in for observation. Amanda's been keeping us informed."

"Amanda! How? She's not…him and her aren't–"

"No, no," said Sam. "Of course not. It seems she's kept in touch with Graham Spellings and he's been seeing Hugh in hospital."

"Oh. So he can have visitors. Which hospital?"

"I suppose so. Colchester District and General."

"OK, Turner Road. I'll have to go and see him. I'm about to leave. It's not that far from where I live." Something occurred to Ali. She said in a small voice:

"But he hasn't tried to get in touch with me I don't think. There's loads of missed calls from you before the battery went flat, but nothing from him. I don't know. Maybe I shouldn't go. What do you think Sam?"

"It's hard for anyone else to know what's best. As far as we know, he's been having tests and he's not very seriously injured."

'So he could have called me, but he didn't."

"I don't know," Sam repeated. "I don't know exactly how ill he's been. Perhaps he couldn't," Sam finished lamely.

"Hmm. Anyway, thanks for telling me. I'll think about it on the way home, whether to try and visit."

"Well, good luck with it, if you do."

ALI drove slowly back to Colchester, trying to decide. Sucker for punishment, instead of taking the more direct route via Sible Hedingham and Halstead, finishing with a dash along the A12, she sometimes took the road through Long Melford and Sudbury and thence onto the A134. There was always some chance that she might catch a glimpse of Hugh driving home. He usually would have turned off the A134 to get to his home near Bures.

In fact, she'd never so far seen him. Was he avoiding the possibility of their cars passing and going home another way?

Tonight she didn't bother with this diversion, taking the A12 as far as the Spring Lane junction with a short run to Turner Road by Cymbeline Way. The traffic wasn't too bad. She made the hospital by seven o' clock.

The ward was busy with visitors when Ali reached it. A queue of people fidgeted and shuffled their feet waiting at reception desk. Ali walked away from the desk and prowled around for a time, her heart in her mouth at the prospect of seeing Hugh. It was very difficult. Some beds had screens pulled right round them, and there were single rooms off the main ward. She could hardly tweak curtains and peer through the windows into the single rooms.

Ali gave up and went back to the queue. At last she was able to speak to someone.

"He's not here. He was discharged today."

The busy nurse started to exchange details about another patient with her colleague at the desk and was about to turn her attention to the next person in the queue.

"But, he was badly beaten and had stitches to his head. He had to have a scan. He was in for observation. He can't have left yet," Ali insisted.

The nurse turned back to Ali.

"Well, he has. Sorry."

That seemed to be it. People behind her were coughing. She had one last try.

"Did he leave a message for anyone. Er, my name's Ali Barrett."

"No. I've got nothing here." The nurses fixed smile focused on the next person in the queue. "Yes? What can I do for you?"

Ali had no choice but to turn and leave.

Disconsolately, she returned to her car. He hadn't contacted her. It seemed like he hadn't even told the office he was out of hospital or Sam would have known. He could have left a note for her, but he hadn't. It was hopeless. She'd have to forget it. She hadn't even time to drive at speed to his house to see him.

She needed to get home. It was her parents' twenty-fifth wedding anniversary and they were holding a bit of a bash for friends and family.

Anyway, he might be staying at Graham's while he recuperated.

CHAPTER 39

"OH hello Ali. You're looking very tanned and healthy. Was it good?"

"Yeah. Pretty OK. Didn't do a lot except sunbathe and go on walks and things. Not much chance of going clubbing or anything with my parents and fifteen-year-old brother. Still it was relaxing and refreshing. What're you working on?"

"The Maddison case. Trying to draft a claim." He was in the firm's small library using a laptop.

"Oh that still. Is there really any chance it'll get anywhere?"

"Peters thinks it will. And the client wants to do it. So we'll have a go I suppose."

Maddison was a so-called celeb, horrified to find that a sleazy alleged journalist had assembled a huge file on her not very interesting activities and more horrified to learn that journalists were able to claim exemption from the normal rights individuals had to gain access to data and records accumulated about them, and to prevent its publication. She had commissioned the firm to research ways that she could at least have access to data about her and then decide what further action to take.

The best course seemed to be to attack the journalistic credentials of the 'journalist'. He had, in fact, never had a serious article of any sort published nor any book or other work of literature. He wrote a monthly column for a local advertiser, which they carefully edited, complaining bitterly about local goings-on, for which he was regarded as a harmless eccentric. That was about the sum total of his output.

He had no visible means of support, he was in his fifties, had long greasy hair, dressed oddly, he was unkempt, he looked unwashed and lived with his mother. He claimed to be ready to publish an article and to be in the process of writing a book with a chapter on Maddison.

It was hoped that he wouldn't have the money to put up

much of a defence and the thrust of the case was that his interest was prurient rather than journalistic, more in the nature almost of a stalker, though he had no criminal convictions at all for any offence.

"What are you working on?" said Phil.

"It's still that surveillance case. It's arguable whether the group will ever be able to prove anything against the company. But if it transpires that they *can* actually prove anything significant, they want to be ready to take action straight away. So I'm supposed to research possible lines of action. I've been putting it off all morning. I haven't found much here so I'm going online in a minute. It's so warm and stuffy though isn't it. It makes me want to fall asleep. To come back from Crete to a heatwave doesn't seem fair."

Phil looked at his expensive watch. "It's nearly one anyway. Pack up and go for a quick one?"

"Why not."

They walked to their usual watering hole. It was heaving. Phil went to the bar while Ali found a couple of seats at a small table for them and he squeezed in beside her.

They discussed firm gossip for a while. He told her what had been happening while she'd been away on holiday. She told him about the spectacular scenery in Crete and what a pain Ed had been most of the time, moaning that he couldn't play computer games or see his mates.

"There's a good party on Saturday. It's my friend's birthday. Fancy coming?" he said casually.

"Oh, I don't know Phil. I'm supposed to be going to a garden party of one the agents in Colchester. The owner's girlfriend is my best friend and I sort of promised."

"Is it in the evening then?"

"Well no, the afternoon. But it might stretch to the evening."

"I'd come over and get you when it's finished if you wanted."

"I don't think so. Sorry Phil, I don't think I can. One party in a day is enough for me really."

"OK. One day you'll say yes. If I keep trying." And he gave

her a friendly smile and gazed into her eyes in that rather dreamy way he had.

Yes, she thought. One day I will say yes. If only Hugh had been so forward at coming forward. They'd probably have got together a lot sooner and maybe they'd still be together if he hadn't made everything so complicated.

Phil was still smiling into her eyes in a heart-melting way to which she wasn't by any means totally immune. She wondered whether to just tell Phil about Hugh and what had happened, to say although she was still heart-broken, she was willing to give it a go if he was, if he was prepared to take it slowly and accommodate a few tears to begin with. It was sorely tempting and any reunion with Hugh seemed as unlikely as ever.

Interrupting her thoughts, Phil was speaking.

"Better be getting back then," he said. And Ali lost her nerve.

IT WAS nearly three months since Ali had quit PWT.

Late August, Sam had texted to remind her about Summer Homes's late summer party to be held on the first Saturday in September in a week's time. She forbore to say that Hugh would probably be attending. She couldn't help thinking, at the risk of stirring things up, that there was still some hope and it was worth one last try to get Ali and Hugh back together again.

Sam sensed that Hugh was unhappy. He normally appeared more or less indifferent to most things and always had. Yet there was a certain moroseness to his demeanour now. It seemed a criminal waste to her that such a full-on affair had come to such an abrupt and dramatic end and all over a stupid misunderstanding apparently. Darren said she should be careful, that she was playing with fire, with peoples' lives in fact. Sam decided it was worth the risk. Perhaps time would have mellowed Hugh.

ALI expected to be free on the Saturday in question and hence had told Sam she would probably be there. She pencilled it in her diary.

The Saturday dawned hot and humid. The Indian summer predicted by the weathermen was holding up. It was such a beautiful day, Ali decided to walk to Summers' office where the party was being held in the walled garden at the rear. She was pretty casual in a tight top, short skirt and wedge sandals. Slim girls could wear these short tight things and look quite elegant. It gave Ali extra confidence. About the only advantage of a broken heart she reflected ruefully. Her dark hair had grown longer with paler highlights from the sunshine and she had a decent tan from being away in Crete for two weeks.

She became pensive as she walked along, oblivious to the admiring glances. She had assumed Hugh wouldn't be going to the party or Sam would never have asked her. Though maybe she shouldn't assume. She was going to have to face things some time. She couldn't hide from her demons forever.

Darren was at the gate to welcome everyone in. He kissed Ali and told her that Sam was in the kitchen.

She found Sam putting the finishing touches to two enormous gateaux, supervising the making of gallons of mayonnaise and telling people where to put the huge plates of canapés.

"Right," she said, "I can be all yours for about half an hour then I'll have to go and check everything all over again."

They sauntered into the garden. Darren certainly could organise a party. Everything was just so. Separate marquees for food and for dancing stood at opposite ends of the garden. The garden was brilliant with late summer flowers, Russian sage, rudbeckia, phlox and crocosmia. What would Hugh's garden look like; would any of her seedlings have been planted? She cast the thought from her mind.

"So you're Darren's social secretary now are you?"

"Well not really. But actually we have got plans for me to leave PWT and become a director of the company. Don't tell anyone will you. Sharon never wanted anything to do with the business. Do you know, in the divorce proceedings she complained that Darren was *too* successful. Can you believe

230

that? It's so interesting. We get on like a house on fire and agree on practically everything. It'll be such fun. We're just waiting for our divorces to become final, then we'll do it."

"Gosh. It seems perfect."

Ali stopped walking and froze. A familiar figure had arrive. Hugh shook Darren's hand before introducing the person with him. She was a willowy blonde in a beautiful, expensively-cut, revealing, but somehow modest, summer number. The girl was young. Younger than Ali. Fresh-faced and gorgeous.

"Who's that?" Ali asked Sam sharply.

"Oh blimey, her name's Fiona something. I never thought he'd bring her with him. Though I suppose he did get her the work experience placement now I think about it. She's only with the firm for a few weeks. Not like you." Sam ended somewhat lamely.

"Not like me," Ali breathed.

"Of course not like you. Oh, Ali, I'm sure it's not like that."

"Are you?"

Sam was about to answer but one of the serving girls came over and asked about the beer and whether there was a new barrel ready to be brought on. Sam had to go and deal with that and she didn't come back.

Moments later, James bounced up to her like a big friendly puppy and kissed her cheek. He then whispered in her ear how wonderful things were going with Maddie and he was so grateful and he hugged her.

"Is she here?" Ali whispered back smiling broadly. Good. She could see Hugh watching them while the svelte Fiona was shovelling food onto plates for them both.

"No," he whispered back, "she had to go to a gymkhana today with her sister. Er, why are we whispering?"

"Not sure." And they both collapsed into fits of giggles. Hugh was stony-faced.

"Come on then. Let's dance," said James and off they went together hand in hand. If getting on well together was the only criterion for a relationship to work, then she and James should by rights be spending the whole of the rest of their lives together.

Sadly, as it turned out, James had to leave after half an hour to do his duty stint at the gymkhana.

Ali wondered what to do. She spent some time doing the rounds of PWT people. Wattsey kissed her and said he was pleased to see her looking so well, though he asked pointedly if he could get her something to eat, perhaps.

She had a laugh with Cathy and Amanda who were much friendlier now that she wasn't working at PWT any longer, with the added bonus that she'd had her heart so publicly broken.

Alison complained that the number of litigants-in-person was on the increase following the withdrawal of legal aid from most matrimonial cases and bemoaned the fact that there wasn't more mediation work about.

Sandra said that that girl Tammy was no better, if anything getting worse and she tutted over to where Tammy was bending to smell a flower and give a young man in a business suit a better view of her cleavage.

By degrees, Ali worked her way back to the punch bowl and was hovering beside it, contemplating getting wasted, when Hugh appeared at her elbow suddenly as if from nowhere. Ali jumped and spilled the rest of her drink.

"How are you, then?" Hugh said.

"Well, you know. Bearing up."

"James not here anymore?"

"Er no. He had to go somewhere. What about you then? I don't see the lovely Fiona in the immediate vicinity."

"Oh," Hugh actually blushed. So that was the way the wind was blowing. It told Ali far more than words could ever say. "Er, she's about somewhere. She's just getting some experience with the firm. She's only with us a few weeks. Not like you." Why did everyone want to tell her that.

"Really."

Hugh drew a deep breath.

"She's just come down from Oxford and thought she might

take a stab at the law."

"Well, it must be wonderful to have one's intellectual equal in the office at last."

Hugh cleared his throat, looked away and ploughed on.

"Her father owns the farm next to the cottage, so he asked me if I could help out – with the work experience."

"My, the things a bloke has to do to get his hands on a small strip of agricultural land." Ali knew it sounded bitchy but she couldn't help it.

Hugh stiffened. "I hope you're not implying what I think you are," he said coldly. Then more levelly:

"Really, Ali, you mustn't be bitter. It doesn't suit you at all."

And he strode off, leaving Ali shaking and wretched.

She could only think of going to find Sam, but Sam was there instantly having watched the encounter hopefully at first, then realising it was all going wrong.

"Sam, I've got to go." Sam steered her to the building and into one of the upstairs rooms.

"It didn't go well then." Sam said.

"That's the understatement of the year. Disastrous wouldn't do it justice. Sam, I've blown it completely. But I suppose it hardly matters if he's sleeping with the fragrant Fiona."

Tears began to pour down Ali's face. She hadn't cried for at least a month and they flooded out now.

"I really don't think so. There's no sign of it in the office."

"Well, my little dalliance with Hugh didn't exactly make the headlines."

"Actually, there was always something there. I didn't realise I'd realised, if you know what I mean, before you told me, but there was some sort of chemistry between you right from the beginning. Especially from his end. The way he looked at you. Oh, and that Christmas present thingy with The Privy sign. It was so intimate somehow. If you want my considered opinion there's no way he's sleeping with Fiona. Still, I could be wrong, though you can bet your life if Cathy and Amanda thought he was, they'd have said something. Did they?"

Ali shook her head miserably. She was sobbing away by

now. "I've blown it anyway. It's all my fault."

"Hang on. It was him who ended it. I don't know what you said to him just now but you're entitled to be miffed at him. If anyone's going to beg to be taken back it should be him."

Ali continued to sob broken-heartedly. Sam disappeared and quickly returned saying she'd asked Darren to order a taxi for Ali. They both came outside with her and fed her into the taxi when it arrived.

"Ali, why don't you come round to our house tomorrow and we can talk about it properly. We're in all day."

"Is there any point?" She checked herself. "But of course I'd love to see you. I didn't mean to be rude. Yes, all right I'll come over some time."

"I just think, well, he wouldn't be so ... touchy, if he didn't care a bit."

"See you tomorrow," Ali sniffed and waved out of the taxi at them.

"ALI, we thought you weren't coming," Sam said, greeting her at the door. "It's gone three."

"Sor-*ree*. You said you'd be here all day. Anyway I had to wait till my face was less bloated from crying and I biked over so it took longer."

"Come and have a cup of coffee. Or perhaps something stronger?"

Ali looked around the kitchen and complimented Sam and Darren on how it had been re-modelled. This house was their new love nest and permanent home and they were thrilled to bits with it.

"You know, I was thinking about Hugh." Sam wasn't wasting any time. "I reckon he's still as stuck on you as you are on him. That's why he was so upset about the Angela thing and why he's so touchy now. I mean, if he'd finished with you because he'd gone off you, then he wouldn't care now would he. But instead I think inside he's devastated to be without you. I think we should try to look at it from his point of view too. I mean if you thought he suspected you of being – I don't know – say, a child molester, well wouldn't that upset you rather?"

"I suppose so. But if he's pining for me it doesn't look much like it. He looks the picture of health. And no signs of having been badly beaten up."

"He's just come back from visiting his family in Australia a few weeks ago so that's probably why. Before that he did look a bit rough actually, I mean before he was injured. Anyway he's a bloke isn't he. They react differently. We stop eating. A bloke shouts and swears, gets drunk with his mates, kicks a football about, goes and pumps iron. Or perhaps in Hugh's case buries himself in law books. Isn't that right Darren." And she turned to her lover for confirmation.

He shrugged. "How should I know? I'm just a bloke. My brains are stuck down in my bollocks."

"What actually did you say to Hugh yesterday to upset him so much?"

Ali sighed. "I suggested that he was sleeping with Fiona to get her father to sell him a bit of land. Or that's what he thought I was suggesting. And I suppose I was."

"So first," said Darren, "he thinks you think he's an attempted rapist. And now, you accuse him of prostituting himself for land. Oh well, that's not going to upset anyone is it!" Sam tutted at him.

"Anyway, it's too late now," sulked Ali. "I won't get the opportunity to see him again. So that's that."

"Actually, at the party he came to try and find you yesterday after you'd gone. He thinks you're going out with James."

"Good. I hope you didn't disabuse him of the notion."

"Well, I was non-committal. You know what he's like. So hard to read. But I'd have sworn underneath all that cool that he was very upset. I'm afraid I had a bit of a go at him actually. I think Victor did as well."

"Huh. I don't want any sort of pity reaction out of him. I'll just have to accept that it really is completely over."

"He's here."

"What? Who?" Ali cast about the kitchen as though someone might be hiding in the cupboards.

"Hugh's here. I said you'd be coming round some time today and he's been here all day waiting for you."

"But I didn't see his car."

"He *ran* here," Darren laughed. "He got us all up at seven this morning. He brought some stuff in a rucksack and he's been down in the summer house at the end of the garden all day working. The kids were intrigued at first. They kept taking him glasses of orange juice as an excuse to go and investigate. And he's been out several times to play ball games with them and chase them about."

"He'd make a wonderful dad," said Sam.

"Too bad I won't get the chance to find out," said Ali.

"Well. Aren't you going to go and see him?" said Sam.

"I can't believe it. I suppose so."

"Try and look a bit more enthusiastic. We've been on tenterhooks all day."

CHAPTER 40

IT was a long, meandering garden. Hugh jumped and stood up when Ali opened the summerhouse door.

"Oh hello, Ali," he smiled.

Ali tried a smile too but found she was much too tense.

"I'm glad you're here," he went on, "I thought you weren't coming."

Ali peered at him suspiciously. "It was a nice day. I thought I'd cycle over."

"Yes. I jogged here."

"Yes, Darren said."

There was a pause.

"Ali, I'm sorry about yesterday. I didn't mean to march off like that. You're entitled to be angry with me. I shouldn't have lost my temper."

"Oh," said Ali, surprised.

"And, er, I just wanted to tell you how sorry I am for what's happened. I've been thinking a lot about things. It was all my fault. And what you did regarding Trish. You did the right thing about it. I was a fool to make such a fuss. And, as for imposing all that secrecy on you, it was the wrong thing to do. It was really selfish of me. It was bound to distort everything." He paused.

"Mostly it was because I didn't know how to cope with our relationship. I ... it overwhelmed me. I felt I needed to keep it battened down. I'm sorry. It was just so immature of me. Anyway, Victor and Fiona made me realise what a fool I've been about Trish."

Ali's eyes went to slits. "You spoke to Fiona about us? Right. Well, she's obviously an understanding girl." Ali looked at all the books and papers spread out over the table. "I'd better let you get on then." She wasn't sure how she was being so controlled on the surface. Underneath she was dying.

She started to exit the summerhouse but Hugh caught her arm. Several thousand volts went through her body. She tried to ignore them.

"Ali. Don't go. Please don't go. I just spoke to Fiona about Trish because I couldn't think who else to ask. I didn't talk to her about *us*. I wanted to know if someone impartial thought I'd been unreasonable. I just couldn't decide myself. Of course you were right not to get involved in what Trish was going to do. I just couldn't see it at the time."

"Right," Ali said again, staring at the floor. She took a deep breath. She was going to say it and clear the air. She'd probably never see him again, but she had to say it. "If I'm really honest, there was a point when I was just open to the possibility that, for some bizarre reason I couldn't work out, that you actually might have gone to Angela's flat that night. Even before Trish told me she saw your car going into Graham's drive."

"I know. That's what hurt so much. I'm glad you've been honest about it. And I'm over it now."

"There were quite a few things that pointed to it. And you know you were so distant at times and gave so little of yourself away. It makes people's imaginations work overtime. But I dismissed it as completely ridiculous."

She didn't say that was after talking to Sam.

"Then when Trish said she'd actually seen your car there on the night, I just thought, because of our relationship, I should stay out of it. We didn't know anything about that awful Symonds character at the time. For heaven's sake if it had come out later that we'd tried to manipulate a witness, well you could have been disciplined and I might never have got my legal career off the ground, not to mention the effect it might have had on Graham's defence. I suppose I thought you'd think the same."

"I wasn't thinking clearly at the time. I'm such a fool. I know people think I'm cold. Robotic even. I suppose I thought you'd see through it all without my having to say anything. I thought we understood each other. I thought you'd understand me because of our times together. I was so shocked and horrified when it dawned on me that you might even have just *suspected* that I'd gone to Angela's flat. But I do understand it now. The secrecy and *me* – the way I am. I've just made such a hash of things.

"And I'm not proud of the fact that I tried to hurt you after we split up by pretending not to care and by giving you back that Privy sign in public. None of it was your fault but I was trying to punish you. And I wanted you to be hurt. That was terribly wrong of me and I'm so sorry."

"Apology accepted." Ali swallowed. "Well, thank you for the opportunity to clear the air. I don't want to get in your way." She turned back to the door. "Good luck, Hugh," she said as she stepped onto the paving outside, her heart bleeding.

She couldn't resist turning around to look at him. He had sat back on the edge of the table. His eyes were tight shut, his arms crossed in front of him hugging his body and he was rocking gently back and forwards. And he started to shake. Her heart somersaulted and her legs turned to jelly. She couldn't bear to see him like that. "Hugh, don't. Hugh, I'll never forget you."

"Ali. Don't go. Please, *please* don't go." She went over to him and stroked his hair, forgetting about the stitches.

"Ali, please don't go. I can't go on without you. Please, *please* say you'll come back to me. I love you so much. Ali I've always loved you since the first time I saw you but … I thought you had a boyfriend. Or you weren't interested in me, or both." He pulled her to him and she buried her face in his shoulder. He smelled wonderful. Just like before.

"Ali. You do love me don't you? You do still love me. Please say you do. *Please, please* say you love me."

Through the haze of pleasure and pain, Ali couldn't help thinking: *Typical of a bloke. He keeps you hanging on forever, then the minute he's ready to declare himself, he demands instant reciprocation.*

"You need to ask! Of course I love you, Hugh." She felt the tension leave her body and she melted into his. "But Hugh, I meant what I said before. I can't live without you. If you leave me again, I wouldn't survive."

"Poor baby," Hugh said with tears in his eyes. "You've got so thin. I can't believe I did that to you. I'll never leave you again, I promise."

"I don't know. I've sort of lost confidence. I thought we had such a wonderful relationship. Secret yes, but wonderful. Wonderful one second and then suddenly non-existent. Hugh, I thought I was going to die. I wanted to die. I wouldn't survive it again."

"Victor ... Wattsey told me the other day about how you were after we split up. He found me mooching about in The Privy when I thought everyone had left."

He didn't mention the angry dressing down Wattsey had given him that had turned to perplexity and total exasperation when he'd caught a glimpse of what Hugh felt like underneath.

"He seems to be very fond of you. I didn't know I'd hurt you so badly. Please believe me. I was stupid. I've been in turmoil too. I've thought about you all the time. In bed at night I've ached for you. Every single night. Your perfect body. Oh Ali."

He was kissing her now. And intermittently whispering her name. She found her hands inside his running top, her fingers digging into him. The shorts and top were so thin she could feel everything through them. All so familiar. His muscular body was pressed to hers, his hands on her bottom and back pulling her close to him.

"Oh, Hugh. Nothing's changed."

"God, I wish I could fuck you here and now."

He swallowed and, gently taking her arms, he put them by her side. "But we can't. Shall we go home."

He wiped her tears away, took out his smart phone and called a taxi. Then he packed up his rucksack and they went hand in hand to say goodbye to Sam, Darren and their four inquisitive offspring. Hugh ruffled Perry's hair and said he should practise with that footwork and he'd be another Ronaldo.

"Is it OK if I leave my bike here?"

Sam was delighted. "No problem. We'll see you soon

hopefully."

CHAPTER 41

A NEW drive had been laid to Hugh's cottage. So he *had* managed to buy the strip of field. It had been rolled and surfaced with clinker. A new post and wire fence along the left hand side separated it from the field beyond. The hedge with the public footpath was still on the right. The taxi dropped them off, turned round on the new gravelled area near the house and drove away.

The borders, Ali was delighted to note, had been dug over and were awash with late summer flowers. "Raised and planted out with love," said Hugh.

"Sown with love too. Shall we go in, then."

It turned out that Hugh's extreme self-control in the bedroom had deserted him for the time being and they came together very quickly.

Afterwards, he shed warm, salty tears over her face and said again and again that he loved her and he'd never leave her ever.

"I hope not," said Ali. He sat up.

"Well, we could always make an honest spider out of Alan and all his children."

"What?"

"We could get married. That's forever isn't it."

"You and me?" she said stupidly.

Hugh looked around the room and peered under the bed. "Yes, I would say you and me would be the primary candidates."

"Properly married?"

"I'm sure we could introduce some improper activities into the union at regular intervals. But yes. Married. Properly."

Ali just stared at him.

"Still not convinced?" He got out of bed, went down on one knee and took her hand.

"This isn't very dignified. Stark naked. But here goes. Aluisha Celia Clayton-Barratt will you do me the huge

242

honour of becoming my wife."

"You know my full name!"

"Since you first came to PWT."

"Well, in that case I can't refuse. Yes. Yes. When?"

"Soon I'd say. As soon as possible. I mean if you want all the church thing, I don't mind. It'd just take a bit longer."

"No, soon is good."

"Hurrah." He opened the bedside cabinet drawer and stirred around, while sitting on the side of the bed.

"I've got something to show you."

He handed her the parish magazine and the clerk's letter, both of which she read open-mouthed.

"Oh Hugh. It's funny. But not funny too. Actually it's pretty sad." She sniffed. "I wish I'd been able to be here with you to share it at that time."

"Tell me about it. I nearly went and topped myself. I certainly became well acquainted with the bottoms of a good number of brandy bottles." He shut his eyes. Ali kissed him gently. "I don't think you realise just how much I love you," he continued. "How much I've always loved you. But why should you. I didn't say anything to you before. I actually actively tried to make you think otherwise. I should've told you then. I shouldn't have allowed all this to happen. I want you to know now. It's more than love. It completely consumes me. In fact, you're probably not going to understand this, but I can't really get enough of you. I don't just mean sex. I want to crawl right inside you. Even when we're screwing I just sometimes think I want to be even closer to you."

Ali looked at him and shook her head. "That's just how I feel. Except that the sex is, well, spectacular. Unutterably exquisite is how you described it after that first time and I couldn't put it any better."

"Oh, Ali. Let me kiss you some more. Come here."

"Hugh." She pushed him away gently. "Why did you storm off yesterday after coming over to speak to me? All this time I've wanted you so badly and you've withheld yourself. Even so recently as yesterday."

Hugh sighed. "When I came over to you yesterday, just standing next to you after all that time, it was as though heaven had opened up. I can't describe what it felt like. You're like a goddess to me. You always have been. I'd felt so open to you. I suppose I'd convinced myself you'd be the same, happy to see me. But you were all closed up. Tight like a drum. You wouldn't let me in."

"Hugh, you unceremoniously dumped me in a car park in front of the whole office. I haven't seen you since I left the firm. I thought you didn't want me all this time. I've just been surviving. Not living."

"I know. I can't begin to apologise enough. I was so, so upset yesterday though. I couldn't believe what you said. I had to say something bitchy back. And then I had to get away. I thought *you* didn't want *me* and I didn't know what to do. You didn't come to the hospital to see me. I lay there hoping you would. Then I thought I'd have another go yesterday to talk to you, but you'd gone and Samantha started raving on at me. And then bloody Victor."

"Hughie. I did come to the hospital the Monday evening but you'd left. You hadn't tried to call me. I'd no idea you'd want to see me but I went to the hospital anyway. I was … it was dreadful. Not being able to see you, not knowing how you were or whether you wanted to see me at all."

"Poor darling," said Hugh, hugging her.

"It won't happen again, will it? That horrible man won't keep on getting his henchmen to have you done over, will he. I assume it was him. Grimsby."

"I'm sure he won't, sweetheart."

"Hugh, we'll have to be honest with each other in future," said Ali. "Not be too proud to say what we think. I mean, I'm only happy when I'm close to you. Otherwise it's awful. I don't know what to do with myself. You don't know what a relief it is just to hold you like this."

"Believe me, I do." And he kissed her softly and a little tearfully, and lingeringly.

"Hugh, just for the record. I haven't been going out with

James. I had a couple of dates with him over Christmas, but nothing happened. He's got a plummy girlfriend from his own set. You know. A better class of gairl and all that," she put on an upper class accent. "In fact I was instrumental."

"Good."

"And?"

"And what?

"What about you and *her*?"

Hugh's expression was one of mystification.

"Oh, for goodness sake, Hugh! You and the delightful, intelligent Fiona."

Hugh laughed. "Heavens, no. Of course not." And he pulled her to him, shook her lightly and said in a mock-villainous voice: "So you think I shag all the hired help, do you? Do you? That I'd violate a girl just to purchase a piece of land? God help any nannies we have to hire." And then he started to tickle her until she screamed. "I always knew that underneath that beautiful exterior you had a mind like a cesspit, but really."

"OK. I believe you."

He rolled back next to her. "Ali, as a matter of interest, are you still on the pill or not?"

"Actually, no. No need."

"So when was the start of your LMP?"

"Er, let's think. About two weeks ago." She looked at him and pulled a face. "Ooops."

"Oh well, it doesn't matter now does it. Well, it wouldn't really have mattered before, either."

"Yeah, well, except if I'd got pregnant just as you were dumping me." Hugh winced. "Honestly, I don't know what I'd have done." She shivered. "It doesn't bear thinking about."

He rolled his eyes. "Oh no. I can't stand to think about it. Don't think about it." He kissed and nuzzled her lower abdomen and said to it: "Well, if you are in there, I love you to bits already."

Then he poked around in his bedside table and brought out a photograph and showed her. It was the Burn's night at Baz's house with Ali and Hugh wrapped around each other.

"Remember this?"

"Do I! I was so embarrassed. I hoped you hadn't seen it at the time. It makes me look as though I'm … *you know*."

"Hmm, it does doesn't it," he said, smiling.

"But I wasn't. It just looked like it. Honestly I wasn't. Not in someone's house in the middle of a dance floor. Really, honestly."

"Well, you are rather prone to it sweetheart, aren't you?" he said, rubbing his nose against hers.

"But I didn't! I didn't!"

"Are you sure?"

"Oh, Hugh. I hope nobody else thought so!"

"Shush. I know you weren't. I was just teasing. I think I might have noticed. Then I'd definitely have asked you out. I did so want to but I didn't know what you thought and I didn't want to get done for sexual harassment. Actually, I thought you were avoiding me."

"I wish you'd asked me out, too. I was – that is, you wouldn't have found me unreceptive. But I was in a complete state. That's why I tried to keep out of your way. I couldn't stop obsessing about you even then. At the time, you know, when you saw the photo, what on earth must you have thought of me?"

"Let's just say it didn't exactly put me off you. Quite the reverse." He kissed the photo, then he kissed her. "In fact just looking at it now Ali darling, I think I'm ready to have another go."

"Oh good. I thought you'd never say. Hugh, I do so love you. I've got to get into the habit of saying it now. I had to stop myself for so long."

"Poor darling. I'm such a pig."

"No you're not."

"Yes I am."

"No you're *not*."

"Oh, but I am." And he started snuffling and snorting all over her while she squealed. Until nature took over.

A WHILE LATER, Hugh looked down at her. "Not that I don't think you're totally gorgeous however thin or otherwise you are, but just in case you really are brewing up a little Barratt-Sutherland in there, you'll have to start eating better. How about going out for a meal to celebrate or I'll go and order a takeaway to be delivered."

"Takeaway please, I want to stay in bed with you a little longer. We can eat it in bed. And talk about us and, you know, the nuptials."

As he padded off to phone for a takeaway, Ali stretched and her hands went under the pillows. There was something there. One hand came out holding a pair of lacy panties. Her blood froze. Then she realised it was the pair she'd been missing for four months. Thank God for that. And how bitter-sweet to think of Hugh nursing an item of her underwear in bed for four months.

"Oh you found them," said Hugh when he came back. "Thank heavens, I don't need them anymore." He chucked them on the floor. "I've got you."

THE END

Please turn the page for a message from the author.

Thank you for reading *The Ardent Intern*. I hope you enjoyed it and would be delighted if you could spread the word about this book and other books of mine. Online reviews would be particularly appreciated on Kindle/Amazon, Goodreads, other sites for book readers and/or your favourite book provider's website.

If you enjoyed reading the book, why not try the immediate sequel to it entitled *Threshold* and get to know other characters better, two in particular, and learn more about Ali and the man she ends up with. In *Threshold*, a person's long-forgotten background rises up, almost as though from the ashes, leading to a serious and dangerous situation in which life is put at risk.

Send me a message any time through my website: https://www.gillmather.com

With my best wishes,

Gill

Printed in Great Britain
by Amazon